Last Call

A
BAD HABITS
NOVEL

A ROMANTIC COMEDY
BY BESTSELLING AUTHOR

STACI HART

BOOKS BY
STACI HART

HEARTS AND ARROWS
Rereleasing in 2017

CONTEMPORARY ROMANCE
Hardcore

With a Twist

Chaser

Last Call

Wasted Words

Tonic

A Thousand Letters—February 2017

SHORT STORIES
Once

Desperate Measures

*To **Kandi** and **Becca**,*
For always being my dearest diary
And shitting rainbows all over my storms.
#GoHomeShirley

Meow

ROSE

My breath came in bursts, heart pounding as Patrick's long body pressed me into the bed. There wasn't an inch between us — we were a tangle of arms and legs, lips and hands, and any will I had to stop him was long gone. I didn't care that I should. I didn't care about anything, not with his fingers stroking my skin like a match, trailing heat in their wake.

He was even better than I remembered.

I opened my heavy lids when he backed away to pull off his shirt, taking a quick second to catch my breath as I skimmed my fingers down his tattooed chest, my eyes roaming over the art that covered every inch of his skin as he watched. It was his soul laid bare — the good and the bad, the happy and sad, all chronicled in black ink so he could remember. As if he could ever forget.

It was a sight I'd missed more than I'd ever confess.

He bent to kiss me, breathing until his breath was mine and mine was his. It was fevered, frantic — my hand against the sharp angle of his jaw, his lips hard, my eyes pinned shut — erasing everything that had happened between us. As if it had never happened.

Patrick broke away to kiss my neck just as a black cat jumped on the bed, and I glanced over with bleary eyes to meet the cat's. He meowed, teeth like tiny white needles against the jet black of his fur.

Patrick didn't stop or seem to notice. His hands slipped up my thighs, tongue brushing my skin, wet lips closing, and my lids fluttered, a sigh slipping out of me as I twisted my fingers in his black hair.

An orange tabby hopped onto the bed and strutted across to sit next to the black one, tail twitching. He blinked at me and meowed.

"What the hell?" I muttered, confusion on my face as another one — this time smoke gray — found its way onto my bed, sat next to the others, looked right at me, and meowed like an absolute bastard.

My face fell as flat as my hope. "I'm fucking dreaming."

This was the moment when my eyes flew open, and I gasped as I woke unwillingly.

Patrick was gone, and so were the cats. My clothes were sadly in place, the room chilly and dark, and my phone alarm meowed at me from my nightstand.

"Son of a bitch," I huffed, heart still chugging as I rolled over to swipe blindly at the screen to stop the noise.

The phone was still in my hand as I flopped back in bed, reminding myself again to change the ringer when I could open my eyes. My roommate, Lily, had set it as a joke weeks ago, and I could never remember to change it back. Instead, I considered options for a payback ringer, top of the list being broken glass, crying baby, and angry hen.

I cracked one eye to glance at my screen. It was eight in the morning, an hour that normally didn't exist in my universe. I'd never been a morning person, which was part of the draw in bartending. Of course, it made adulting kind of hard when you didn't get up until two, but luckily, I didn't have to adult very often. Jury duty being an unavoidable, annoying, and despicable exception.

I thought real hard about the two-hundred-fifty dollar fine I'd get nailed with if I didn't show up.

Real hard.

But it wasn't worth it. I'd get out of bed for two-hundred-fifty bones. Hell, if you fed me enough tequila and I had on a pretty bra, I'd probably take my shirt off for that kind of money.

I sighed and flipped off my comforter before reaching over to turn on my lamp. My room was always dark thanks to blackout curtains that aided and abetted my reverse sleep habits. The only time they were opened was when Lily wanted to torture me out of bed before lunch.

She was spared a sudden, gruesome death only because she's my best friend.

I peeled myself out of bed and shuffled into the bathroom in nothing but a Cub Scout T-shirt and panties, rubbing my face as I yawned, trying not to think about how warm my bed had been. Definitely trying not to think about Patrick's lips — or his hands, or jaw, or tattoos or his —

He dumped you more than seven months ago, Rose. Get over it.

Stupid asshole dreams.

Let me give you some relationship advice. Don't date the guy down the hall, because when he dumps you, you can't get away. Definitely don't date a guy in your group of super tight-knit friends, because then you *really* fuck yourself. Especially if he was your best friend, and *especially* if he never stopped looking at you like he'd devour you if you'd say the word, even months after he dropped you like a bad habit. Really makes it hard to stick to your guns.

But stick to my guns I did. Patrick and I were an unwieldy, knotted up mess, so when it ended for good, that was it. I didn't even know how to approach fixing it because it was fucked up beyond all repair, so I threw up the wall. And once the wall is up, there's no scaling it. It's like nuclear lockdown — gates don't open for two-hundred years, so go get yourself a Snickers and pull up a chair because we're going to be here for a while.

I glanced in the mirror and yawned again, hazel eyes watering as I twisted my long, shaggy black hair into a rope and tossed it over my shoulder, feeling grumbly as I washed my face and hands. I needed to at least look presentable, wear something professional-ish, which was a problem since ripped up jeans and combat boots made up a large sum of my wardrobe. So I sighed heavily and made my way into Lily's room to find something 'normal' to wear. She was the light to my dark, the optimist to my cynic. The 'normal' to my 'not.'

I stopped dead when I stepped into her room.

A body shaped lump was stretched out in Lily's bed under her covers.

The problem: Lily hadn't slept at home in months.

My pulse exploded in a burst as I tried to figure out who it was because that lump was too big to be Lily. Obviously the logical leap was that a homeless guy wandered in and crashed in her bed. Or maybe it was a tired burglar. A lost little old man? Maybe the nursing home was looking for him. Or the police. Or his kids, looking for their inheritance.

I stood frozen next to the bed with my brain tripping over what to do. Call the cops. Scream. Run. Fight. I blinked and looked around for a weapon, eyes lighting when I landed on Lily's nightstand.

My lips pursed, eyes on the lump as I opened the drawer silently and grabbed Philmore Dix.

I stepped closer to the pile of bedding, breath frozen in my lungs as I extended it slowly to poke the lump in what I thought might be its shoulder.

The covers flew up with a yelp of the man underneath, and I screamed as the lump rolled off the bed and hit the floor.

Patrick was wild-eyed, black hair a mess, tattooed chest heaving as he blinked up at me. My heart kickstarted with a thud, and all the blood rushed to my cheeks and ears.

"Tricky! What the fuck?" I yelled as I threw the hot pink vibrator at him.

He put up his hand to stop Phil from hitting him in the chest. "Fuck, Rose. You scared the shit out of me."

I gaped. "*I* scared *you*? What the fuck are you doing here?"

"Sleeping."

"Obviously," I shot as I hung a hand on my hip, trying to keep my eyes on his instead of his body. I wondered briefly if he was naked. My heartbeat ticked up a notch. "Why are you sleeping *here*?"

He sighed and ran a hand through his dark hair, putting it in place elegantly. "Ever since Lily started sleeping over, I haven't had a full night's sleep. Three in the morning, every morning, like clockwork. First the moaning. Then the headboard banging. I've tried everything, Rose. You've gotta know this was the last resort. I wouldn't have done it if I wasn't desperate for sleep."

I regretted the fact that he had a key to our place, along with regretting a hundred other things as I glared at that beautiful asshole, sitting on the floor of Lily's room, wrapped in pretty, frilly bedding as he stared up at me with sad, intense eyes, eyes that begged me to understand. What pissed me off the most was that I *did* understand.

I felt that pull to him, in the moment. His eyes always did that to me — I swear if he looked hard enough, he could see straight through me.

I shoved my feelings on the matter back down into that dark corner of my heart and kicked its door closed.

My eyes narrowed, teeth clenching once. "How long have you

been sleeping here?"

His face tightened in the smallest increment, but I saw it just the same. "Over a month."

I ran a hand through my hair, not even sure what to say. "Jesus Christ, Tricky. You should have asked me."

"Lily suggested it. I told her we should ask you, but she said you'd flip out." He smirked a little, since she was right and all.

"That bitch," I breathed, only like forty-two percent serious, but that forty-two percent was *really* serious.

He was still smirking just a little, that dick, even though he had those eyes of his on me like sexy lasers. "Come on, Rose. I mean, I've been here for a month and you didn't even know. I'll stay out of your way, I swear."

My jaw was set, but I was torn. Everything pointed to picking him up my his scruff — naked or not — and tossing him out. I just wasn't sure how much of that was irrational. So I put on my hardass, scowling a little for effect. "It's way too early to have this discussion. I need coffee, or whiskey. Or both. You work today?"

"Yeah, until six."

"I have jury duty, but meet me here after and give me the day to think about it."

"Fair enough." The shadow smirk bloomed into a full blown crooked smile. He picked up Philmore, turning it over to inspect it as his brow climbed. "You were going to assault me with a pink vibe?"

I shrugged. "It was the closest blunt object."

He snuck a glance down at my legs. I'd forgotten I was nearly naked, and another little burst of adrenaline shot through me as I watched him look me over.

I was all of a sudden very glad I'd done laundry a couple of days ago and had my top-shelf undies on instead of the days of the week panties I reserved for periods and trips to the laundromat.

I turned for Lily's dresser to rummage through her clothes with clumsy hands, hiding behind my dark hair to cover the flush in my cheeks. When I turned around, business casual in hand, he was still staring at my body. I ignored the shot of heat that ran through me and made a face somewhere between a scowl and a glare.

He looked up at me without the least bit of remorse.

The light streamed in through a crack between the curtains, a slice of sunshine across his angular face and curves of his shoulders, illuminating his blue eyes as tiny specks of dust danced in and out of the beam.

I realized I wasn't breathing and clutched the clothes in my hands with sweaty palms, needing to get out of that room before I suffocated. "All right … well, I'll see you tonight, Tricky."

"Sure." His voice was tight, the smile somehow gone from his face without me realizing when it had left.

I wondered if he was as affected by me as I was by him, just before I walked away from him with only one other thought.

This cannot be good.

No Questions

PATRICK

I **stared at rose's ass shamelessly** as she blew out of the room, breathing a sigh when she was out of sight.

It could have gone worse than dagger eyes and vibrator assault. She didn't say no when I asked to stay, and I counted that for something.

I gathered up Lily's comforter and climbed back into bed, slipping a hand behind my head as I listened to Rose swear her way through the apartment. Best to stay out of her way — it was too early to press my luck any more than I already had.

As I waited in the otherwise quiet room, I replayed the encounter in my mind, pictured her standing over me. Even barely awake, she looked like something out of a dream. The light shone in, illuminating her dark hair to look red, glowing like embers. The small, tight tee hitched over her hip on one side, the Cub Scout logo stretched across her breasts. Her long legs, the tattoo on her hip and thigh that I'd done myself, a mark I'd made on her that could never be erased.

Outside, she was cool and confident. Inside, she was on fire.

Nothing had been easy between the two of us since we'd broken up. I shouldered the blame for that, and it wasn't something Rose would let go.

We'd been friends first, good friends, and for years. There was a night, a moment when I knew I felt more for her. No, it wasn't even that — I'd had a thing for her ever since I'd met her. It was that I realized that she felt the same. Something in her eyes asked me for more, and when I kissed her, her body told me it was true.

We made a deal: We'd take it one day at a time, and if it ever became too much for either of us, we'd say the word and end it, no questions asked.

And that's how the happiest months of my life began.

I'd been alone for most of my life, no room in my heart for anything serious. But Rose and I were easy. We slipped into a pattern of togetherness, every day, every night. I remembered coming to this apartment under much different circumstances, sleeping across the hall in her bed, spending every moment with her that I could, all under the umbrella of a bullshit, poisonous mantra: 'No questions asked.'

It seemed so simple, at the time. A way to lower expectations and pressure. An easy way out wherein we could retain our friendship and respect for each other. We thought, at least. At the end of the day, it made no difference.

Sometimes, you have the whole world in your hands, and you don't realize it until it's shattered, left crumbled and sparkling in your palms. That you don't know that you've lived your best days, not until they're gone. Not until you look back. That day — the day I walked away — was one of my greatest mistakes, and I've made more than my share. It's the only one I counted as a regret.

It wasn't her fault that I was afraid, that the days and nights and togetherness I'd come to want and need all of a sudden seemed big and serious and terrifying. It wasn't her fault that I realized I loved her, that I'd let her in deep enough that if she left me, I could never repair the hole it would leave.

So I ended it. And when I sat her down, when I told her simply that I wanted out, she accepted it just as simply. No questions asked.

I mistook her acceptance for apathy, and that apathy nearly killed me. She didn't care, I convinced myself, then convinced myself that I didn't care either. Repeated it in my head as I asked Veronica — another tattoo artist where I worked, one who'd been signaling her interest to me for months — if she wanted to go on a date. To Habits, the bar where we all hung out. The same bar where Rose bartended.

Like I said. Regrets.

The look on Rose's face when I walked in with Veronica wasn't one I'd ever forget. I think she was too shocked to hide her hurt, her anger, and that's when I knew she'd been fronting, giving me what she thought I wanted, just as I presumed to know her feelings.

That night was a long one. It wasn't long before it was too much to bear — the tears she blinked back, her body tight, the way she avoided looking at me, like if she did, she'd turn into a pillar of salt. I ushered Veronica out and apologized, an apology that earned me a verbal lashing, one I accepted and deserved, then watched her storm off. It was weeks before she'd even really speak to me again, and the first words she spoke were a joke at my expense, a good-natured joke that served as an olive branch.

I'd gone back to Rose's place, waited on her couch to come clean. Beg. Do what I had to to get her back. But it wasn't enough. I knew as she stood before me, hands shaking, tears streaking her cheeks, eyes full of betrayal. She told me never again. She told me I wasn't forgiven. She told me it was over for good. Forever. And I believed her.

So I'd spent the last seven months wishing I'd done things

differently. Waiting in the wings. Watching her for an opening, looking for any sign that there was a chance for us.

But if Rose was anything, she was stone cold. One chance. Just one. And I'd wasted mine.

I heard her come out of her room and pause in front of the doorway to Lily's for only a second before she turned with a huff, and her footsteps grew quieter until the door opened and closed, marking her exit.

I imagined her walking down the hall grumbling, wondered how likely it was that she'd actually let me stay.

I sighed and climbed out of Lily's bed, making it like I always did to leave it just like I'd found it. I found myself looking over the painting I'd done for her years before, after I went to my first ballet. As a principal dancer for the New York City Ballet, dance was her life, a devotion I understood. A sacrifice of her time and body for her passion. Shoes from various shows hung on her wall around the painting, all noted with the date and performance. The piece was almost entire black with the edge of her body and tutu visible in the softest whites, pinks, peaches and yellow, painted in oil with raised brush strokes. I always noticed what I saw as flaws, wished I could pick up a brush and just apply a little paint here, a little over there, make it perfect.

But perfect didn't exist. It was a lesson I'd learned long, long before.

I pulled on my sweatpants and T-shirt just as my phone alarm went off, and, once dressed, I made my way through the apartment, which was as familiar to me as my own. For four years, we'd lived down the hall from each other — me and West, Rose and Lily. We all had keys to the others' apartments, for emergencies like running out of coffee filters or milk. Plus, the girls had cable and we didn't, so it wasn't at all uncommon for any of us to find the others in our place. Although, I'm the first to admit that sleeping in Rose's apartment without her knowledge crossed the line.

My only defense was that I was desperate for sleep. And that it was Lily's idea.

Two months ago, Lily and West got together, and she started sleeping over. A month ago, I stopped sleeping.

West and I shared a wall, and when the headboard started pounding in the middle of the night, every night, the first thing I did was move my bed across the room. Every night, it seemed to get a little louder, a little longer, and every morning I'd wake up a little more exhausted.

I'd tried everything I could think of. Earplugs drove me nuts. Music was too distracting. I think there was an electrical problem in our apartment because every white noise machine or fan I bought didn't last more than a day or two before shorting out. So when Lily offered me her old bed, I took her up on it, eventually. After she twisted my arm, convincing me it wasn't creepy because she'd given me permission, after all. There was no need to tell Rose, she'd said.

I'd barely slept for a week at that point. Desperate times, and all that.

It was so quiet that first night when I snuck in while she was work, and I slept like I was dead. There was no going back after that.

Keeping it a secret was easy enough. Rose didn't get in until late, usually around three when the bar closed, long after I was asleep. And she never woke up before noon, well after I was already gone.

Until today, at least.

I padded down the hall, opening the door of my apartment to find West and Lily at the table with two bowls of oatmeal between them like there was no one else in the world.

I couldn't help but smile.

They glanced over when I closed the door.

"Hey, Tricky," West said with a smile from behind his dark beard.

"There's breakfast on the stove, if you're hungry," Lily added with a smile of her own, pushing her long, blond hair over her shoulder before taking a bite.

"Thanks." I made my way through the kitchen and grabbed a bowl, savoring the secret about Rose for only a moment before throwing it at them casually. "So, Rose just caught me."

Everything grew still, and I smiled, my back to them as I spooned the oatmeal into my bowl.

"Shit," Lily said. "What happened?"

"She tried to brain me with your vibrator." I dumped a spoonful of brown sugar into the bowl and turned to find them both staring at me. "What?" I asked innocently as I took a seat.

Lily's cheeks were pink. "You're serious." It wasn't a question.

"Dead serious," I said with a smirk. "That's a pretty impressive piece, Lil."

"Oh, my God," she groaned.

I chuckled. "Anyway, we scared the hell out of each other. She was wielding that thing like a nightstick. I don't know how much damage it would have done, though."

She laughed, trying to cover her embarrassment. "You'd be surprised at how much destruction a silicone dick loaded with a couple of C batteries can do." She abandoned her spoon for her coffee mug, wrapping her long fingers around the cup before bringing it to her lips. "What did she say?"

I raised a brow and stirred my breakfast. "Besides '*What the fuck are you doing here?*'"

She rolled her eyes. "Yes. Besides that."

I shrugged. "Just wanted to know why I was there, so I explained myself and asked if I could stay for a while."

Lily watched me expectantly. "And?"

"She said she'd think about it."

West leaned back in his seat, smirking. "Well, I'd call that a win.

Better than death by vibrator."

Lily snorted. "Depends on how you're using it." Her smile fell, and her bottom lip slipped between her teeth. "How mad is she at me?"

"I don't know if she's mad, but she's definitely not happy about it. I told you we should have asked her," I said as I took a bite.

She made a know-it-all face. "Well, if she wasn't so prickly when it comes to you, we could have. I'm not using my bed, and you're not getting sleep. It makes sense. Anyway, better to ask for forgiveness, right?"

"Hopefully she lets me stay."

Lily gave me a reassuring smile. "I'll see if I can convince her."

I smiled back. "Thanks, Lil." I scooped up another bite. "So, what are you two doing today?"

West set his napkin on the table and let out a satisfied sigh. "Absolutely nothing."

"Glorious nothing," Lily added, her face mirroring his. "I'll start rehearsals for the Saratoga summer season next month, but otherwise, it's just a lot of this. I'm still holding out for a weekend trip to the Hamptons. Cooper better come through on that for me." She smiled and stood, picking up her bowl.

West chuckled. "Hell hath no fury."

She made a face at him, still smiling as she moved to pick up his bowl.

He stopped her as he stood, taking the bowls. "I got this, babe."

Lily handed over the bowls and reached up on her tip toes to kiss him on the cheek. "I guess I'll go get ready for the day, then. Leave you boys to gossip. I've got to prepare my ass for Rose's reaming."

"I'm sure it won't be so bad," West said half-heartedly as he rinsed off the dishes.

She snorted. "Yeah, right. I'm prepared for her to eat my face off like a piranha."

He looked over his shoulder at her. "Sounds scary."

But she waved a hand. "Nah, I can handle it. Plus, I earned it."

And with that, she turned and headed into the bathroom.

I took another bite as West set the bowls in the drying rack. He turned and leaned against the counter with a dish towel slung over his shoulder, shaking his head at me, smiling proudly. "Staying with Rose. How about that?"

"Hey, man. She hasn't agreed yet."

He folded his arms. "Yeah, but she will."

"How can you be so sure?" My brow climbed.

"Because there's no good reason not to."

I chuckled and poked at my breakfast. "Yeah, I'm sure Rose could find a reason or two."

"Or three or four, but in the end, they're all bogus, and she knows it. Don't worry, man."

"I guess I could always try to sleep in my own bed," I joked. "Maybe kick you guys out, send you to christen Lily's bed and keep Rose up instead."

West laughed. "Like anything could keep Rose up when she's fully immersed in the cave."

"Perfect. So when are you moving?"

"We actually talked about it. I mean, it made a lot more sense when Maggie was sleeping in there. There's not enough money in the world to convince me to sleep with Lily eight feet away from my little sister. Plus, I have a full-sized bed, and Lily has a twin. Not to say we couldn't move the beds, but that's … well, that's *moving*. I just don't know exactly what we're doing yet, you know?"

"Yeah, I get it. It's fine. I'll keep paying rent here, Lily can keep paying rent there, and we'll figure it out when we have to."

He nodded. "All right. Rose will come around. Maybe in more ways than one."

I raised a brow. "Somehow I doubt that."

West smirked. "Oh, ye of little faith. Lily and I have a theory."

"Oh?" I took a bite, amused.

"Yup. The only thing in between you two is the two of you." He looked proud of himself.

"Well, I'm glad you have the answer," I said flatly. "Should be easy to solve."

"I'm just saying that maybe this will be good for the two of you, bunking together. But maybe you can find a way to get through the other side and into something new."

I wished it were true, wished it wholeheartedly. "It's more complicated than that."

He made a face. "You're not the only people in the world to ever break up."

I nodded and spooned some oatmeal into my mouth, pausing for a moment. "That's true. But I burned the bridge with her. She doesn't want to forgive me."

His dark brow arched. "And you know because you've asked?"

"I asked after I brought Veronica to the bar, yeah." I set down my spoon and sat back in my chair. "Look, here's the thing. I get where she's coming from. Being with her was like …" I looked away at nothing in particular. "It was like seeing in color for the first time after a lifetime of black and white. It was too much, too big, so I broke up with her because I was scared of how I felt. And after everything with Veronica … well, there was no going back. *She doesn't want to forgive me.* She tolerates me at best."

West wiped his hand on the towel with a disapproving look on his face. "So, what, you're just giving up?"

"I'm just being realistic."

"Rose can be worn down. Lily does it all the time."

I chuckled. "Yeah, I've seen it. But the same physics don't apply to *me* and Rose as they do *Lily* and Rose."

He hung the towel up and took a seat at the table again. "I'm not suggesting you go full white knight and try to get her back, but maybe you can at least to find a way to remind her why she didn't used to merely tolerate you."

"If I agree, will you drop it?" I took a last bite of my breakfast and pushed away from the table.

He smirked. "Probably not. It's leg day today. Meet you at the gym after work?"

"I'm supposed to meet Rose to talk about our sleeping arrangements, so I might have to skip it," I said as I washed out my bowl and set it on the rack.

He pointed at me. "Don't puss out. You'll end up with chicken legs."

"Who needs a trainer when I have you?"

"Exactly. Good luck with Rose, man."

I chuckled. "Thanks. I'm gonna need it."

I walked through the apartment and into my room, feeling … displaced would be a good word, I guess. It was my home, the only place I'd ever called my own, but I felt foreign there lately. Lily had moved in all but officially, and as much as I loved the two of them, and as happy as I was for them, I felt like a voyeur most days. As if I were intruding, even though they never put that out or treated me as an inconvenience. It just all of a sudden felt like *their* space. And that underscored my loneliness.

I'd been alone my whole life, but I'd never been lonely, not until I found love in my friends. Because once you have something, you can lose it. It almost makes you wonder if it's easier to be alone.

Solitude had always been a part of who I was, and it was a place where I found comfort. When I was a kid, I spent hours alone sketching, painting, learning mediums. Just me and my headphones. I was used to isolation, used the time alone to recharge. Find my center.

I made my way into my room, which was more of an art studio than bedroom. A rubber mat covered almost all of the hardwood, and my easel stood close to the window with an unfinished charcoal piece waiting for me. Canvases stood stacked against every free inch of wall space, some blank, mostly not, and my bed and dresser stood against the only wall not otherwise occupied.

I pulled open a drawer, rummaging around for jeans, then headed to the tiny closet, which was only big enough to hang a few shirts, deciding on my short-sleeved houndstooth button-down, thinking about Rose.

But then again, I was always thinking about Rose.

How do you move on when she's the only thing that feels right? I'd been looking for the answer for seven long months, since we'd gone our separate ways.

Except we didn't go our separate ways.

Rose was everywhere. Habits. Down the hall. Every day, always. She lived in my thoughts, in my heart, present in nearly every moment of my life. She was my ghost, haunting me, and I couldn't escape. I didn't know if I even wanted to.

It was my penance.

I stared at my reflection in the bathroom mirror, jaw set as I combed my hair back. My face was just about the only part of my body not covered in ink, and I saw the hardness in my brow, in my eyes. As if the tattoos were my warning label. *Damaged goods. Beware. Turn back now.* I saw them as a reminder of all I'd been through, though I knew it was in part to keep people away. They told you what you'd get, if you dared take the chance. And most people weren't willing to take the chance.

Maybe West was right. Maybe Rose and I could find a way through, even though I'd conceded to exist in the state of purgatory we found ourselves in. Maybe there was a way out. Maybe this was a chance.

A flicker of hope ran through me.

If I got the chance, I wouldn't waste it.

Flesh & Ink

PATRICK

Summer in new york was in full effect, though it was early enough that we weren't to the unbearable humidity that made most New Yorkers flee to Long Island at the first opportunity. I smiled as I approached Tonic, the tattoo parlor where I'd worked for almost ten years. The sign over the door was black and white filigree, like an old apothecary label, and I pulled open the heavy black door, greeted by the sounds of Nirvana playing on the overhead speakers.

I jerked a chin at Shep, standing behind the counter as I walked across the planked floors and to my booth near the front of the shop.

Tonic was one of the top shops in Manhattan, in business since the late 90s. The talent that Joel and his younger brother Shep had acquired was noteworthy enough to have won a host of awards, and we were all booked out weeks in advance.

I counted it as absolute luck that Joel had taken a chance on a skinny, quiet, eighteen-year-old junkie. I didn't realize it at the time, but I was looking for more, looking for something real, and I found it when I walked into Tonic. If you can imagine a father figure, a big brother, and a best friend, all rolled up into one, that was Joel. No telling where I'd have ended up, if it weren't for him.

I set down my bag and took a seat on my red leather stool, grabbing a pair of black rubber gloves to start setting up. I rolled over to the antique cabinet where my supplies were kept to gather ink cups, ink, and needles, using the sketch I'd done — a cobalt photo-realistic butterfly framed by a set of complex geometric lines — as a guide for sizes. I glanced in the speckled old mirror next to my cabinet to see Shep air drumming "Smells Like Teen Spirit," and I shook my head, smiling.

Our booths lined one side of the shop, each separated by low walls, keeping the shop open. The walls were either black or covered in velvet damask wallpaper all the way up to the brick and exposed piping, and each booth was decorated per the personality of the artist who filled the space, though all with a macabre, Victorian feel. Mine featured an oil painting of a skull I'd done, taxidermy crows, the speckled rococo mirror, and a series of smaller acrylic paintings I'd done of Victorian girls in corsets, all in elaborate, oval frames.

Joel walked up from the back and leaned on my wall, smiling. He was thirty-eight, though if I didn't know better, I'd peg him much closer to my age, a decade younger than he was. His beard was thick and dark, hair long on the top, shaved on the sides, and he was covered neck to heel in tattoos, with bright eyes and a comforting smile.

He smirked at me, which was the expression he wore most of the time. "How's it going, Tricky?"

I smiled. "Can't complain." I fed my machine's cord through a plastic cord bag and hooked the end on my tray. "How about you? Did you go to that show last night?"

"Paper Fools, yeah." He threaded his fingers together, jumbling the letters tattooed there to say *TSHHAIT* rather than *THIS* and *THAT* like they usually did. "Dean always sends me passes when they're in town. Perks of being his tattoo artist."

"Perks are never bad." I picked up my grip and inspected my needles.

"Well, not these kinds, anyway. Yeah, the show was great. Shep and Ramona came too, and Ramona brought some chick to set me up with. Tara, I think. No ... Tina." He still didn't look sure of himself.

"You bang her?"

Joel snorted. "Of course I did. I'm alive, aren't I?" He eyed me, still smirking. "So, what are you doing Thursday night?"

I gave him a flat look. "I don't have any plans."

"Great. We'll go to Habits for your birthday, 'cause you know I didn't forget."

"Of course you didn't." I said as I bent the needle I'd use for the line work and fed it through the grip.

"Perfect. Glad you agree that it's a good plan. See? Now, that didn't hurt, did it?"

"Only my soul, Joel. Only my soul."

He laughed, and it was a big, comforting sound, full of amusement at my discomfort. "Invite West and everybody, and make sure Rose is off so she can hang out with you." He waggled his brows.

I grabbed a couple of rubber bands and wrapped them around my machine before covering it in plastic. "You're just as bad as West and Lily, you know that? Bunch of shitty matchmakers you are."

"You still sneaking in to sleep over there?"

I sighed as I set down my machine and started filling the plastic ink cups. "Yeah, but the jig is up. She busted me this morning."

He sucked in a breath through his teeth dramatically. "She put you out?"

"Not yet. She wanted the day to think about it, so we'll see tonight. I mean, it's not like I don't have somewhere to go. Like my own place."

"You can always crash with me, if you need a place to stay," he said, suddenly a little more serious.

"I know. Thanks, man. But you've done enough for me over the years."

"Psh, letting you surf my couch for a couple of years isn't exactly worth sainthood."

I met his eyes. "No, but saving me from myself is."

He shrugged, looking away. "You would have done the same. Anyway, here's to hoping Rosie sees the light and lets you stay. God know the two of you just need to lock yourselves in a room until you make up." His brows raised. "Hey, new birthday plans."

I laughed.

The bell over the door rang, and Penny, Ramona, and Veronica walked in, laughing. Another thing our parlor was known for — the three hot chicks who pierced and tattooed there. All three of them had been featured in tattoo magazines and calendars. They were roommates and best friends — Penny, whose hair was shamrock green this month, Ramona, tall and blond, and Veronica, the raven of the three.

"Morning, ladies," Shep called from behind the register.

"Hey, Shep," they answered in unison, then broke out laughing.

The girls dispersed, Penny making her way back to her piercing booth as Ramona strutted over to Shep.

He leaned down and tapped his cheek. "Knock me one right here, gorgeous."

She smiled wide and obliged. When she turned, she hung a hand on her hip. "Hey, Joel, are you gonna call Tricia after last night?"

His face lit up like a light bulb, and he snapped his fingers. "Tricia. That was it. And no, probably not."

She rolled her eyes. "This is why we can't have nice things, Joel."

He shrugged.

Veronica walked past us and into the booth behind mine, and Joel and I watched her like a couple of cats. She was gorgeous — pitch black hair pulled back in a twist that looked straight out of an old movie, green eyes always lined and winged. Her pretty little nose was pierced with thin gold rings, twice in one nostril and her septum, with another in the center of her bottom lip, right at the swell. She had sleeved arms and smaller tattoos behind her ear, along her collarbone, down her thighs, visible through her ripped up tights she wore under her shorts.

Like I said. Gorgeous. Somehow hard and soft, her body modded to make her look like walking art. Too bad I wasn't even remotely interested in her. Even worse — I'd dragged her into the mess with Rose, knowing full well that I wasn't really into her.

Don't look at me that way. I really thought I knew what I was doing.

She smiled at us as she set her bag down. "What's up, Tricky? Joel? You two are looking good."

Joel nodded at her. "Not looking so bad yourself, Ronnie." He pushed off from the counter and stepped into the middle of the room. "Listen up, everybody," he announced.

Drew, Max, and Eli, the other artists, walked out from the back, and everyone turned their attention to Joel.

"So, Tricky's birthday is in a couple of days, and he told me the one thing he *really* wants is a party. One where everyone is there just for little old him. Preferably one where we all sing him Happy Birthday in public."

Everyone whooped and laughed, and I shook my head, smiling.

"Let's all go to Habits to celebrate. If you all embarrass him properly, I'll buy lunch for the shop the next day. Deal?"

Everyone chimed, "Deal."

He smiled at me like a bastard and walked to his station, which was right in front of mine, just inside the window so people could see him work from the street. Everyone dispersed again as a couple of clients walked in, making their way to Shep at the counter.

Veronica was busy covering her tray in plastic wrap, but she glanced over at me as she worked. "So, Habits, huh?"

"Sounds like it."

"Didn't have much say?"

"Do I ever?" We shared a look, and she chuckled.

"Classic Joel." She eyed me a little warily. "So, I'm guessing Rose will be there?"

I nodded and rolled back to my desk, hanging my elbows on the surface. "Probably."

"Because I haven't seen her since …"

"I'm sure it'll be fine," I said, hoping it was the truth. "She's cool."

She chuffed. "I'll take your word for it."

I raised an eyebrow, and she raised one right back.

"What?" She reached for the paper towels and began to tear and fold pieces, stacking them in the corner of her tray. "I guess I can't I blame her for being frosty to me when we met. You should have told me what was going on before you took me there that night."

Regret. There it was again, rising to the surface unbidden, with no warning. "Yeah, well, there are a lot of things I should have done."

Her face softened. "They say that's how we learn. But what the fuck do 'they' know, anyway?"

I chuckled.

"So, what do you want for your birthday?" She slipped her machine cord through a plastic tube and hung it on the edge of her tray.

I crossed my ankles with a sigh. "I guess 'to be left alone' is out."

"If Joel has anything to do with it, yeah."

I thought it over, and a simple answer dawned on me. "How about your favorite book?"

She smiled as she gathered supplies and lined them up on her tray. "You're a big reader? Who knew?"

"Yeah, well, you don't live with a Lit student for four years and not learn to love it."

She tsked and shook her head. "Tricky Evans, full of surprises."

The bell over the door rang, and I turned to find my first client walking in. I applied the stencil and laid her down in my chair, pressed my hands against her skin, machine in my hand as I drew and shaded the lines and dots, slow and steady. Needles and blood, raw flesh and ink, all to the steady buzz of the machine in my hand, making my mark in a way that would last as long as the body under my hand.

Sausage Stack

ROSE

To say my day was long would have been an understatement. I sat for hours in very uncomfortable clothes in a very stiff chair, which stood packed into a very quiet, very full room. My only armor against boredom was my book, except I couldn't *concentrate* on the freaking book on account of Patrick.

I tried not to think about his naked chest, or the swell of his lips as he asked me to stay, or his eyes that burned a hole in my resolve, just like they always did. But I was Rosie: Extinguisher of Flames. Particularly Patrick flames. I'd become a pro over the months. Ice Queen, extraordinare. Cool as fuck. What happened between us was water under the bridge. In the past. He asked me to stay, and I'd think about it logically.

I could be logical and reasonable and leave all my feelings out of it. Probably.

Then I remembered that his naked chest had been sleeping twenty feet away from me for a month, right there, right across the hall, which sent me from logical to totally-not-logical-ever-because-fuck-him.

Of course, he wasn't the only one to blame for the sneaky fuckery going on. Lily gave him permission without talking to me. She let my ex sleep in my apartment without my knowledge, which was creepy and shitty and not okay. I couldn't figure out what would have convinced her to sanction that. I'd get to the bottom of it, but first, I'd make her sweat. I hadn't messaged her, and I knew she knew I knew, and I *also* knew she knew I was pissed.

Sometimes the best way to say what you feel is silence.

I put my book away and replaced it with my notebook and pen. First I doodled a variety of images to depict my mood: a hand flipping the bird, a gun shooting a flag that said *No*, cartoon flames, and a brontosaurus with its head in a tub of popcorn. I glanced at the clock. It had been fifteen minutes.

So I turned the page and stared at the blue lines until they were blurry.

I would see Patrick tonight, and I had to give him an answer. There wouldn't be time for a conversation with Lily. I had to decide on my own.

I wrote two word in the top margin: PROS and CONS.

Then I chewed on the end of my pen for a really long time.

Personally, the pros were few. Maybe more naked chest. I wouldn't really have to see him, if he kept up the sneaking like he had been. He wasn't really hurting anything. Not really.

There was really only one con, but it was too real.

I don't trust myself around him.

As much as I liked to pretend that I was completely over Patrick, the truth was that I missed him. I missed my friend. I missed the man who'd woken me with a kiss and left me with a smile. I missed his touch. His words. His presence.

But I wasn't allowed to miss him. Not after he dumped me and brought the hottest girl I'd ever seen to *my* bar when I was working. And then he tried to backpedal. He was sorry, he'd said. He begged me to see that he'd made a mistake.

The hurt was indescribable. He was right. He'd made a mistake, but there was no way I'd open myself up to him again, and that's exactly what I told him, just before I told him to get out.

We'd never spoken of it again.

It was weeks before I even made eye contact with him.

Why so cold, you ask? Isn't he so damaged and beautiful and *sorry*? And the answer is yes, he is. But he hurt me deeply enough that I knew there was no way I'd let it go. There was no way to fix *us*, not with that amount of baggage on both sides.

See, I don't do a lot of third chances. You read that right. You want a do-over, you get one and only one. If Patrick had come back to me before Veronica and changed his mind, I would have welcomed him with open arms. Granted, I would have been more wary the second time, but I would have taken him back in a heartbeat. In fact, I felt deep down that he'd come back to me. But then he paraded a girl in front of me not twenty-four hours after we'd broken up.

There are things I'll forgive, but that humiliation is not one of them. And being cold was the only way to insulate my broken heart.

I glanced back over my list, realizing that I didn't have a single reason to say no, nothing that I could stand up on, at least. It wasn't my room. It wasn't my bed. So I could put my feelings in the backseat and be a grown up about it, rather than saying no just because he made me itchy.

I closed my notebook with a sigh, feeling better only because I'd made a decision. The decision itself was another thing entirely, but my mind was quiet enough that I was able to pick up my book again, throwing myself into the escape of the story. At least that would have a happy ending.

Mercifully, I wasn't chosen for the jury, and I made my way home through rush hour traffic, grateful that I didn't have a normal job. Bodies packed into the train, wall to wall, some fortunate enough to have a seat, the rest of us doomed to stand next to each other, in a space that smelled of metal and people, avoiding eye contact at all costs. The doors opened and closed at each stop, and streams of people poured in and out before we'd move again.

By the time I was climbing the stairs of my building, my mood had reached an epically sour, smelly state. I had an hour before Patrick would be over, so I could at least change and maybe have a drink before I had that conversation. I felt a little better at the thought, though I still grumbled as I unlocked my door and dropped my purse, closing the door a little harder than I meant to.

Patrick popped off the couch, and my hand flew to my chest, eyes wide. "Jesus, Tricky!"

He yawned and rubbed his smooth jaw, seemingly unaffected. "Sorry. You said you wanted to talk, so here I am."

I fumed as I kicked off my shoes, taking a deep breath to vent the heat. "I thought you said you were off at six?"

"My last appointment canceled." He looked apologetic. And gorgeous. "I didn't mean to scare you."

"It's fine."

He moved to the end of the couch, waiting for me to sit next to him, so I did, despite my crawling nerves and thumping heart. I caught a whiff of him, the clean smell of soap and laundry, and found myself leaning in to breathe him deeper.

I course-corrected, turning so my back was against the armrest as I eyed that pretty bastard, wishing I wasn't in this position. "All right. Here's the deal."

He relaxed a hair, which irritated me for some reason.

I tried not to scowl. "I can't think of a single reason why you can't stay here, so I feel like I should say yes."

He nodded, looking a little less comfortable at my phrasing.

"Lily's obviously fine with it, and it's her bed and her room. I'll agree to it, but I have three conditions."

Patrick shifted. "Let's have it."

"Try to be gone or asleep while I'm here, okay? I don't want to worry about whether or not I have a bra on, or if I'm going to walk in on you in the john."

He smirked. "All right."

"No moving your stuff in. You sleep here, that's it. Got it?"

"Got it."

"We're not roommates, okay? So no —" I waved a hand as I thought about how to phrase it. "I don't know. *Bonding,* or whatever. Just be a ghost."

He nodded. "Consider me invisible."

I sighed, hoping this wasn't going to be a huge disaster. *You can do this. It's fine. Totally fine. Boundaries are defined.* "So, that's that. I'm meeting up with Lily in a bit and need to change. If I don't get out of these clothes, I'm going to freak out."

He smirked, and my eyes narrowed.

I pointed at him. "Don't crack a bad joke, Tricky."

Patrick put up his hands. "Who, me? Never." He smiled, and the urge to slap him crept in. Slap him and then kiss him for being charming when I wanted to hate him. "So, I know I'm invisible and all, but I hang out here for the cable regardless. Is that still allowed if we're not," he made a hand gesture like I had earlier, "*bonding*?"

"Fine," I answered, doing my best to not make it sound like one of those other F-words before standing to make my way to my room.

"Rose?" he called after me.

I turned. "Yeah?"

His eyes burned hot on mine, blazing and intense. I don't think he even knew he was doing it — he just existed in a constant state of smolder. "Thanks."

I smiled, hoping my knees weren't about to buckle under the weight of his stare. And then I cranked up the freezer. "You're welcome."

Getting out of that room became priority one. I tried not to hurry away, letting out another heavy breath as soon as my bedroom door was closed and there was sheetrock and timber between us.

Priority two was getting the polyester off my body.

Seriously — I never wanted to work in a profession where I had to keep the words "slacks" and "blouses" in my fashion vocabulary. I folded the dark pants and button down neatly. They were a little wrinkled — our closets are so small, there's no way to hang anything up in there, not really. But there was no way in hell I would have ever been convinced to iron that morning.

Lily and I were going to Habits, my home away from home, one of my favorite places to hang out, even though I worked there. Some people hate going to work when they're not working, but Habits was never like that for me. Maybe it's the vibe. Maybe there's some magic about the bar that made me feel like I was somewhere I belonged. Either way, I never minded.

I had no intention of dressing up for the occasion, especially since I knew I'd be peeling Lily's grape. So I pulled on a pair of black leggings covered in what looked like bleach spots, a black V-neck, and my favorite flannel. Cotton. Glorious cotton and elastic waists as far as the eye could see.

I sat at the foot of my bed and stuffed my feet into my combat boots, sighing as I pulled my hair back to get it off my neck.

That's better.

I felt a little more like myself when I walked out of my room, beelining for my bag as I tried to avoid eye contact with Patrick.

"Have fun," he said, his voice deep and velvety.

I grabbed my bag and pretended to look for something. "Don't sit too close to the TV or you'll ruin your eyes."

He chuckled.

"See you later, Tricky," I said politely and left the apartment before I made it any more awkward.

Three steps down the hall, I remembered that I was pissed at Lily — I'd been too distracted by Patrick. In half a dozen more steps, I was banging on the door as a warning before opening it with a scowl on my face, ready to blow.

Lily sat in West's lap in the armchair, long legs slung over the side, arms around his neck. They seemed to just be talking — talking and smiling and looking absolutely perfect. Which they were. We all knew they *would* be perfect together, and long before they realized it.

My anger abated at the sight of them together. Not entirely, but enough that I felt more wry and less stabby.

"Hey, asshole," I said, mostly to Lily, as I closed the door firmly. "You ready to go? Because I'm pretty sure you owe me a drink or nine."

Her cheeks flushed as she looked up at me. "I mean, if that'll make it better, I'll buy you a bottle." She turned her attention back to West just long enough for them to share a simple kiss and a lingering look before she stood.

"You mad at us, Rosie?" West said with that easy smile of his.

I flipped him off, and he chuckled.

"Aw, you know we mean well."

"Which is exactly why I only shot you the bird instead of shooting you in the face."

He snickered.

Lily sighed grabbed her bag. "Come look for me if I haven't texted in an hour. There's no guarantee she's not still packing heat."

I rolled my eyes. "I hate you."

"Lies." She waved at West, and we stepped out into the hallway. "So," she started, overly cheery, "how mad are you? On a scale of one to homicide?"

I shot her a look. "Somewhere between maiming and dismemberment."

"Well, then things could be worse," she joked, but her smile slipped. "I'm sorry I didn't tell you about him sleeping there."

"I mean, what the fuck, Lil?"

"Well, we thought you'd—"

"Yeah, yeah. You thought I'd freak out, right? Well, here we are, and I'll tell you *this* freakout is way worse than the freakout I'd have had if you'd asked me."

"But you would have said no, and he needed rest, you know?"

"Well, *maybe* you could stop banging like monkeys all night long so he could sleep."

She put her hands up as we walked down the stairs. "Seriously, we aren't *that* loud. And anyway, why does it matter if he sleeps there?"

"Because it does. I mean, what was your endgame? Did you think I wouldn't figure it out?"

She wrinkled her nose and sniffed. "I dunno. He pulled it off for a month."

I made a noncommittal noise.

"I kind of hoped you'd be okay with it."

"I mean, Jesus. You should have just gotten me drunk and convinced me to do it. At least then I wouldn't have tried to pistol-whip him with your vibrator."

She busted out laughing, and I couldn't help it — I laughed too.

"Fuck, it really was ridiculous. His eyes looked like freaking pool balls." I peeled my eyelids open and stuck my face in Lily's.

She was still laughing as she pulled open the building door. "I would have paid money to see that."

"I kind of wish I'd hit him. Give him a big ol' mushroom stamp right on the forehead. Bam." I slapped my hands together.

Lily breathed out, trying not to giggle anymore. "God. I really am sorry I didn't tell you."

I shrugged. "Whatever. It's done now, and you were right about my reaction."

"What'd you end up telling him?"

"What else could I say? I told him he could stay and gave him some ground rules. Which he actually immediately broke by asking me if he could stay and watch TV," I realized.

"Well, it's not like that's a new thing."

"I know, but I don't want to hang out with him, dude. I need him away from me."

Lily nodded and said "Right," like she didn't mean it.

I shot her a look. "What?"

"Nothing." Her voice was a little high. "I mean, keeping away from him hasn't really done you any favors, but you know what's best for you."

My eyes narrowed. "Ugh, don't get all passive-aggressive on me. Just say what you mean."

She shrugged. "I'm just saying maybe you'll get over it if you're around each other, that's all."

I scoffed. "Yeah, right. Just get over it. Sure."

"Anyway, new topic, since this one is obviously sore and worn out. How was jury duty?"

"About as fun as I'd imagine stapling my lips together would be," I said as we walked toward Habits. "At least I didn't get picked."

She nodded. "Bright sides. I like it."

"What have you guys been doing all day?"

"Nothing. It's been amazing. Is it weird that I never really got why people took vacations?"

I gave her a flat look. "Yes."

She chuckled. "I mean, theoretically, I get it, but all I've ever known is dance, twenty-four-seven, ever since I can remember. Plus, I've just never had anyone to really go with, to share it with."

I flagged a hand. "Uh, hello? Chopped liver, nice to meet you."

She laughed again. "Right, because you always go on vacation."

I shrugged. "I'm just saying. I would have gone with you."

"Well, thank you for that. Good to know."

I laughed and bumped her arm.

"Anyway, it's given West and me a ton of time to hang out."

I smiled at her. "God, you're such a mush."

"I know," she beamed. "It's so weird. Like, he was my best friend—"

I gave her another look.

"—*Besides* you—"

"Thank you."

"—But it's like I didn't really know him. Not like I do now."

I snorted. "Oh, like on the biblical level?"

She flushed. "I mean that, obviously, but just … I don't know. All of him. Everything is different and the same, like I unlocked something in him and he did in me. Does that make sense?"

My smile this time was knowing, though I knew it held a hint of sadness. "It does."

"But, I mean, the biblical level is pretty rad in itself. Definitely not the worst thing ever."

"Ha. I'm sure, especially given the fact that you get all porno every night. Tricky can't even handle your super loud fuckery anymore."

She made a stinky face. "That's awkward."

My eyebrows climbed. "Well, maybe if you two brought it down a notch, I wouldn't have my ex begging me to sleep in your old room."

She looked down her nose at me dramatically. "Look, we have needs, and those needs must be fulfilled. I can't say I'm sorry for that.

It really does suck for Tricky, but I don't care if he sleeps in my bed as long as you're okay with it. I'm not using it."

I gave her a hard what-the-fuck stare.

"What?" she asked like I was the crazy one. "I mean, sure, he's your ex, but it's not like you guys aren't still friends."

"Can we put that in air quotes? Because I don't really feel like we're legit friends. I feel like 'we're friends who dated and ruined everything but are still trying to be friends, except it's bullshit.'"

"That's a really long title. I'm not calling you that."

My pause was heavy, my words quiet. "It's a big deal, and you know it."

She nodded. "I know. I just wish it wasn't." We walked in silence for a moment. "Honestly, I think it'll be good for you two. I think you just need to push past the awkward I-miss-your-junk phase and get to the we-cool phase."

I thought about it for a beat. "Maybe you're right."

She looked pleased with herself. "Of course I'm right. I'm the queen of right."

I smiled slyly and stood a little taller. "I know just how to get out of the I-miss-your-junk phase."

"Oh?" Her brow raised.

"I just need to find myself some new junk to worship."

She cackled. "I just pictured you doing hoodoo over a dick shrine."

"I told you to stop going through my things. You're so nosey."

The cackle turned into a sort of sheepy noise.

I snorted. "Oh, my God. You sound like you belong in a barn."

She pushed me in the arm. "Takes one to know one. Your donkey laugh takes the cake."

I pushed her back. "I don't have a donkey laugh."

"Do too." She pointed at me. "I'm getting you whiskey drunk and recording it so I can blackmail you with it. Anyway, I think it's adorable." She pinched my cheek. "So, do I hear this right? You're going to start dating?"

I shrugged. "Why not? Maybe that'll help me un-jam."

She shimmied her shoulders as we approached the bar. "Oh, I'm sure you can find someone to help you *un-jam*."

"Man, you're on a roll." I pulled open the door for her.

"Well, you keep setting me up,' she said with a shrug. "So, what, are you going to get on Tinder and just look for a sausage stack?"

"When you say it like that, how could I not?" Nothing about the statement was enthusiastic.

She rolled her eyes as we walked through the bar. "I don't know, Rose. I skipped the whole dating thing. I just know it's impossible to meet people in New York, so online dating makes sense, even if it's like the Wild West."

I waved at Shelby as we passed, pointing to the back tables. "I'm a bartender, so it's not like I don't get hit on, but it's too close to home or something. I don't want someone to know where I work before our first date, you know? Like, what if he's a creep? Then he can stalk me at work where I can't get away from him."

"Fair enough. All right, so no one who goes to Habits. So … Tinder?" she asked hopefully.

I laughed as we sat in a high booth in the back. "Maybe. OKCupid? Ugh, I don't know. The whole thing makes me twitchy."

Her face lit up and she shook my forearm. "Download the app and let's troll for boys."

"I don't know if I'm ready for that."

"Stop being a baby. It's not like you're agreeing to the sanctity of holy matrimony. If nothing else, just get some play."

I rolled my eyes. "Some play? What are you, a dude from the 90s?"

She ignored me. "Just set up a profile so we can look and see. Look, you don't even have to answer any of them."

"Obviously. But by even having the profile, I'm basically asking for dick pics and creepy propositions."

"Welcome to dating. Come on. Just download the app and let's window shop."

I sighed. "I need a drink for this."

She grinned and slipped out of the booth. "Done. That app better be on your phone by the time I get back, or I'm holding your whiskey hostage."

"Bossy."

"Wuss."

I had a stanky look on my face as I waited for the app to download, and I'm pretty sure it got even uglier when I opened it.

Welcome to OKCupid. Choose your username.

WhiskeyRose9er. Dread crept in, followed by trepidation as my fight or flight kicked in, but I forged on, motivated by whiskey.

I'm not proud. It had been that shitty of a day.

I went through the signup process, and by the time Lily came back, I only had the horrible task of choosing a photo left to undertake.

Lily set down our drinks as she slid in next to me, craning her neck to see my screen. "Oooh, profile pic. What are you going to use?"

"I don't know. You decide."

She grabbed my phone. "I was hoping you'd say that." She opened my photos, and I picked up my drink to take a long swig. "This one. It's slutty *and* classy. Perfect do-me eyes to cleavage ratio." She handed the phone back to me.

I sighed. "All right. Now what?"

"Now, we search!" She was full-on grinning.

"You are way too excited about this." I chose from the search options, and we waited— me nervously, Lily was bouncing — while it pulled up matches. The screen filled with a long line of hotter guys than I'd prepared myself for.

Lily blinked. "Wow. I'm actually kind of impressed."

"This is how annoying it is to meet someone. We all have to resort to a catalog." I swiped through the list.

She pointed at one. "What about that one? *TylerStack88*?"

"Too 'bro.'" I swiped again.

"Oh, my God. *SacredSnake*? Please tell me that's not a reference to his dick."

I looked closer at the photo. "Based on his jizzed up bathroom mirror, I'm going with probably."

"Hmm," she hummed as she took a drink. "Ooh, What about him? *SkateTreason*? He's cute, his picture's good, and he skateboards, look. Click on him."

I did and we read through his witty profile. He sounded cool, but I paused. *Too good to be true.* "I'll save him for later. Let's see what else Cupid has hiding." I kept swiping. "Look at this guy. *UndyingArt*. I love this picture of him, so cute. Nice jaw. Tattoos."

"Wow, Rosie," she said, her voice heavy with sarcasm. "Artist with a nice jaw and tattoos?"

I smiled sweetly. "Fuck you, Lil. I have a type. Anyway, he's blond, so it's basically nothing like Tricky." I opened up his profile and read his well-worded bio. "Says here he makes furniture."

"A man who works with his hands. He can build you a bed and then bang you on it."

I snorted. "I'm intrigued."

"Message him."

I made a face again. "Shouldn't I, I don't know, think about it for a minute? Keep browsing?"

"Just message him and ask him for coffee. If you find a better one, ask him out too."

I wrinkled my nose.

"It's just coffee for chrissake. You're not asking him for his DNA."

I contemplated his profile again, not at all sure of myself. Look, as hard as I played, and as much as I wanted to move on, it wasn't that easy. But I needed to do something. It was time for me to really move on, especially if he was going to be staying with me. After all this time, if we were going to be friends, I had to change, do something different. It was the healthy thing to do, I told myself.

"Well, Operation Get Over Tricky's Junk is off to a great start."

I rolled my eyes. "You suck."

"You're the one who won't pull the trigger. Maybe you're just not ready."

"Am too."

She folded her arms. all sassy. "Prove it."

I threw the shade right back at her. "Fine, pusher." I clicked message button and paused for a long second, swinging back and forth between jumping and running.

"Chicken."

I glared at her, then turned back to my messages. *Rip off the Band-Aid, Rose.* I typed out a message, hoping I didn't sound desperate or dweeby, reading it over once.

I'd love to meet up for coffee, you free tomorrow?

Short, simple, to the point. I hit send and half-tossed my phone onto the table. "There. Happy?"

Lily grinned again. "So happy. Want to look for more?"

I picked up my drink. "I want to get wasted and hide under a rock."

She laughed. "It's not like everyone doesn't do this."

"Then why does it feel so pathetic? Shopping for a date online is exactly like buying condoms. You stand there scanning eighty different packages, trying to hurry because of some lingering shame, topped with the worry that someone might see you. I mean, what do you get? Ribbed? Extra sensitive? Fire and Ice? You never know what you like until you try one, so you take a risk on some shit like Fire and Ice and it ends up being a burning crotch nightmare."

Lily burst out laughing.

"Seriously, whose idea was it to put Icy Hot on your genitals? I'm pretty sure that cautionary tale has been in every teen movie ever." I took a drink. "Like I said — it's exactly like online dating. I don't want Fire and Ice in my lady parts. I just need some nice, normal, no-gimmick business that won't get me pregnant."

My phone buzzed in my hand.

I gaped when I saw the message. "Oh, my God. It's UndyingArt. He says he's free tomorrow."

She squealed like a pre-teen who just got the newest *Tiger Beat* in the mail. "What are you going to say?"

"Well, it'd be kind of weird to say no at this point," I said as I answered him, setting the place, and he agreed almost immediately. Butterflies took off in my stomach. "We're meeting at Roasted tomorrow afternoon." I set down my phone and smiled at her. "A date with a cute artist."

"How do you feel?"

I bobbed my head, rolling the feeling around. "Good, I think. That was way easier than I thought it would be, and kind of a rush. I thought it would take longer to find someone I wanted to go out with than four-point-two seconds."

"Well, no one would ever accuse you of being indecisive."

I raised my glass. "That, my friend, is very true."

Negative Space

PATRICK

wasn't sure how late it was, only that it had been long enough that the voice in the back of my mind told me I should probably leave or go to bed before she came home. But I couldn't bring myself to do it, just recrossed my ankles with my eyes on my sketchbook, telling myself I was just comfortable. That the next time I got up, I'd go to sleep. That I definitely wasn't waiting for her to come home so I could see her.

Music played softly from her portable speaker, a beat to drive my hand as it guided the charcoal across the page in heavy strokes. A curve and a line for her lips. The swoop of her hair. The angle of her jaw. The smallest smile resting just in the corner of her mouth as she looked away.

I knew every detail of Rose's face, every expression.

I pictured her in moments permanently imprinted in my mind.

As she lay in bed next to me on some otherwise unmemorable morning. After I kissed her for the first time. When I told her I wanted to end it, her face as flat and smooth as glass. I thought she didn't care.

Wrong.

It wasn't her fault, what had happened between us. I just didn't know how to handle what I felt for her. I didn't even know what my feelings *were.* Not until it was too late.

And now, after everything, I somehow found myself bunking with the girl I couldn't let go. I pushed away the thought that this could be my chance, not wanting to hope. In my experience, hope led to disappointment. But if nothing else, maybe Rose and I could at least find a way to mend things on some level. I blew it up, so I figured it was up to me to figure out how it all fit back together, one piece at a time. Even just friends would be better than nothing, better than what we'd been over the last few months.

I knew what nothing felt like, and I never wanted to go back to that.

Life could have been so much harder than it had been for me. I never went hungry. I was never beaten or abused. I had a roof over my head and clothes on my back. But I couldn't say I ever felt loved or wanted. Not that I could remember, anyway.

My father — The Sergeant, we called him — was in the Army, and it suited him almost too well. I sometimes wondered if he could have survived in a civilian life, a civilian job, the quiet, hardened man I knew who valued structure and order over everything. I suppose it was why we never saw eye-to-eye — I had the rebellion gene, thanks to my mom.

Sometimes I think I remember what it was like when I was very young, though part of me thinks it's just a recreation of an old photo, a retold story from someone else's memory rather than one of my own. But I remember us happy, even though it's a fleeting feeling — as soon as I touch the thought, it's gone. I remember the three of us laughing, holding hands as we watched the giraffes with their long black tongues, necks stretched to reach the green leaves near the viewing platform.

I was nine when she left us, and I think she took the best part of him with her. Maybe she just normalized him somehow, or maybe she was a buffer that made everything feel like it was fine. Either way, he was never the same after she left. I don't think he really knew what to do with me, and we never understood each other. Temperamentally, he and I were very much alike — stoic, avoiding what we didn't know how to deal with, leaving things unsaid and unresolved. I stayed out of his way, and he stayed out of mine.

Art was my only constant, the place — the *only* place — where I could be open and honest. Over the years, I filled sketchbook after book, never taking classes, never expecting it to amount to anything. It was just what I did, something to fill my soul and the silence of my life. We never lived anywhere for more than a year before we were re-stationed, which meant I never really had a chance to make friends. So I was the weird, quiet kid who wore mostly black, with charcoal-smudged fingers and hard eyes, smoking under the bleachers.

When I turned sixteen, The Sergeant announced we were moving again and it just hit me. I didn't want to go. I didn't want to live with him. I wanted to go to New York, start a life for myself.

He didn't even put up a fight when I told him, just gave me a couple grand and told me to call him if I got in any trouble.

I never called. Neither did he.

It had been more than ten years since then. Sometimes I wondered about him. If he found a new wife. Had more kids. If he was happy. Sometimes I wondered if he wondered about me. But usually I didn't think about him at all.

I'd taken a bus from Fort Rucker, Alabama, to New York with nothing but what was in my dad's old canvas army-green duffle bag, used the money to rent a room at the Vanderbilt YMCA for a month, and found a job at an Italian restaurant bussing tables.

It was there that I met a gangly blond kid, a couple years older than me with a smile like Christmas morning and the ability to make me laugh like no one I'd ever met. Seth was my first friend, the first person to make me feel included. It was the first time I'd ever been happy. He lived with his buddies, Danny and Sarah, and said they had room for me, if I wanted to stay. And of course I wanted to stay. I wanted to stay forever.

But what I thought was good and real was just an illusion. I followed Seth down the rabbit hole all the same.

I'd done drugs before — smoked a little weed, tripped on mushrooms — but nothing like what I walked into with Seth. Molly — ecstasy — was the first step for me, the easy push, something to make you feel like everything was going to be just fine, the overload of serotonin that made all of my problems, past or future, seem small and trivial. Then it was ketamine, heavy limbs and stretched out nights spent just existing. And through it all, I felt like I finally had a home. That I had a family. That I belonged. And I was so in love with the idea that I sacrificed myself to hang on to the feeling.

One night, Jared, our dealer, came over and brought a needle kit. Free samples of China White. Like nothing we'd ever felt before, he said, and he was right. It was like nothing I ever felt again, even though I chased it every time I put a needle in my arm.

The next two years were a blur, days and nights running together like dripping paint. The four of us split rent in a shitty two-bedroom in Hell's Kitchen, working so we could get high. Then Seth started peddling for Jared, and the cycle went around and around, faster, deeper, darker — until we were all lost.

I remember the day I *woke up* in both senses of the word. The metallic tang of unwashed bodies hung in the thick air, still and stagnant from long, slow breaths and closed doors and windows. I didn't know what time it was, what day it was, as I opened my heavy lids, mouth sticky. I looked over at Seth, hanging half off his rumpled bed, the knuckles of one hand dangling just over the floor. His face was turned to mine, eyes closed, ringed with dark shadows, hair more yellow than golden, dark and thick with oil. His needle kit lay on the bed next to him, the cigar box open, contents strewn around it.

I didn't recognize him. I didn't recognize myself. And it was then I knew I needed more out of life than I was giving myself.

I didn't have a diploma, so my job options were slim. But I could draw. I saw an article about Tonic in a magazine and wondered if being a tattoo artist was a possibility. You didn't need a diploma or degree, you just apprenticed and practiced and *became* what you wanted to be.

And that's exactly what I did. Walked into that shop where — I learned later — it was nearly impossible to get a job. I showed Joel a couple of my sketchbooks, and he hired me on the spot. Even offered me a place to stay, helped me get clean.

People may call me Tricky, but the best things in my life have come to me by sheer luck.

The door opened behind me, and I closed my sketchbook, looking over my shoulder to find Rose with her bag in the crook of her elbow, foot on the door as she pulled her key out of the lock.

"You're still here." It wasn't an accusation or a question, though I couldn't quite place her tone, like she was happy and pissed at the fact.

I stretched. "Just about to go to bed. How was Habits?"

She set her bag on the table and took a seat in the armchair., propping her boots on the coffee table. "Good. The usual."

I watched her twist up her hair, noting that she was concentrating a little too hard for such a simple task — lip between her teeth, eyes narrowed with focus. I realized then that she was drunk.

"I didn't expect to see you tonight," she said as she settled into the chair.

I leaned forward to set my sketchbook on the table by her feet, glancing up the line of her legs to meet her eyes. Mine lingered there. "Yeah, sorry. It was just getting late, so I figured why leave and then come right back?"

"I have a date tomorrow," she blurted, looking somehow nervous and determined all at the same time.

My heart stopped for a long moment, though my face was still as I leaned back to settle into couch again. "Okay."

Her cheeks flushed as she picked something invisible off the arm of the chair. "Not that I need your permission, or anything. I just thought you should know, you know? Like you staying here doesn't mean—"

I smirked, covering for the fact that she'd called me out. "Are you trying to convince me or yourself?"

Her mouth opened and closed again, and my smirk climbed. Stone-cold Rose, caught off guard. I wondered if it was my lucky day.

"I know what it doesn't mean, Rose. Funny that you'd assume I didn't, though," I joked.

Her flush deepened. "It's not like that. I just wanted to say it out loud."

"I get it. I wasn't planning on making a move."

It was true. I hadn't planned on it, but I wouldn't ignore an opportunity. I'd never admit that to her, though, and she needed reassurance that I wasn't going to make it weird. So that's exactly what I gave her. "Look, it's been long enough that we've danced around each other like this. Maybe we can find our new normal. Move on."

I said it like it was simple, but it was just another lie to keep us both standing.

I veered us away from that subject and into the last thing I wanted to talk about. But I had to play it cool, pretend I was fine with it. I had a feeling I'd be doing a lot of pretending in the days to come. "So, a date, huh? You excited?"

She relaxed into her chair at the mention, looking a little weary. "I don't even know, man. Mostly, I'm nervous. It's been a while." Her eyes darted to mine, like she'd forgotten for a second it was me she was talking to.

I stared at her bottom lip where it was pinned between her teeth — lips that were mine. Lips that had said words I wished they would utter again. Lips that had smiled only for me, that had kissed my own, that had delivered her to me.

Lips that were my deliverance.

Lips that could be kissing some other guy within twenty-four hours.

I smiled reassuringly through the fire in my ribs. "I know the feeling. What's his story?" I asked, not wanting to know.

"He's an artist named Steve. I don't know too much else."

"What's his medium?" I was genuinely interested, only because I hoped it was something I could hold against him.

"Not sure, though I know he makes furniture at least."

I nodded, impressed despite myself. "Lots of math, which is why I never got into it."

She laughed. "Right? My high school algebra teacher was a friggin' liar. I've never once had to solve an algebra problem as an adult."

"Try learning it on your own. Joel attempting to help me while I was getting my GED was a fucking riot." I snickered at the memory.

Those smiling lips again. I couldn't look away. "Oh, my God. I can only imagine the swearing involved in that."

I chuckled and rested my arms on the back of the couch with a sigh. "Shep's actually the mathmagician of the family, so at least I had him to step in and save the day when quadratic equations got the best of us."

"So," she said as she leaned forward to untie her boots. "I think everyone's going to Habits night after next. Maggie and Cooper are even going to be there." She made a mock surprised face.

"It's a miracle."

Her eyes were on her fingers as they unlaced the first one enough to slip her foot out. "It's been so weird lately. Everyone's so … busy."

With each other, was the rest of that sentence. "For sure. I feel like I haven't seen Cooper and Maggie in weeks."

"Because it has been weeks." She wiggled her toes before getting to work on the other boot. "We've barely seen them since they moved in together after like four seconds of dating."

"Who would have guessed?"

She chuckled and shed the final shoe, dropping it with a thump. "Certainly not West. I'm surprised he only decked Cooper once for nailing his sister."

"West has two rage buttons: Lily and Maggie."

"Truth. It'll be good to see everyone, since they're all taking a break from being grownups, or whatever." She wrinkled her nose.

I shook my head, thinking about how much had changed over the last couple of months. "It blows my mind that Cooper, playboy of the century, the guy who never took anything seriously, has a live-in girlfriend and a real, adult job. At an investment firm. Where he wears a suit and tie to work every day."

"Playboy to professional. At least he has somewhere to wear all those fancy suits of his."

I chuckled. "Like Coop needs an excuse."

"True. And then Lily and West are just together all the time. It's so strange to be here alone all the time now," she added, partly to herself.

"Mine's the opposite. It's strange to feel like you have nowhere to go. Though it's not like I haven't been through that before. At least I'm not a kid this time, and at least it's not like I really have nowhere to go." I watched her for a beat. "Thanks again for letting me stay, Rose."

Her face softened. "You're welcome. I'm glad I can help, even though you're still a dick for not asking first."

I put my hands up in surrender. "Hey, blame Lily for that."

"Oh, trust me. I do." She stretched and groaned. "Man, I'm beat. Getting up at eight in the morning is horse shit."

I laughed. "You get used to it."

"Who said I wanted to?" she asked as she stood.

I grabbed my stuff and followed her to the bedrooms. "Hey, don't knock it. You'd be surprised at how much you can get done when you're awake during the day."

Rose yawned one stretched-out word. "Pass." She turned in her threshold and looked up at me with dark eyes, most of her hidden in shadows of her dark room. "Sleep well." The words were soft, full of some emotion I couldn't quite place. I only knew I wanted to cross the small space between us and kiss her until she was breathless.

But instead, I stepped into Lily's dark bedroom. "You too," I said quietly. And I closed my door as she closed hers, putting the walls between us as we always did.

Save Me

ROSE

woke the next morning to the damn cats again, though at least this time they didn't break up contraband dreams about certain sexy ex-boyfriends who happened to be sleeping in the next room.

Not that it mattered. I had a date with a cute guy in a few hours, and I was optimistic. Maybe he wasn't as hot as Patrick Evans, but who was? I was sure Patrick was some superhuman, unreachable by mere mortals like me. He was on another planet, in another universe. Completely unattainable.

I knew he was still attracted to me — he was about as subtle as a car alarm — but I didn't know if what he felt went deeper than that. The man was written in a language I didn't understand. I thought I did through the things we didn't have to say. But he was otherwise closed to me. I could see the pieces of him moving behind his eyes, but the meaning was lost on me. The attraction was the only thing that was simple. The only thing that made any sense.

And today, I felt better and worse about him. Last night marked the first real conversation between the two of us since we'd broken up.

Look, I get that it's crazy. We hang out all the time. But I'd conditioned myself to ignore him, which I think might have made him crank the intensity. I don't even think he knew he was doing it. He just looked like that. Lily called it resting smolder face.

I called it trouble.

My date was in a few hours, and I was still nervous. It was the kind of morning I'd usually find Lily and curl up in her lap like a cat so she could pet me, but Lily wasn't here. So I shuffled out of the apartment and down the hall in my pajamas, knocking on the door in warning, opening it when I didn't hear any protests.

"Lil?" I called.

"In here," she said from the bedroom.

I closed the door and walked toward their room. "You decent?"

"For now," West said, and Lily laughed.

"Don't scare her away. Come in."

I smiled when I walked into the room. They were stretched out in bed wearing pajamas even though it was ten, which might as well have been four in the afternoon to them.

"Aww, look at you bums," I said, the words gooey and sweet.

West had a full-sized bed, and Lily scooted, shuffling West against the wall to make room for me. "Pile in, Rosie."

I climbed in and slipped under the covers.

West propped up his head and smiled. "Maybe I'll go make breakfast so you two can make out."

I laughed. "What a gentleman."

"Just be sure to give the nanny cam over there a good show, all right?" He made a show of it, angling his head to peer at his bookshelf, pointing in its direction.

We giggled, and West kissed Lily on the cheek and climbed out of bed, stretching his long body and twisting his dark hair up into a knot.

"Thanks, LumberWest," I called. "I'll have bacon and eggs, please."

"You got it." He winked and left the room.

Lily's cheeks were rosy, her smile soft and sweet. She looked like a princess — wide, blue eyes, long blond hair, creamy skin. And I'd never seen her so happy, not in all the years I'd known her.

"I miss you." It just slipped out — I hadn't meant to get all sappy. But I couldn't help it. I really did miss her, and was feeling sentimental. I might have also been PMSing, or as I sometimes called it, the Filter Deteriorator.

"I miss you too, Rosie."

"I wish you'd been there last night when I got home. Tricky was sitting in the living room almost like he was waiting on me."

She raised a brow. "Oh? How'd that go?"

I sighed as she moved back to West's pillow, relinquishing hers to me. I gave it a solid punch to fluff it before settling in. "Well, I told him I had a date, which wasn't weird at all."

"That bad?"

"I mean, I guess it could have been worse. He asked me polite questions about it with his face like a statue or a robot or something. Then we talked for a little and went to bed."

She rolled her eyes. "Boring."

"You're the worst. What do you expect us to do? Make out?"

"Just take off your clothes and parade your goodies around for him," she said cheerily.

"I'd rather not have sex with my ex, Lil." The words were as flat as my face.

She gave me a look.

My eyes narrowed. "You're really not helping."

"I know. I'm sorry," she said with a sigh. "I just know that you two care about each other, and you're both important to me. I want you to be happy. And the thought of double-dating with you guys makes my brain explode."

I chuckled. "Well, don't hold your breath."

"Don't tell me what to do, Rose Fisher." She pulled the covers up so we were in up to our necks and smiled innocently. "So when are you meeting Sexy Steve?"

Nerves fluttered through my ribcage at the thought of meeting a stranger for a date. "In a couple of hours."

"So, dating again."

"Scary. I don't exactly have a stellar track record when it comes to guys."

She chuckled. "Who does?"

"Hell if I know. I swear, bad luck with guys must be a Fisher thing. Like, my cousin Ellie. Every guys she's dated ends up being a jerkwad asshole. She called the other day, I guess this latest one is a real piece of work. She thinks he might be cheating on her."

"Ugh."

"And then there's me. The guys I've dated have either been completely unavailable or egomaniacs. Take Jack, for instance. You don't know rock bottom until your boyfriend and roommate leave town and steal everything in your apartment that wasn't nailed down."

She raised an eyebrow. "No, but I did get suckered by the biggest douchewhore in the New York City Ballet."

"Nice try. Blane at least brought you to West."

She smiled. "And Jack running off with Liz brought me to you."

I chuckled. "God, I'm glad you answered my Craigslist ad and not some psycho."

"You had me at *Vaginas only. Penis denied on entry.*"

"Seriously, you could have been a serial killer," I said with a laugh. "Let's just agree that ninety percent of all humans are assholes. Statistically."

"You're so cynical."

"I know. I can't help it. Growing up in LA ruined me, and people like Jack and Liz just drove the last nails in the coffin. I mean, I moved here *for* Jack, and then he fucked me over so hard." I shifted my voice into jerk-boy tone. "*Come on, babe. The LA scene is tired.'* It sounded like an adventure at the time. And then he wanted to turn around and go back when he got picked up by that Indie label in Burbank. I felt like a rubber band."

She shook her head. "Jack was a dick."

"That's true. But he was so pretty," I said wistfully.

"Douchesparkle. Lead singers of bands have it all over them. You can't see the douche for all that hair and musical talent."

"Honestly, I don't think it would have been so big of a deal if my best friend hadn't left with him."

"Yeah, because clearly she was an awesome friend."

"Who stole my shit."

She nodded. "Who stole your shit, exactly. No wonder you love me. The bar was pretty low."

I laughed. "It was just a reminder that people suck. Probably not one that I needed. I mean, I did grow up in LA. I think they issue *Fuck Everybody* T-shirts to all California residents at the DMV."

"Sounds like New York and LA aren't so different after all."

I snorted. "Shhh, don't say that too loud. Wouldn't want to start a fight."

"Well, let's look at it this way. Maybe you've put in your dues on shitty guys. Maybe it's time for the Fisher luck to turn around. I mean, you've got a hot date today, and if things don't go well, a hot guy is sleeping in your apartment."

"Ha, ha."

"Do you know what you're going to wear?"

"Duh. That's obviously what I did when I was trying to fall asleep last night." *When I wasn't thinking about Tricky like twenty feet away. With no shirt on.*

"So are you going to do a three date bang? Does he need to buy you dinner before you give up the goods?"

I cackled.

"What? You've got to have a game plan. It's not Tinder, so at least there's no unspoken expectation that you're only meeting to bone."

"I'm pretty hard up, but I'm not that hard up. I have plenty of Tumblr porn and batteries to get me by without having to resort to Tinder. I think I'm ovulating too because I'm super lucky in the uterus department. Do you know how shitty it is to have PMS *and* raging ovulation hormones? I was watching anime the other night and totally got a ladyboner. An anime ladyboner. What has happened to me?"

"Anime dudes are sexy, ovulation or not. I don't know what it is about them."

"The emotional unavailability?"

She shrugged. "Probably."

"I don't know, but clearly I'm extra frisky, which sucks because Tricky is a trigger."

She waggled her brows. "Yeah, he is. A real pistol."

I rolled my eyes.

"Sorry."

"You're so full of shit."

She giggled. "I know. So, *Steve.*"

"Yes. Steve. Thank you. So, I think definitely a three-date situation sounds right. Make sure he's not nuts. Unless he's fairly normal and really, really hot. Then I can't be trusted because it's been a long, long time."

"I approve."

My mind skipped through scenarios of the date, kicking up my nerves. "I wish I could put you in my pocket and take you with me. I don't want to do this alone."

She smiled. "You'll be fine, Rose. It's like riding a bike."

"If you say so. Will you be here when I get home?"

"I don't think so — we're going to have a late lunch and go to a movie."

I pouted. "Well, damn."

"Text me and let me know how it goes. We can talk at Habits tonight too," she assured me.

"For sure. I'm excited to have everyone in one place tonight."

"And if your date sucks, we'll all be there to make fun of him with you. And then we can pick out your next guy. Group effort, and all."

I raised a brow. "And what if I don't want to go on another one?"

"Aw, come on, Rosie. Don't be a party pooper."

I chuckled.

"Bacon's ready," West called from the other room.

I peeled myself out of bed. "Now *that* is something I'll get out of bed for, no questions asked."

few hours later, I approached Roasted, wiping my palms on my jeans. My last first date was over a year ago and with one of my best friends, taking its viability as 'first date' consideration down a couple of notches. And despite my steady stride and don't give a fuck expression, I was nervous.

Real nervous.

UndyingArt, otherwise known as Sexy Steve, stood when I entered, smiling. He was a good looking guy, tall and blond, with neatly combed hair. His Henley sleeves were pushed up to his muscular forearms.

I noted that he was wearing a scarf. It was June. Apparently there's no hipster-o-meter on OKCupid.

"Rose?" he asked hopefully.

I smiled and extended a hand in greeting. "Hey, Steve."

Rather than take my hand, he grabbed me by the shoulders and pulled me into a hug. My eyes widened, nose burning from the scent clinging to him, something chemical and sharp. I pulled away first, and he reluctantly let me go.

He sort of smirked down at me. "Sorry. I always say you can tell a lot about a person by their hug. Test number one." He winked, and I gave him what I was sure was an awkward smile.

Not gonna lie. I was super uncomfortable. I was not one of those people who hugged strangers, especially not strangers who smelled vaguely of a funeral home. My eyes darted to the door.

"Want to sit over here?" he asked.

"Sure." I followed him to a table by the window, hoping I was just overreacting or nervous, ready to give him the benefit of the doubt, though I really wished I'd planned an escape call with Lily.

Steve took a seat and leaned back, folding his hands over his stomach. "Man, I didn't even ask you if you wanted coffee or anything. Maybe a lemon bar? I know you like those."

A tingle crawled up the back of my neck. "How did you know that?"

He waved a hand. "Oh, I spent a couple of hours checking out your Facebook. You took a picture of one the last time you were here. Your entire profile is public, did you know that?"

The tingle found its way up to my face. "No. No I didn't."

Steve chuckled. "Anyway, just let me know if you want a little something. And sorry if I smell like formaldehyde. I swear, it won't wash out."

I raised an eyebrow in surprise, part of my brain relieved at making the connection to the smell while the other was really glad I'd met Steve in such a public place. "I thought you made furniture?"

"I do. *Taxidermy* furniture. You know, stuffed chairs, beds, divans."

I had been looking forward to telling Patrick what his medium was. Not anymore. "Wow, that's … fascinating," I said flatly.

Steve nodded, looking really proud of himself. "I've always loved dead things. My mom stuffed her schnauzer, Mitzi, when she died, and man, I was so into it. I used to keep her in my room. Like, I love the idea that you could preserve something forever."

I turned on my bartending skills, which are largely pretending skills, looking for an opening to leave. "It's cool you get to do something you love for a living."

"Right? Not everyone gets to have a job they love, you know? But I get to work with my hands. Create something that makes a statement." He leered a little. "Plus, who knew you could sell a potbelly pig ottoman for three thousand bucks? The market is growing, and I'm ahead of the curve. The Kardashians are about it right now. They bought four pieces from me last week."

I blinked and cleared my throat, morbidly curious and genuinely shocked that this seemingly normal guy could have such a high creep factor. "So, ah. Where do you get them? The dead animals?"

He shrugged. "All over. The things you learn. Like, do you have any idea how hard it is to find a dead grizzly bear? Shipping from Alaska is insane, especially for hazardous materials. I'm sure you can imagine. I just got a shipment of dead armadillos from Arizona for an order of custom purses. People just can't seem to get enough of them." He smiled, and it was a nice smile, for a serial killer.

"So, who buys these purses?"

"Texans, mostly, but also some hipsters who eat steak." He sat back in his chair. "So, you're a bartender?"

I tried to answer without reacting physically. "Yeah, for what seems like forever."

"Are you in school?"

My least favorite question. I shifted in my seat. "No, no school. You?"

He shook his head. "I have a business degree from NYU. I mean, everyone should have a degree, right? If you don't, you just end up working at a movie theater or drugstore or something. Gotta prove you can finish what you start, you know?" He didn't wait for me to respond, or seem to realize that he'd basically just called me an idiot. "Anyway. my art is all I'll ever need. Can you imagine working a job in some cubicle on Wall Street? That's like the place where dreams go to die."

I sort of laughed. "Yeah, but … novelty furniture? That can't last forever, can it?"

He looked at me like I was crazy. "Why not? Taxidermy is an ancient art. It's not going anywhere."

"I dunno. Just seems a little irresponsible to count on that as income," I answered honestly, dragging the awkward conversation down a flight of stairs.

He scoffed. "And bartending is, what … stable?"

My eyes narrowed at the dig, but I smiled. "Has been so far. I mean, I don't make three thousand a pop pouring shots, but at least I don't smell like death."

He seemed confused. "Well, what are you passionate about?"

"Is whiskey an option?" I joked.

Serial Killer Steve didn't laugh. "No."

And then, my mouth took off with no fear or foresight. "How about teen movies from the 90s? I mean, it's not nearly as exciting as having my hand up a dead grizzly bear's ass all day, but it's got to count for something, right?"

He made a face, finally catching on to my sarcasm. "I didn't mean it like that."

"Yeah, you did. Didn't even wait to see if I was kidding."

"Were you?"

I folded my arms. "Does it matter?"

He shrugged. "I just think it's sad, is all. I can't imagine living my life without something I was passionate about."

I just looked at him for a second with flushed cheeks, imagining myself kicking him in the face. But instead, I smiled tightly. "Well, it was nice to meet you, but—"

"Hang on, wait. We're not going to hook up?" His face fell.

My hackles rose as I stood with a sardonic smile on my lips. "Listen, *Steve*, I'd love to take this back to your murder room so you can show me your knife collection, but I think I need to go wash my hair since I smell like a morgue. I really hope you and your *passion* are super happy together."

He rolled his eyes. "Well, at least I didn't waste money on your coffee first."

"Unbelievable," I muttered, and then I walked the fuck out of Roasted like my boots were on fire.

What Goes Around

PATRICK

I **smoothed the last piece of** tape over the girl's shoulder blade, covering her fresh tattoo as she looked over her shoulder at me.

"Leave the covering on for the next four hours, then toss it. Don't cover it up again, okay?" I handed her a care sheet. "You'll want to wash three times a day with a non-scented mild soap. I really like baby soaps. It's going to start itching in a few days, but don't scratch it, all right? Just slap it."

She raised an eyebrow as she sat up and righted her shirt.

I smirked. "Trust me. It works." I rolled my chair over to my cabinet and grabbed a small apothecary jar. "Use this balm after you wash it to keep it moisturized."

She batted her lashes as she took it. "All right."

"Any questions?"

"Can I, ah, call you?" She bit her lip. "You know, if I need anything?

I mean, about my tattoo?"

I smiled, choosing my words carefully. "Sure, you can call the shop if you have any questions."

"Thanks, Tricky," she cooed.

I was already breaking down my station. "You got it, Cherice."

She walked to the counter as "Siamese Dream" blared over the shop speakers, Billy Corgan wailing his lament as she paid. I was peeling the plastic wrap off my tray when she made her way back and leaned over the low wall, giving me an eye level view of her cleavage.

"Thanks again," she said with a smile and handed me a couple of twenties.

"Any time."

She looked me over once more before turning and strutting out. I glanced at Joel, who watched her from behind the counter. He shook his head and shot me a smile.

The bell over the door rang, and I looked back, expecting Cherice again. My hands froze, needle gun in my hand.

I hadn't seen Seth in nearly a year, when he'd called me for help. He needed money, which was the immediate reason he'd called. But more than that, I knew he needed to get clean. I'd been trying for years to save him. But he didn't want my help, not then. He just needed someone to bail him out, get him a fix. Three days, he'd been high. And we fought. And I'd left him where I found him in his apartment, trying not to think about the knobby joints of his arms, his grey skin marred with bruises and track marks.

We hadn't spoken since. I didn't even know if he was still alive, didn't realize how much it had weighed on me, not until that moment when I saw him walking into the shop whole and felt the rush of relief.

He looked more like the kid I met so long ago than I'd seen him in years — clean and smiling, blond hair combed, green eyes bright. I think his shirt was even ironed.

I glanced at Joel, whose eyes were narrowed as he watched Seth approach me. I set down my machine and stood, stepping around to greet him.

He laughed, pulling me into a hug. "Goddamn, Tricky. It's good to see you."

I hugged him back, feeling the warm weight of him in my arms. "It's been too long, man."

He let me go and stepped back, looking me over. "Way too long." He glanced over at Joel. "Hey, Joel. Shop's looking good."

Joel had the good manners to smile and play along, even though I knew he disapproved. "Thanks. You're not looking so bad yourself."

He smiled back, looking proud and together. "Yeah, well. A lot's happened."

"Looks like it."

Seth turned to me. "I was in the neighborhood, wanted to see if you were here. Got a minute?"

I nodded. "A few. Walk with me to Roasted. We'll grab coffee for the shop."

"Sure."

I pulled off my gloves and tossed them. "Joel, text me what everyone wants."

"You got it, Tricky," he said, watching Seth like a guard dog.

I took a breath, not sure what to expect as we walked out of the shop and into the sunshine, still battling the shock of seeing him and the wariness I always felt when it came to Seth. Wary, but protective. Because no matter what had happened between us, I loved him. And if I could shake the habit, so could he.

I glanced over at my first friend, my oldest friend. My friend who I had been sure had been beyond saving, but was somehow standing next to me with no signs that he was using, twenty pounds heavier than usual, no listing, ringed eyes.

He looked sober.

Seth slipped his hands into the pockets of his jeans and looked down at his Converse. "How's life treating you, Trick?"

I shrugged. "Can't complain. You look good, man."

"Thanks. I'm straight. For real, this time. The yo-yo's out of string."

I nodded. "How long?"

"Six months. It's the longest I've ever gone." His voice was a little distant, touched with wonder. "It feels good, man. I get what you've been selling me all these years. The other side." He waved a hand like he was displaying a movie marquis.

I smiled. "Finally. Rehab?"

"Nah, couldn't afford it. I went to NarcAnon, made the choice. How many times have we talked about it? A thousand?"

"At least. How did you handle the come-down?"

He shook his head. "It was … it was bad, man. Two weeks before I felt like I wasn't going to die. I tossed my stash, even broke my phone so I couldn't call anybody. I was too sick for most of it to even get out of bed or I would have found my way to Jared or somebody, anybody. I don't know how you quit cold turkey like you did."

"If I hadn't had Joel to take care of me, I don't know how I would have either."

His eyes were sad. "Yeah. You're lucky for that. But anyway, I just wasn't ready before, you know?" Seth sighed, shaking his head. "I was lying there in my bed, shaking and sweating in between puking into the trashcan next to my bed, and I stared at the ceiling and realized I didn't want to die, and I'd been killing myself for years. I just didn't know it. I finally got what you've always said. I can't quit for anyone but me."

"Yeah, I know." And I did. That choice changed the course of my life. Sometimes you find yourself at a crossroad, and the path you choose determines everything — when you find love or lose it, if you live or die. The choice I made, the choice made possible by Joel, was something I woke up thankful for every day.

He took a heavy breath and continued. "So, yeah. I got clean, got a real job, scheduling deliveries for a courier company. Basically, I listen to the radio and yell at messengers all day. Life could be way worse."

I chuckled.

"I mean, not that bussing tables at Bartalotti's wasn't swanky as fuck. Remember Bartalotti's daughter?"

"How could any of us forget Gia?"

"Right? The curves alone." Seth shook his head and sighed, smiling. "You haven't lived until you've nailed Gia Bartalotti in the walk-in."

"Next to the tubs of bolognese," I added.

"Man, I miss the free bread."

I gave him a look. "Pretty sure it wasn't free."

He shrugged. "Free for me. Anyway, my sponsor found this gig for me. Feels like a fresh start. Like a get out of jail free card. Been there six months — I think that's the longest I've held a job since Bartalotti's too."

I smiled over at him. "I'm proud of you, man."

He smiled back, but there was pain behind his eyes. "Does it get easier?"

I thought about it as we walked for a moment. "Yes and no. I don't think about it as much, not anymore. But every once in a while …" I let out a breath. "Sometimes you can't hide. It's part of who you are. You just have to want to be sober more than you want to use."

He nodded as we crossed the street. "That's what I'm afraid of. I quit drinking and everything though. I don't even go out, which is fucked up. I basically just watch Netflix every night."

"You found normal."

Seth laughed. "Jesus. So what the fuck is new with you?"

"Same old. Working a lot. Painting."

"You still at our old place with West?"

I thought I picked up a little bitterness at the mention of West, but when I looked over, it seemed to be gone. After I'd left Joel's, Seth said he wanted to get clean, so we moved in together. Within a year, I had to kick him out, which was when West moved in. Seth never forgot it, either, that I'd made a new life, one without him, without drugs. "Yeah, still in the same place. Sorta, at least."

He raised a brow. "How's that work?"

"Long story. I've been crashing at Rose's."

He smirked. "Oh, man, Rosie Fisher. Tell me you're banging her."

I sighed. "Not anymore."

He gaped at me. "Shut the fuck up, man — are you serious? You bastard. I remember when she dated Jackie boy, that fuck." He shook his head, smiling wistfully. "It feels like a million years and yesterday. It's been a blur, the last few years especially." He paused for a beat. "Remember that cat Sarah and Shane had?"

I chuckled. "King Fluff? How could I forget?"

"He was the fattest motherfucker I'd ever seen. Best cat I ever met." Seth shoved his hands into his pockets and cleared his throat. "Shane called. Sarah … she passed."

Cold snaked through my chest. "Yeah. He called me too. Have you seen him?"

"Not since before I got sober. We were on a bender. She looked bad, man, even then. Shane too."

I nodded, feeling somber. "You don't go that hard for that long and make it out the other side in one piece. It's what I've been trying to tell you."

"She looked like she was already dead. Her arms were so thin, and her face …" His brows dropped, pinned together. "I've been around junkies half my life, but to see Sarah and Shane where they were, after knowing them when we started this? When we were young and …

I don't know. I looked in the mirror and I didn't know myself." The words were quiet. "I'm sorry, Patrick. For everything I've put you through, for everything I've done. You don't owe me anything, and I don't want anything from you other than to try to make it right."

We walked in silence. I wasn't sure what to say.

"You're the best friend I've ever had, and I let you down, over and over again. Now, I'm clean. Now I can be the friend to you that you were to me. I just wanted you to know, in case you wanted to take me up on it."

I looked over at Seth, the kid I met when I was sixteen, alone in the city, in the world. When I had no one, I had him. The friend I'd been trying to save for the better part of ten years.

I couldn't deny him. I never could.

"Of course. You know I'm always here."

He smiled, his eyes shining. "I won't let you down. Not this time."

I smiled back. "So, we're going to Habits for my birthday in a couple of days, if you want to swing by."

"Fuck yeah. Still have the same number?"

"Yeah." I nodded. "Hit me up."

"I will."

"Tricky?"

I looked up to find Rose barreling toward us looking pissed. "Hey. You okay?"

She huffed and rolled her eyes as she came to a stop in front of us. "Yeah, just finished with my—" She glanced over to see who I was with, and her face bent in confusion. "Seth?"

"Hey, Rosie," he said with a smile, and she smiled back, head tilted.

"Man, it's been forever. You look great." She stepped up to give him a hug, shooting me a what-the-fuck look over his shoulder as they embraced.

"It's good to see you," he said as he backed away.

"Yeah, ah, you too. What are you guys doing?" she asked.

The question was loaded, I knew. "Just getting coffee," I answered. "What are you doing over here?"

"I just came from there. For my 'date.' Which was a disaster, in case you were wondering."

I was. I found myself smiling. "Did you get lemon bars, at least?"

She huffed. "No, that's the worst part. He was creepy as shit, so I didn't get coffee *or* lemon bars, which is basically the only reason I come all the way to Roasted."

"Well, we're going there now. I'll grab you a lemon bar."

She smiled, seeming to feel better at the offer. "Thanks. Oh, and get this. The guy's medium? *Taxidermy.* The guy makes furniture out of dead animals."

We laughed, and I winced. "Wow."

"Yeah. It was a nightmare." The conversation lulled, and she looked between Seth and me with questions behind her hazel eyes, eyes that looked more green than usual. She shook her head just once, small, and smiled. "Well, I better get going. Have fun, guys. I'll see you later, Trick."

My eyes were on her. "See you, Rose."

She blushed, just a little, just enough. And then we parted ways.

Seth shook his head and glanced back over his shoulder. "Damn, dude. I can't believe you and Rose. I just always saw her as … I don't know. Unavailable."

I shrugged. "People say that about me too."

He chuckled. "Because you are."

"Maybe that's why we worked. For a minute at least. Being friends was easy."

"Yeah. I mean, we were friends too, but I thought pretty much every dude was friendzoned. Only available to doucherockets like Jackie, and I guess broody art-types like you."

69

I snorted as we came to a stop outside the coffee shop.

Seth hitched a thumb over his shoulder. "I've got to get back to work, but damn, is it ever good to see you."

I smiled, feeling hope for Seth for the first time in a very long time. "You too, man."

He hugged me again, and we clapped each other on the back. "Later."

I stepped into the coffee shop and to the counter, ordering coffee for the shop, waiting as the lattes were frothed and espresso shots made, reeling from what had just gone down, the shock of seeing Seth sober ruling every thought.

He was clean. It was what I'd always wanted for him. I just didn't know if he'd hang on this time. It was maybe the most hope I'd *ever* had for him, as tenuous as it was, and I contemplated what it would mean for him. What it could mean for me, to have the friend I'd always known he could be.

I was still lost in thought when I walked back into the shop to find Joel at the counter, arms folded, lips downturned.

"Did I just see that right?" His brow was low.

I sighed and set the coffee carrier on the counter. "Sure did."

"What did he want? Money?"

I rubbed the back of my neck. "An old friend of ours passed."

His face softened at the news. "Patrick, I'm—"

I held up a hand. "It's okay. I hadn't seen her in years. Sarah, the girl we used to live with. I'm surprised her boyfriend was sober enough to even call to tell me."

"Doesn't make it any easier."

I unpacked the coffee, lining the cups up on the counter. "No, but I let all that go a long time ago. It was too hard to see them all living that way, but there was nothing I could do about it. You can't help somebody who doesn't want help. I don't make a habit out of arguing with brick walls. If Seth taught me anything, it was that."

"Is that really all he wanted?"

"That's all, he said. He's six months clean." I leaned on the counter and grabbed my cup, spinning the cardboard sleeve around.

He shook his head and gave me a hard look. "You know it always starts out like this."

But I met his glare with one of my own. "I do know. This time feels different, but I'm not letting my guard down."

Joel rubbed the back of his neck and sighed. "I'm sorry, man. I don't mean to be a dick about it, but this is what he does. He comes back and burns you the second you get close. Seth holds the power to fuck you up more than anyone. Even Rose."

"Yeah, I know."

"I know you want to help him. Just know I only want to help you. Must be something about those puppy dog eyes of yours." He shook his head. "The day you walked into the shop, barely eighteen, skinny and dirty, and you opened your sketchbook right here to show me your work, I knew I'd be patching you up for a good while. Never even thought twice about taking you in. I knew you'd work hard. I knew you had talent. I knew you were good, Patrick. Always did."

I smiled, my heart full of gratitude that I'd ever found someone to believe in me. "We're just a couple of suckers, you know that?"

He snorted. "Do I ever."

Death Grip

ROSE

Awkward date aside, it hadn't been a horrible day.

I came home from the ordeal annoyed and changed into shorts, a tee, and my Vans, blowing out of the apartment with my longboard under my arm and earbuds blaring. It was a gorgeous day, the sky high and cornflower blue, without a cloud to be seen, and everything just felt good, right, as I cruised around Central Park, happily alone with my thoughts.

So Steve was a disaster, but one bad date wouldn't stop me. Not with my shades on and the wind in my hair.

Patrick crossed my mind, the surprise at seeing him unexpectedly flashing through me again. Sometimes, I think my brain toned down how beautiful he was in my memory because seeing him always took me a little by surprise, like the real, live version of him had so much more presence and grace than my mind could store and recall.

I realized I'd been seeing a lot of unexpected Patrick lately. Part of me hoped it wouldn't become a thing. The other part … well, I told her to shut up and sit down, let's just say that.

But what I couldn't get over was seeing Seth. It had been years, and he'd definitely changed for the better — today was the first time I'd ever seen Seth not *looking* like a junkie, and I could see that Patrick was amazed at the fact. But Seth was bad news, always had been. Every six months or so, he came around needing money, a job, a place to sleep — Patrick was the one Seth called when he was in trouble. He had no family to speak of, no other friends who weren't junkies, and Patrick was always there for him, sometimes at great personal cost. Like this: a few years ago, he'd been thrown in jail overnight alongside Seth. Guilty until proven otherwise. Guilty by association. But he'd gotten out without charges, an unfortunate mistake. Wrong place, wrong time.

After that, Patrick tried to distance himself as much as he could.

The thought that Seth would be hanging around made me nervous. Patrick had suffered enough in his life without someone like Seth taking advantage of the loyalty he felt for the people he loved. I figured he saw some of himself in Seth and just wanted to save him. Fix him. But some people were beyond saving.

By the time I came home that evening, I was happy to find my apartment empty, no Patrick to be found. I had to admit, it was nice to have somebody around — I hadn't realized just how alone I'd been — and I felt better about him, about *us*, than I had in a really long time. Like there was a glimmer of hope for our friendship. I just wished there was another way, one that didn't involve him being in my apartment every day.

But for now, it was quiet, and I was blissfully, consciously alone, just like I wanted. Or at least that's what I told myself, as if I could repeat the mantra until it manifested into truth.

So I turned on my radio, made some ramen from my favorite Chinese market, and sat down at the table with my book, which happened to be a romance novel. I was in for what was hopefully a long evening of reading, devoid of talking and ex-boyfriends. I opened my book with excitement flitting through me — the hero had this huge secret, and the heroine was about to figure it out, which meant a blow up was imminent.

That was always the best part.

You're surprised? Just because I'm a cynic doesn't mean I don't love love. I just didn't think I was cut out for it or that it would ever really happen to me. I had hope for a moment in time with Patrick. I thought he was my happy ending, but really he was just another shitty chapter.

See, the reason why I love a good romance is that life sucks. It's harsh and cruel and ugly. Only the lucky ones get their happy endings, like my parents, or Lily and West. But that was the standard I held love to. Not that it had to be a fairy tale. Not that I expected perfection. I just expected respect. The trouble is, most people don't deliver that. But I'd been fooled enough.

So I chose to read about it instead.

It's supremely satisfying when the good guys win and the bad guys lose. When the guy gets the girl and everyone lives happily ever after. Reading is the greatest escape. Where life is unfair, fiction can be perfect. The appeal is infinite, and the reason why I read at least three romance novels a week. If I can't have it, I may as well imagine it.

I opened my book and began to read as I spun my fork to twist the ramen up, blowing on the steamy noodles before stuffing them in my mouth.

The door opened, and Patrick walked in. My face fell as my pulse ticked up a notch. Solitude, destroyed.

"Hey," he said and dropped his keys in the dish like he lived there.

"Need something?" I asked with an eyebrow up and my eyes still on my book.

He pulled off his jacket and tossed it on the back of the chair. "Just got off work. Brought you lemon bars."

I felt like a dick for being a dick when he'd brought me my favorite pastry, and I glanced up as he smiled and passed the small bag across the table to me.

Patrick had a dozen smiles for various emotions, with only a couple that showed his teeth. There were sideways smirks and small smiles where only the edges lifted, a small degree of what he was willing to share. But when he laughed — really laughed with abandon, when he let go — those smiles were brilliant. They changed his face, the stoic, sharp features shifting into pure joy, so rare to see that it was blinding.

I pushed my musings away and smiled back gratefully. "Thank you. I'd been thinking about going back all day."

He took a seat. "What'd you do all day?"

"Skated. Just got back a bit ago." I looked into my bowl as I twirled my fork in my noodles again, avoiding his eyes, feeling a little trapped. Like I couldn't get away from him. "So, I can't help but notice you've been here every time I am. Not that I mind a little company, but this was exactly what I was talking about when I said we weren't roommates."

He smirked, leaning back in the chair as he folded his arms. "So, twenty-four hours in and you're already done?"

My brow dropped. "I'm just saying, you keep just *being* here. Like yesterday after jury duty."

"You asked me to come over to talk."

I abandoned my fork in the bowl. "Yeah, but I didn't know you'd be here when I got home. If this is going to work, I need boundaries. It's no secret that I'm not exactly thrilled about all of this, and I asked one thing of you. Just one. You're sleeping here. You don't live here."

He watched me, blue eyes burning, full of honesty. "Yeah, I know. But, Rose … when I go back to my place, Lily and West are always there. Don't get me wrong — I couldn't be happier for them. It's just …"

"But how did it end up that I have to deal with the fallout of what they do and how you feel about it?"

"I know it sucks, trust me. Do you think I want to be sleeping in Lily's bed instead of my own? Or that I want to be here, in your space after you've been doing your best to ignore me for months? I'm not trying to push you into something you don't want, so if you want me to go, I'll go. Just say the word."

I let out a heavy breath and poked at my dinner with my fork, feeling like a dick again because I was one. It wasn't fair for either of us. "No. I'm sorry, you're right. It's just … this is a little stressful."

"I know."

"But if the tables were turned, if they were in my space, loud fuckery or not, I know it would be really weird. Like, even just walking in and seeing them hanging out feels like an intrusion. I'd want somewhere else to be too, if I were you. I love them, and I love them together. I just can't handle the reminder that I'm alone. And now that they're both free for a bit, this is almost the only place to be alone. So I'm sorry for putting up a fight about this. It's just … it's not easy, that's all." *Because I hate you, and I love you, and I hate that I love you.*

His smile was small, with a hint of sadness.

Just do this, Rose. It's the right thing to do. Accept it and find a way to deal. I took a breath and did my best to let it go, or at least loosen my death grip on it. "Well, you have my permission to come and go at will. Not that you were waiting on it," I said with a smirk as I loaded my fork and brought it to my lips. "How was your day?" I took a bite, anxious to change the subject.

"Full of surprises. Like Seth coming by the shop."

I swallowed my noodles like they were made of sawdust. "Yeah. What was that all about?"

He watched his fingers as he picked at the edge of the placemat in front of him. "A friend of ours died. He wanted to know if I knew."

I lowered my fork, my eyes searching his face. "I'm sorry." I said quietly.

He shook his head, eyes still down. "It's all right. He looked good though, didn't he?"

"He really did. So, what did he want?"

Patrick chuckled. "You sound like Joel."

I shrugged one shoulder. "Well, Joel's a smart dude. Seth always wants something."

"I don't think he does. Not this time. He's clean, has a real job. He's coming to Habits for my birthday in a couple of days."

I made a butthurt face. "Thanks for the invite."

"It was Joel's idea," was his defense.

"And Seth got an invitation before me. I see where I sit on the food chain. Maybe I'll change my locks after all," I joked.

He smiled. "I really did forget about the party. I don't think about my birthdays. As far as I'm concerned it's just another day."

"But it's not. It's *your* day. I don't care if The Sergeant didn't give that to you. We'll make a big deal about it. Always."

His eyes were hot again. "You don't miss what you never had."

My breath was shallow, and I turned my attention back to my noodles. "Who's going?"

"The Tonic crew for sure. Hopefully you guys."

"And Seth."

He watched me, fiddling with the placemat again. "And Seth."

I set my fork down, trying not to be pushy. But I couldn't just sit by and watch him get tangled up in another mess. "Do you really think it's a good idea to get mixed up with Seth again?"

"I'm not getting mixed up with anything," he said simply and leaned on the table. "He's my oldest friend. You have to get that."

"I do, but he's only brought you pain and drama."

He shook his head. "That's not true. He gave me hope at a time in my life where I had next to none."

"So did Joel."

"And I'd do anything for him too." It was a simple truth.

I frowned, not willing to accept his logic. "The difference is that Joel wouldn't take advantage of you. Seth will."

"I'm not putting any expectation on Seth. I'm not going to fuck this up, Rose. But he came to me and said he's sober and apologized. I'm not letting him in, but I'm not shutting him out, either. Just trust me, okay? I'm not going to get suckered into anything. I know how he works, and I'm smart enough to know better than to pin my hopes on him."

I nodded reluctantly, because what else could I do? "Okay. I'm sorry."

His face softened, and he smiled. "Don't be. Thanks for looking out for me."

"Did you eat?"

"Yeah, I grabbed something after work. You work tonight?"

I shook my head. "I'm off again. What are your plans?"

"Didn't have any. Was just going to chill, maybe sketch, but I don't know. West and Lily are camped out in the living room."

Damn them. I sighed again in resignation. "Well, you can hang here."

"I promise I'll be good and quiet."

I laughed. "No wild dance parties?"

"Only if you want one." He pushed away from the table and stood. "I'm going to grab my stuff. I'll be back in a bit."

"All right," I said as he walked out, leaving me alone again.

I sighed again, book abandoned as my thoughts circled around. If I'd thought things were complicated before, it was nothing compared to where we were headed, and I felt my control slipping away. I couldn't deny him, and part of me didn't want to. But the louder, pushier part of me knew better. Knew that with every inch I gave, the more danger I was in. I couldn't fall again — I still hadn't healed from the last time.

I finished my noodles and cleaned up, settling into the couch with my book just as he came back, taking a seat next to me at the end of the couch. Music played, filling the silence, the comforting quiet of just being together. His feet were on the coffee table, and I leaned on the arm of the couch on my end, legs stretched across the cushion between us, trying not to think about him, though I snuck glances when I could. I always loved to watch him draw — his eyes trained on the page, the muscles of his forearms fluttering, making waves in the tattoos across his skin.

After a while, my nerves had quieted, and I found myself absorbed in my book. My legs stretched out incrementally until my toes and the tops of my feet were hooked behind his bicep and part of his back. Then his arm moved to rest behind my calf, pulling my leg into his side. As conscious as I was of him, it felt easy, natural, without intention or expectation, and before very long, I was so content, so comfortable, that I didn't even realize I'd fallen asleep next to him.

Whenever

ROSE

A **knock rapped at the door,** but it sounded so far away, and I was so warm. I nuzzled into Patrick's neck and sighed, and his arms tightened around me in answer.

My eyes flew open.

Patrick.

I jerked away from him like I'd been electrocuted, arms and legs flying as I rolled off the couch and hit the ground with a thump, elbow first.

"*Shit,*" I hissed as the knock came again.

I glanced around, eyes bleary, rubbing my elbow, heart pounding as I looked back at Patrick — his eyes barely open as he looked around, confused. It was barely daylight, and I realized we'd slept on the couch. Together. All night. Somehow, we'd ended up twisted around each other like ivy.

"Roooooooose? Hellooooooo? Anybody home?" The voice from the other side of the door was muffled, but I knew it, and as I shuffled to the door, I tried to wrap my sleepy brain around what was going on.

I pulled open the door, my surprise settling in as I took in the sight of my cousin, Ellie, standing in my hallway with an innocent grin on her heart-shaped face.

Ellie Fisher was just over five feet of porcelain skin and soft, curvy body. The barely twenty-one bombshell had the body of an adult, the face of a teenager, and the brain of a second-grader, with the biggest heart, bless it.

"Rose!" She rushed me, hugging me with more strength than I expected.

"Ellie?" I sputtered and pulled away. "What are you doing here?"

She smiled and pushed her long, copper hair over her shoulder. "I came to visit!"

"I can see that. But why are you here? And at —" I glanced at the clock. "—Six in the morning?"

Her brow quirked. "You said I could come see you whenever, so I did." She put her hands up in the air. "Surprise!"

"But…" I started, trying to make sense of it all. "Did I miss a message from you? I mean, you didn't leave me a voicemail, right? Because you know I don't use my phone for that."

"No, you said whenever, so here I am." She was still smiling sweetly as she grabbed the handle of her suitcase and brushed past me.

I sighed. "Come on in."

"Thanks, Rosie." Ellie stopped just inside the door and gaped when she saw Patrick.

He sat up and rubbed his face, smiling at Ellie as he blinked his eyes open. "Hey."

Her eyes went wide. "Oh, my God, Rose. Is this that guy you used to date that you said did that thing in bed where he—"

I laughed super loud to cover whatever she was about to say and grabbed her by the shoulders to present her to Patrick. "Tricky, this is my cousin Ellie. Looks like she's going to be staying with us for a while."

His jaw was a sharp line, the corner of his mouth drawing up in a smirk. "Nice to meet you."

Ellie's brows knit together in confusion. "Wait, he lives here? Were you guys sleeping together? I thought you guys broke up?"

My cheeks were on fire, and I wished to God she picked up on body language, particularly mine as it told her to stop talking. "Ah, he's just staying here for a little while."

"But where's Lily?"

"Staying with West, so we sort of swapped roommates temporarily. Tricky here has been sleeping in her old room."

She snickered. "Not what it looks like to me. I can sleep on the couch, as long as you guys aren't using it." Her eyebrows climbed.

Patrick shook his head. "Don't worry about it. Take the room. I have a bed at my own place."

"I'm down for whatever," she said with a shrug.

"You take the room. I insist." He smiled, but I could see how bummed he was, and I'll admit — I hated seeing him like that, knowing he was contemplating more sleepless nights. Not enough to demand he sleep on my couch, though. I'd offer it, but no way would I push him to stay. Especially after last night, or this morning, or whatever time we ended up cuddling on the couch. Like I needed shirtless Patrick in my house any more than was absolutely necessary.

I tried not to think about how good that had felt, being close to him. Being in his arms, his skin against mine, his —

Stop it, goddammit.

I smiled. "Couch is always free, Trick."

"Thanks, Rose."

I turned to my cousin and took a breath, still a little flabbergasted.

"I'm just so surprised to see you, El."

"Good, that was the idea." She was still smiling like she'd slept for nine hours and had the best night's sleep of her life. "I took the redeye out of LA and slept on the plane, so I'm ready for a day of New Yorking! What should we do first?"

I blinked. "I have no idea."

"Okay, well you take a minute to think it over and wake up while I go get me and Valentino settled in."

I stopped and looked over at her, realizing she had a small crate attached to her suitcase. "Valentino?"

Ellie smiled, rolling her eyes dramatically. "My cat, silly."

I cocked my head. "How long are you staying, El?"

She shrugged and rolled her way into Lily's room. "You know, just however long," she said noncommittally.

Ellie disappeared into the room, and I turned back to look at Patrick, who shook his head.

"I have no idea what's happening," I muttered.

"Looks like you got a new roommate."

"And a cat."

He smiled. "And a cat."

"Just what I never wanted."

As if on cue, a very fat, very fancy black cat strutted out of Lily's room, sizing Patrick and I up with judgy, green eyes. His fur was black, though his paws and chest were white with a black marking just under his neck, which made him look like he was wearing a tuxedo. He hopped up on the table and sat, wrapping his fluffy black tail around his paws.

I reached out to scratch his neck. "Hello, there, Valentino."

He lifted his jaw, looking away with a meow, giving me his permission to pet him.

I couldn't help but laugh. "This cat is fancy as fuck."

Valentino looked less than impressed at the likes of Patrick and me.

Patrick padded into the kitchen to make coffee, and I sat down at the table, feeling overwhelmed.

I ran my hand down Valentino's silky back, and he arched his spine into my palm as I watched Patrick pouring the water in the tank, putting in the filter, pouring in the grounds, all while bugging the fuck out.

I'd just woken up in Patrick Evans' arms.

Those were words I never thought I'd utter again, even if only in my mind.

I couldn't remember how it happened, if he'd fallen asleep first or if I had. It was just like it used to be, the two of us wound together — we always slept like that, *before*. Part of me wondered if he'd planned it, wondered if he was fucking with me or something. But I watched him, standing in my apartment, looking like he belonged there, making coffee like he used to, making me feel like I used to. Making it harder to keep my feelings in check.

He hurt you, Rose. Don't forget that.

The truth of the matter was that it meant nothing. It didn't change the fact that we weren't together. It didn't change anything that had happened between us. It didn't mean he was forgiven, or that I was wanted.

It didn't change anything.

There was only one solution: to pretend it didn't happen.

So instead of dealing, I'd throw myself into planning Ellie's day.

I got up and made my way to the couch, digging through the cushions until I found my phone to text Maggie.

Hey, hope it's not too early to message on a Saturday, but I just had my cousin drop in unexpectedly, and I was wondering if you still had your sightseeing list?

She texted back a minute or so later as Patrick took a seat next to me, setting my cup of coffee on the table in front of me.

Hey, no worries, we're up. I have the list, or if y'all want, I can come with. Just let me know!

I sighed, relieved. "Thank God for Maggie." *That would be so great. Maybe we can meet at Genie's and put together a plan?*

Sounds good. I'll head that way.

"Hey, Ellie," I called into the other room, "you hungry?"

"Starved."

"All right." I pulled up Lily's name in my texts and invited her too, then exchanged my phone for the coffee, sitting back on the couch with another sigh.

Next to Patrick.

He yawned, which made me yawn.

I sipped my coffee feeling squirrelly and tired and confused, repeating to myself that nothing had changed, nothing had changed, nothing had changed. I felt him watching me and looked over, meeting his gaze.

Time seemed to slow down. I don't know what it was … something in his eyes that called to me, something that scared me. Because if he'd asked me anything in that moment, I would have said yes.

Ellie walked in, and our heads swung around to look at her. She smiled like she'd just caught us doing something more than sitting in a quiet room together. "So, breakfast?"

"Yeah," I said as I hauled myself off the couch. "Give me five minutes to get ready." And I hurried out of the room, wishing I could erase him from my heart so easily.

Patrick

I *parted ways with Ellie and* Rose in the hallway, catching Rose's eyes once for a long moment, wondering if she knew what I was thinking, if she knew what I wanted. If she understood that I wasn't going to wait quietly in the wings anymore.

All this time, I thought she didn't want me. I thought I couldn't have her. But this morning, with her body against mine, I knew. When she looked at me, eyes wide and open, I was sure. She wanted me just as badly as I wanted her, and this time, I wouldn't stop. Not until she was mine again.

My determination echoed in every beat of my heart, every footstep, every thought, as I showered, changed, walked the blocks to work. I needed a plan, because I couldn't go into this guns blazing and just take her. Not yet. If I wasn't careful, I'd blow it, and this was it. My last bullet.

I'd win back her trust, and the second I could make a move, I would.

By the time I walked into Tonic, I felt more sure of myself than I had before, maybe ever. The shop was mostly empty — I was on the early bird crew — though Joel was at his desk in his station. He looked up and looked me over, one eyebrow climbing.

"What set your boots on fire?"

I smiled. "Rose."

"What'd you do?"

I walked into his station and leaned on the short wall. "Nothing, yet."

"Well, don't hold out on me. What happened? Tell me everything."

"I'm gonna get her back."

He waited for me to elaborate and huffed when I didn't. "Stop being cryptic, goddammit, and tell me what's going on."

My smile stretched wider, though I struggled to find the words. "I'm not even sure how to tell you, Joel. When we woke up this morning, I just knew I had a shot. I felt so stupid for not seeing it before, but ..." I rubbed my jaw. "I thought she didn't want me, but that was a lie. I can get her back. I've just got to prove she can trust me again."

"Hold up, back up. When you woke up? Together?"

"Yeah. We fell asleep on the couch last night, and this morning she just looked at me, and I knew. It was just a glimpse, but it was there."

"Well, what are you going to do? Ask her out?"

My smile fell a little. "She's doing some online dating thing. I ran into her yesterday after one of her dates."

He folded his arms and shook his head. "Man, I told you this would eventually happen. Now it's going to be even harder to get her back, you realize that, right? She's going to meet her dream guy and forget all about you."

"She won't."

"How do you know?"

I smirked and leaned forward. "Because I'm her dream guy."

A laugh boomed out of him. "I can't argue with that, Tricky. I really can't."

"I just can't fuck it up this time."

"No, you can't. I suspect if there is a chance for you here, it's the last one. Last call."

"Last call," I echoed, knowing it was the truth. I had to step up and order or walk out. And I wasn't ready to leave.

It's Tricky

ROSE

pushed open the door to Genie's after breakfast, and the girls filed out behind me.

"So," Lily started, "we'll get Ellie a thirty-day MetroCard, and hop the train to Times Square. After that, we'll walk to Rockefeller, then to Grand Central and take the train back up to Saks."

"Perfect, Mom," I said cheerily. "Did you print up itineraries for us?" She stuck her tongue out at me.

"Sounds good to me," Ellie added, looking up at the buildings as we headed toward the subway. "Now that's all settled, can we please talk about how you were sleeping with Tricky when I got here this morning?"

Lily and Maggie's faces whipped around with identical expressions, and I felt my cheeks heat up.

"Uh, what's that you say?" Lily asked.

"Whatever, it was nothing. He was hanging out last night, and we fell asleep on the couch. End of story."

Ellie laughed. "Looked like more than that to me."

I made a face. "We were fully clothed."

No one spoke.

"We didn't even kiss!" I added, frustrated.

"Did you want to kiss?" Maggie asked.

"No, of course not," I lied.

"He sure looked like he wanted to kiss you," Ellie said as she stepped off the curb.

"Thanks for that, Ellie. It's not a big deal guys. So I'm attracted to my ex, and he's staying at my place because *somebody's* getting nailed like a porn star every night."

Lily rolled her eyes.

"We fell asleep on the couch. It's not like I banged him."

Lily shook her head at me. "You mean to tell me that you're not at all conflicted about hanging out with Tricky all night and sleeping with him? Like, nada? No feelings on the matter?"

"I mean, sure, it was weird, but it didn't mean anything. We didn't even talk about it, and I'm dating, remember?"

Maggie eyed me. "So you don't know if it was a big deal for him, though, right?"

I scoffed. "Of course it wasn't. Honestly, I think he just feels guilty about how things ended and probably wants to bone me just as bad as I want him to bone me. That's all. That's the extent of it." I said it like it had to be true, because if it wasn't true, I was in deeper shit than I thought.

Lily snickered. "You want to bone him."

"Who *doesn't* want to bone Tricky?" I asked, flustered. "Have you *seen* him?"

She laughed. "Nice try. It's okay to admit that you enjoyed sleeping with him, you know."

"Sure. It was nice. Amazing, even. He smells like heaven, and his arms are so sexy, they could have their own Tumblr. But he's not mine, and I don't want him."

Lily raised a brow.

"Okay, I refuse to want him." We trotted down the subway stairs in silence for a second before I continued. "Seriously, this changes nothing, okay? It was just a weird thing that happened and it's over. Later, we'll pick out a new guy for me go out with, because I'm *dating*. I'm gonna date some guy so hard, he's gonna get whiplash. I'm gonna date the fuck out of that guy because I'm over Tricky, and he's over me, and it's *over*, okay?" I rambled, taking a breath as soon as I could.

"Fair enough," Lily said as we walked up to the MetroCard vending machine, seeming to answer for everyone.

"Thank you," I huffed.

Ellie's face scrunched up as she inspected the machine. "How's this work?"

Lily smiled and stepped up to the machine. "Here, I'll do it for you."

I sighed, feeling the pressure of the conversation leave a little as I turned to Maggie. "How are you? I haven't seen you in an age."

She beamed, pushing her blond, curly hair our of her face. "Oh, I'm good." Her Mississippi accent was thick as honey. "Just so busy. Work has been nuts at the shelter. I'm so happy for the promotion, but man, they have me workin' like crazy putting together reading curriculums for homeless shelters across the city."

I smiled proudly. "That's amazing, Mags."

A blush bloomed across her freckled cheeks. "Thanks. It's my dream job."

"All right," Lily said, "We've got it. Let's go."

We headed toward the turnstile. "How was Greece?"

"Oh, Rose, it was the most beautiful place I've ever seen. We started in Athens and sailed to Mykonos, Rhodes, and Santorini. That one was my favorite. I could have stayed forever," she said with a dreamy sigh. "Anyway, Coop is good too, he's just been working like crazy like me. I swear, we get home every night, order in, watch a little TV, and pass out. I miss y'all though. You doin' okay?"

"Yeah, I'm doing okay. Just the usual, you know. Work. Sleep. That's pretty much it."

"And Tricky's staying with you. That's new."

We stopped at the platform. Lily and Ellie chatted, and I dropped my voice a little. "Yeah. It's the right thing to do, and I want to help him, but it hasn't been easy."

"No, I can't imagine that it has been. Seriously, those eyes he gives you … I don't know how you're still standing."

I chuckled. "Some days I don't either."

The train pulled up, and once the doors opened, we filed on. It was early enough that we found seats together.

"So," Ellie said, turning in her seat, "I'm kinda fuzzy on how all you guys know each other. Like, didn't Maggie live with you for a minute, Rose?"

"Musical roommates," Lily said with a laugh.

I laughed. "Seriously. Everyone's lived with me except Cooper and West." I turned to face Ellie. "Okay, so it's a little complicated, so tell me if you get lost."

She settled in and put her concentrating face on. "Okay."

"All right. So, the first person to move into the building was Tricky. He lived there with his friend Seth for about a year. And about halfway into that year, I moved in with Jack and Liz."

Her eyes were narrowed in thought. "Got it. Also, fuck Jack."

I held up my hand for a high five, and she slapped it. "Yes, fuck Jack. So, when Seth moved out, West moved in."

"Wait." Her nose wrinkled up. "How did Cooper know Patrick?"

"They met at some club opening and hit it off. When he found out Tricky was a tattoo artist, he sent West over to the shop because he wanted some work done, and when they got to talking, it came up that Tricky needed a roommate. So did West, he and Coop were moving out of their dorms at Columbia, and West didn't want to live on the East side, penthouse or not."

She snorted. "Yeah, I think I'd take the penthouse."

Lily laughed. "Well, West's nothing if not practical."

"Okay," I continued, using my hands to make a diagram in the air. "So West moved in with Tricky, and then Jack and Liz took off. Then Lily moved in."

Lily raised her fist in solidarity. "Flower power."

She nodded. "I'm still with you."

"Then Maggie moved here a few months ago and stayed with us for a minute. Or, me I guess, since Lily wasn't really sleeping at home anymore. And she's West's sister."

"Right. Okay." She paused for a second, and I could see the wheels in her brain turning. "Okay. I might have followup questions, but I think I'm good for now." She snapped her fingers. "Wait, Lily has a sister too, right?"

Lily grabbed the pole in front of her as the train pulled to a stop. "Yeah, Astrid."

Ellie's eyes widened. "Oh, right. Astrid Thomas. The model, duh. Like I haven't seen her in USWeekly."

"That's my sister," Lily chimed. "She wanted to come today, but Times Square on a Saturday is like a paparazzi nightmare. She'll be at Habits tonight, though."

Ellie perked up even more. "I can't wait to see this bar after everything I've heard."

"And," Lily said, "Tonight's the night we pick out Rose's next date, since her last one was a disaster."

My face was flat. "He stalked my Facebook and surprised me with facts about myself."

"Hooooohmygod." Ellie's mouth was an 'o.' "No."

"Oh, yes." My eyes darted to Lily. "Lil, I forgot to tell you — I ran into Tricky when I left Roasted, and he was with Seth."

Her eyes widened. "Seriously?"

I nodded.

Ellie and Maggie watched us. "That's bad?" Ellie asked.

I nodded again. "Very bad. Tricky's a recovering addict, and Seth has been trying to get clean for years. Unsuccessfully."

"Oh."

"What did he want?" Concern was written all over Lily's face.

I sighed. "Nothing, he said, but who knows. He'll be at Tricky's birthday party."

"Oh, God. Should Habits hire a bouncer for that night? When Seth drinks …" Lily didn't finish, just gave me a look.

"I know. Tricky said he's totally sober, so at least no one will get their nose bloodied."

"Unless somebody pisses off my brother," Maggie added, trying to lighten the mood.

Lily chuckled. "Yes. Unless that happens."

The train pulled into the Times Square station, and we walked the blocks north until the street opened up, buildings stretched high, covered with lights and billboards and videos. There were people everywhere, cabs stopping and going in yellow streaks as we stood in the middle of New York, and even the most hardened of us couldn't help but take a quiet moment to appreciate the beauty of the city we loved so much.

We made it back to the apartment that afternoon with aching feet and a little bit of sunburn. I almost wasn't surprised to find Patrick there, eating a sandwich in my kitchen.

"Hey," he said. "I was just about to head to Habits — West and Cooper are already on their way down."

"Oh," Lily said, smiling as she hooked her arm in Maggie's. "Want to just go now?"

"Sounds good. We'll see y'all there." She waved, and the two of them left.

Ellie stretched. "I guess I'll go change. Be right back." She disappeared around the corner and into her room.

"I guess I'll walk down with you and Ellie."

There was no escaping him. Not anymore. I tried to smile. "Sure."

My mood sank again, down into the sour depths. I had to be PMSing, because I snagged a lemon bar from the bag on table and ate it in three bites before I'd even made it to my room. It would also do a lot to explain my mood swings. Not that Patrick couldn't manage kicking my mood up and down like a see-saw on his own, but the raging hormones didn't help.

My cousin showing up out of the blue didn't help either. I loved her, but in that moment, tired and smelling like New York with my gorgeous ex sitting at my table, I just couldn't deal.

I reminded myself that Patrick and I were in the same boat. He was bearable. Maybe even a little enjoyable. It reminded me of what it used to be like. Before.

I pushed the memories away before they had a chance to settle in.

I emerged from my room a few minutes later in black jeans, combat boots, and a black, low cut tank, feeling a little more like myself. Liner was winged. Lips were red. Necklaces were shiny. Hair was big. And it was time to make that cheese.

Patrick was still at the table, and when he looked up at me, we both sort of froze. Everything moved slow and long like it had that morning. The light over the table cast deep shadows on the angles of his face, almost shielding his eyes, but they glinted, caught on mine like a lifeline.

I cleared my throat and grabbed my bag, turning to him once I'd collected myself enough to be coherent. "I'm sorry. About Ellie jacking your bed. I mean it — if it's too bad over there, you can always stay here."

His deep voice rumbled through me. "Thanks, Rose."

I took a breath and tried to put on a passable smile, like he didn't hijack my ability to keep my shit together. "No problem."

Ellie came out of Lily's room in a sparkly top, a very short skirt, very high heels, and a full on arm party of bracelets, with Valentino in her arms.

One of my brows climbed. "Uh, you may be a little overdressed for Habits, El."

She shrugged and kissed her cat. "Not worried about it."

"You're letting your LA show."

Ellie laughed and put Valentino down. He watched us as he walked away, probably to judge his new digs, as Ellie picked up her bag. "California girl until I die, Rosie. I once saw a chick at a Target in The Valley in a floor length fur coat. LA don't care."

"True," I said as we left the apartment. "I swear, LA is the only place where you would see a guy in a grocery store wearing a full blown tux at eleven in the morning on a Tuesday, right next to an old lady wearing rainbow tights, booty shorts, and a crop top. And the best part is that no one looks twice."

Patrick chuckled. "It's not like New York doesn't have its own weird."

"That's true," I said, "but it's a different kind of weird. Different vibe."

Patrick's hands were in his pockets as we descended the stairs. "I've never been. It's one of the only places I haven't lived."

Ellie flipped her hair. "Moved around a lot?"

He nodded. "My dad was in the army. Mostly grew up in the Midwest."

"What was your favorite place to live? Besides New York?" she asked.

He thought about it as we turned on the landing and headed down the last flight. "Kansas, weirdly. It seemed to have just the right everything. Seasons. Landscape. It was the most classically normal place I ever lived."

"And the worst?" I asked.

He made a face and pulled open the building door for us. "Killeen, Texas. I mean, I'm sure not all of Texas is bad, but that was the hottest summer of my life. When the thirty-foot walk from your front door to the car leaves you wringing out your shirt, it's too hot. I swear to God, it was like living in hell."

Ellie laughed. "Screw that. There are usually like two weeks in the summer in LA where you want to die, but otherwise it's not so bad."

"Is this your first time to New York?" he asked.

"Yup. Lily came home with Rose once, so we've met. The rest of you guys I've only heard of."

I smiled. "Ellie and I grew up pretty close to each other. Our dads are brothers. Hers was the wild one."

She snickered. "And yours was the goodie."

"Maybe by comparison. Couple of surfers out of Venice Beach. El and I grew up together, which was nice since I'm an only child."

"I wish I was. But instead, I have two older sisters — one engineer and one chemist."

Patrick looked impressed. "Not bad."

"Ha. Unless you're me. No pressure, right? At least I'm the baby, which means I get away with murder." Her lips curled into a smile.

I laughed. "It's true," I said to Patrick. "She can pretty much do anything at all and her parents are over the moon."

"I thought they were going to kill me when I told them I wanted to model, but they just clapped and cooed and paid a zillion dollars to have head shots done. Honestly, I think they were surprised my sisters went all intellectual. I mean, Dad's smoked so much weed in his life, I'm surprised he can remember his last name most days. And Mom is more interested in her shoe closet than most other things."

"They mean well," I said, smiling.

"They do, which is why it's tolerable. My sisters are uptight. Pretty sure they think the rest of us are all flibbertigibbets."

I laughed. "Ooooh, good word."

She giggled. "I know. It's so fun to say. *Flibbertigibbet.*"

Patrick opened the door to Habits for us, and we stepped into the bar where I'd worked since I moved to New York. It was clean and modern, with white subway tile and dark, planked floors, a long, dark bar taking up most of the space. The piping was exposed, the tiles all gone to open it up, give it some air.

It was my home away from home.

Shelby stood behind the bar, a sandy-haired, freckle-faced pixie who flashed a mega-watt smile at me. West and Lily were already sitting at the bar with Cooper and Maggie, and we waved our hellos.

"Cooper, West, this is my cousin, Ellie."

"Hey," she answered with a twiddle of her fingers.

"Nice to meet you," West said. "What are you doing in New York?"

"I came for a visit," she said with a smile.

My eyebrows were up, though I was smiling. "With her cat."

Cooper looked between Ellie and I. "So a quick visit, then?" he joked.

Ellie shrugged. "I couldn't leave Valentino with Darren, that asshole.

He'd probably kick my poor baby out. Maybe drop him into the LA River just to be a dick."

Cooper laughed. "Sounds like you could use a drink."

"Let me go put my stuff away and I'll be right back." I walked past Patrick and into the office to clock in and stow my bag. By the time I took up my station behind the bar, they were all sitting, and Astrid was there too, sitting right next to Lily.

I smiled down the line of my friends. Mine was the best seat in the house. "So, what's everybody drinking?"

They ordered their drinks, and I poured accordingly. It was second nature. Glass, ice, booze. I knew the bar so well, I didn't even need to look at the labels, just reached for everything by memory. Heaven help any asshole who didn't put shit back where it belonged.

Astrid turned to Ellie. "So, what brought you to New York, Ellie?"

She took a sip of her vodka tonic. "I dunno. Just wanted out of LA. I walked in on Darren nailing this bitch Sasha, who was clearly not my friend. On *my* brand new duvet. I was *this close* to tweeting her real name, which she shouldn't have told me, but she was drunk on appletinis in Hollywood one night and I convinced her to tell me. Honestly, I would have just stuck with Susan, but that's just me." She rolled her eyes and took another drink. "Anyway, I was trying to figure out where to go and was just like, 'Duh. Rose.' So, here I am." She smiled.

Lily and I shared a look. "How long are you staying?" She asked.

Ellie shrugged. "I was going to maybe start looking for a job."

"So, you moved here?" Lily prompted.

She giggled. "I guess I kind of did?" She waved a hand. "I'll find another place if I decide to stay. Just tell me if you're over it, Rosie."

I smiled because what else could I do? If it were anyone else, I would have flipped. She could drop a house on me and I'd give up the ruby slippers without a second thought. "It's fine, Ellie. What did your mom say?"

Ellie rolled her eyes. "You know her. She's on some new juice diet and started selling cosmetics so she can fund a new line of dog clothes for her Yorkie. She's going to Cabo with Dad and just bought a bunch of clothes that even I wouldn't wear. And I'm a slut."

Maggie almost choked on her drink.

"Anyway, she didn't care, not when I told her I was coming here with you."

"Well, now you're here," I said, "and you've unlocked your Times Square achievement. What do you want to do next?"

She looked up at the ceiling. "I'd like to go out, for sure. Shopping, that's a must. Definitely need some D. And then, I don't know." She squinted. "I'm thinking a piercing."

I laughed. "Oh, Ellie. It's good to see you."

She smiled. "You too."

I looked down the row of faces in front of me again, realizing how much I missed everyone being together like this. It used to happen organically, though now it required several days of texting and coordination to get together. But any way I could get it, I was happy to take it.

I beamed at them. "I'm glad you guys all came out. It's been too long."

"It has," Maggie said as she pushed her curls out of her face. "I feel like we've all just been so busy."

Lily popped her head around West and pointed at Cooper. "Not too busy for sailing, though. You promised me sailing, Cooper. I need the Hamptons in my life."

He chuckled. "I'll deliver. I promise. How about Fourth of July? Everyone's invited."

A chorus of agreement rolled through us.

Lily jerked her chin at me, smiling like a traitor. "I think you should tell the boys how your date went yesterday, Rosie, before the tribe picks out your next one."

I glared at her. "Oh, it was great, if you love a good horror story."

"How bad was it?" Cooper asked, and Lily made a rim shot sound with her mouth. Everyone else leaned forward, and Patrick's eyes were on me like a magnifying glass. I avoided looking in his direction at all costs.

"Trust me. It was bad. He went on about his deep interest in dead animals and his 'passion' for taxidermy. Then he judged and insulted me for not having a 'passion' of my own. He said whiskey didn't count, so clearly he knows nothing."

"Hear, hear," Cooper cheered and raised his glass.

Everyone chuckled and took a drink, and I shook my head with a sigh. "It's so dumb. I don't know what I want to do, but why should that matter? I'm happy where I am. There's nothing else I particularly want to do. So who cares if my job is my passion? I mean, how many people get to say they're passionate about what they do?"

But then I looked at all of their faces, realizing each of them *did* work their passion: Maggie in charity work, Cooper in his family business, West a literature grad student, Lily a professional ballerina, Patrick an artist, and Astrid a model. And then there was me. And Ellie, I guess, too.

Maybe being talentless was a Fisher gene defect.

I actually laughed out loud at the realization.

Cooper took another drink and leaned on the bar. "Well, I mean, everyone has something they love. What about you?"

I leaned on the bar too. "I dunno. I love to skate, but it's not like I can be a pro skater at twenty-six, if I were even good enough. I'm good at bartending, and I like the hours. The money's good. It just works for me right now, in life."

"What else?" he asked.

"I love movies and reading. Usually romance, all kinds."

He raised his brow. "What about running a bookstore?"

I thought it over. "Could be fun, but I don't think I'd do well with any corporate shit. It would have to be my own thing." I smiled at the thought, imagining what it could be like. "What if it was just romance?"

His brows climbed higher. "What if you sold comics too?"

My eyes widened. "What if it was *a bar*?"

Lily gasped. "Oh, my God. What if you did like singles mixers? Comic boys and romance girls, finding love?"

I was gaping, my mind skipping through ideas. "Holy shit. That would be amazing."

Cooper tipped his glass toward me. "I would back the fuck out of that."

I laughed.

"I'm serious, Rose." He leaned a little closer. "You know how to run a bar — you've been working here for years. I know comics. You know romance. I'll put up the money, and you run it."

My ears were hot, and I kept laughing. "That's crazy. But it would be amazing. Who doesn't want to get drunk and hang out around books? I could do like special events for book clubs, or even run a monthly book club, alternating between romance and graphic novels."

Lily was amped up. "Seriously, think how hard it is to meet people in the city? That sounds like the perfect bar for some hard core matchmaking."

"What would you call it?" Maggie asked.

"Whiskey and Words," West called out.

"Whiskey Rose?" Lily added.

I shook my head. "Nah, doesn't really say books. Paper Cuts?"

"Ooh, I like that." Astrid raised her glass. "Books and blood. Your tag line can be '*Suck it when it bleeds.*'"

"Hmm," I hummed, enjoying playing along. "What says romance and comics and booze?"

"Plot Twist," Ellie said.

"Book Drunk," Cooper said with a laugh.

"Book Wasted," Lily shot. "Word Wasted."

"Wasted Words," Patrick said, and we locked eyes as everything came together, clicking into place.

I smiled at him, feeling the warmth of his gaze wash over me. "That would actually be perfect."

Cooper smirked. "Well, now it has a name. The hard part is done."

I shook my head, still daydreaming. "It's fun to think about."

His smile stretched a little higher. "Just think how much fun it'll be to run."

I rolled my eyes and laughed. "Okay, Cooper. Now, who needs another drink?"

I poured another round while everyone talked, my mind still savoring the thought of running my own business. It would be fun. Hard, but fun. But I'd never let Cooper bet that much on me. Who knew how I could ever pay it back. Who knew if I could even do it without running it into the ground.

It sure was fun to dream about, though.

West leaned on the bar, talking around Maggie to Patrick, so she slipped off her stool and made her way down to the other end of the bar to sit with the girls. So naturally, so did I.

Lily smiled conspiratorially. "Time to pick date number two."

"I haven't even had time to recover from date number one."

She shrugged. "Gotta get back on that horse, Rosie." She held out her hand and wiggled her fingers.

I sighed and pulled my phone out of my pocket, slapping it into her palm.

Lily grinned as she pulled open the app. "I don't know why you don't enjoy this. It's so fun."

I laughed. "Maybe for you. You're not the one who has to meet the guys. After Serial Killer Steve, I have to say I'm a little gun-shy."

Ellie waved a hand. "One time, I met this guy on Tinder who had like thirteen dogs. I didn't stay to bang because who wants that many dogs in your ass while you're hooking up?"

Astrid snorted. "I can't even use dating sites. The gossip mags would have a field day. Talk about dogs in my ass. So my dating pool is limited to other models and socialites, which is basically the worst subset of dating population ever."

Maggie shook her head. "I've dated two guys ever — Jimmy, who never kept it in his pants, and Cooper. I am not at all equipped to weigh in on this."

I smiled at her. "The only equipment you need is a vagina, and you have one of those."

Lily scrolled through, holding my phone out so we could all see. Patrick seemed to know what we were doing — I could feel him every single time he looked over. Something was different with him. I mean, he'd been staring at me from the other side of this bar for months, but now it was different. Deeper. Like I could feel him calling me.

He was like a sexy tractor beam. So I did exactly what I could — I ignore him. Okay, I pretended to ignore him. I may have also stuck my butt out at what I thought might be the sexiest angle and been overly conscious of my hands, but whatever.

"Oh," Ellie said, pointing at the screen. "Hang on, go back up. Who's this guy? *DesignerDan*?"

"No more artists," I said flatly.

Lily chuckled. "What about *KingTaco*?" She clicked on his profile.

"Points for the screen name, but working out is listed as a hobby."

"That just means he's probably got abs. I mean, *they* all work out." Lily nodded at the boys.

I rolled my eyes. "Well, yeah, but they wouldn't list it as a *hobby*. Also, he says he's looking for '*Someone who's awesome.*' Next."

STACI HART

Astrid snickered. "*BavarianCream*? There are too many jokes to even list."

Lily squinted at the screen. "*Hrywshs*? Is that like, hairy wishes? Hurry washes?"

"Heinous wooshes?" I added.

"I'm going with hairy something. His beard connects with his chest hair." Ellie pointed to his picture with her face jacked.

Lily laughed. "Dude, look at *YankeeBro*."

My nose wrinkled. "Too real. Is he wearing a Ed Hardy shirt? I thought those went out of style like six years ago."

Astrid shook her head. "Like, he actually thought that was cool. He put the word bro in his screename and was like, 'Nailed it.' I'd think it was clever if it was a joke, but the guy has Swarovski crystals on his shirt."

Lily kept swiping with a confused look on her face. "Why are there so many pictures of guys with dogs?"

"I automatically assume those guys are players," I said.

She laughed. "You are such a cynic. What about this one? *DollarsAndSense*?" She turned the screen.

I bobbed my head. "Cute, and points for word play, but that bow tie is a no."

Lily frowned. "What's wrong with his bow tie?"

"It makes him look like he's twelve. It's not like when, I don't know, say Patrick wears one."

Astrid nodded. "Oh, yeah. There's not much that can top that. The bar's too high."

"So high," I added with a laugh. "What about that one?"

Markalark's profile picture was gorgeous — the light streaming in from a window as he looked down at his fingers on the neck of his guitar. He was a musician without any morbid hobbies, or at least nothing he wrote about on his profile, which the four of us combed over.

Lily raised a brow. "Are you sure you want to give a musician a shot? I thought you swore them off forever after Jack."

I shrugged. "I'd give him a coffee date to prove me wrong."

She handed me my phone, smiling. "Message him."

I took it and fired off a message, trying not to feel nervous, figuring I could keep searching. *SkateTreason* crossed my mind, that hot skater boy I'd found the other day, but before I could look him up, my phone buzzed in my hand.

I gaped. "Holy shit, he already responded."

"Bam," Ellie said, breaking open her hand like she had thrown a bomb.

Hey, Rose. Nice to meet you. I'm available to hang whenever. When are you free?

"He wants to know when I'm free. What do I say?"

Astrid picked up her gin. "You don't want him to think you're desperate, but it sucks to wait to something that's not a sure thing, too."

I chewed my lip. "So tomorrow's too soon?"

Ellie shrugged. "Fuck it, I say. Not too soon at all."

What's your day like tomorrow? I asked. *I know of a great coffee shop nearby.*

My phone buzzed a second later. *Perfect. Just let me know the address and time, and I'll be there.*

My cheeks were hot, an involuntary smile on my lips. "It's on for tomorrow."

Lily grinned eagerly. "Are you excited? You look excited."

"I am. I mean, anything has to be better than Serial Killer Steve."

"Maybe Music Mark will be a hit," Maggie said, smiling before sipping her bourbon.

I glanced over at Patrick, meeting his shadowed eyes. "We can hope."

Eventually

PATRICK

Maggie, cooper, and astrid left, but the rest of us closed down the bar, waited for Rose to clean up, all while my mind rolled over what my next move would be. I felt ambitious, maybe a little foolhardy, unwavered by the girls swiping through a dating app, aside from the flashes of jealousy. I'd resisted the urge to pull a movie scene hero move and hop the bar to kiss some sense into her, ignoring the visions of her being with another man — in *any* sense of the word — because I knew she'd come back to me if I was patient. I didn't know how I knew, but I did.

The way she looked at me this morning triggered something in me, the briefest glimmer of what she'd been hiding behind a wall of apathy that told me she still felt it. I'd calmed down from my cavalier high, knowing I couldn't be rash or hasty, as much as I wanted to be.

So, slow and steady it would be. The more time that passed, the more the wall would crumble until it was gone.

It was late, the bar locked and dark behind us, when we found ourselves walking up broadway, pizza in hand.

"Mmm," Ellie groaned, mouth full. "The pizza here is way better, but I still would have preferred a taco truck."

Rose nodded. "Seriously, finding good tacos in New York is impossible. I've been looking for years. There's one that's amazing, but it's in Union Square. No way am I taking the train seventy blocks to Midtown just for tacos, no matter how bad I want them."

Lily chuckled, angling her pizza for a bite. "May as well be in Jersey."

"Or Brooklyn," West added.

"I dunno," I said. "Pizza is the best drunk food. It's got everything you need — carbs, dairy, protein. Grease. Can't do without that."

Rose smiled at me. "Chase it with a glass of water and some ibuprofen and you're hangover free."

I smiled back and took a bite, wishing I hadn't refused sleeping on her couch. Maybe there was still a way back over tonight. She didn't want me to stay. No, it wasn't that — I could see it in her face. She was afraid to let me stay. Afraid she'd give up any more of her resolve than she already had.

When we reached Rose's door, Lily and West said their goodbyes, walking on to our place. Their place. West's place? I didn't even know anymore. I hung back, waiting for the girls to get inside.

Ellie headed straight to her room with a wave over her shoulder, and Rose turned to me as she pulled her key out of the lock and stuffed her hands in the pocket of her leather jacket.

"Are you sure you don't want to stay?"

I looked into her eyes, trying to decipher whatever was behind them, though it was just beyond me. I wanted to tell her I wanted to stay forever. I wanted to tell her I needed her. I wanted to touch her lips and tell her that she was mine, and I was hers. But I smiled, not saying what I wanted to. Just like old times.

Slow and steady.

"I'll survive. See you around, Rose."

She nodded, lips parted, her eyes on mine like she understood on some level, a level she wasn't willing to acknowledge. "All right, Tricky."

I backed away, watching her as she closed her door, and then I turned for my apartment.

West and Lily were still shuffling around the living room. He looked over his shoulder as sat on the couch, bending to untie his shoes. I took a seat in the armchair, propping my feet on the coffee table with a sigh.

"It's been too long since everyone came out. That was nice." Lily set her bag down on the table and sat next to West, smiling at me conspiratorially. "So are you gonna tell us what happened with Rose last night?"

West leaned back and wrapped his arm around her, pulling her into him as they settled into the couch with a brow raised. "Uh, what's this?"

I smirked. "What'd Rose say?"

"Well, she didn't give up much, but given how flustered she was and how many times she said it wasn't a big deal, I'm guessing it was definitely a big deal."

"It was accidental. We were just hanging out and fell asleep, but when we woke up ..." I looked at the bookshelf across the room, packed with books two layers deep and any way they could fit. "There's a chance for me."

Lily's cheeks were flushed, her smile bright. "It's kind of what I've been telling you. There's absolutely a chance for you. Are you going to take it?"

I met her eyes. "I have to."

"Well, what the hell are you doing over here then? Get back over there."

I chuckled. "As much as I want to just go over there and get her, you and I both know she's not ready for that."

She wrinkled her nose. "No, probably not. Whats your plan?"

I sighed and stretched. "I haven't figured it out yet. I definitely think I need to be over there as much as possible — it's the only only way I'm going to get her to trust me. But I gave up your bed to Ellie, and … I don't know. I knew she wanted me to try to not sleep on her couch, so here I am."

"Use us as an excuse," Lily said.

I raised a brow.

She grinned as she sat up and leaned forward, resting her elbows on her knees. "Seriously. That's been the excuse all this time, right? Well, get back over there and tell her we're just too loud and horny and inconsiderate for you to sleep here."

"Like, right now?" I asked, thinking of three reasons off the top of my head that going over there at that moment was a terrible idea.

"No, not right now." She waved a hand. "Not until she's asleep. It won't be long — it's so late. So in like a half-hour, just go over there and crash. Problem solved."

West laughed. "Aren't we just a bunch of conspirators?"

Lily shrugged and hitched a thumb over her shoulder. "I mean, West and I can go in there and get crazy if you need us to."

I put out a hand. "Yeah, no. I'm good." I paused, thinking it over, weighing it out.

Lily rolled her eyes. "Oh, my God. Just do it. Come here, West. Tricky needs motivation. Stick your tongue down my throat." She grabbed his face comically and pulled, smushing her lips against his, making exaggerated moaning noises. West laughed against her mouth.

I chuckled, shaking my head at them. "All right, all right. I'll go."

Lily stopped being gross and smiled, looking proud of herself. "I'm happy for you, Tricky. I hope it works."

I smiled back as I stood. "Me too. 'Night, guys."

"'Night," they called after me as I headed into my room.

I turned on the lamp next to my bed, an island of soft light in the dark as I pulled off my jacket. Untied my boots. Unbuttoned my shirt and tugged off my jeans. And then I slipped into bed, sinking into the comfort of my own sheets, my own pillow.

Rose had another date tomorrow, and I wasn't even ashamed to say that I hoped it was a disaster. I hoped it bought me more time. Brought her closer to me. Maybe this year I'd get what I wanted for my birthday. I closed my eyes for a moment, imagining it — the first kiss, the first touch, the feeling of her in my arms.

I think I drifted off for a moment because when I opened my eyes, the light was a little too bright, my body heavy as I dragged it out of bed. I wrapped myself in my comforter and shuffled down the hall to Rose's, laying down on her couch that was a little too short to really be comfortable, staring into the dark room, though everything came into focus eventually.

Eventually.

The word defined so much of my life. Eventually she'd come around in one way or another. Eventually I'd need to figure out what to do with myself. Eventually, I'd need to get the girl or move on. But we were all caught in a transition, and the only way out was time. The dice were in the air, and we were all waiting for them to hit the table and roll to see if we'd won or lost.

Joan Jett

ROSE

I leaned over the counter in the bathroom the next afternoon, lips stretched in an O as I lined my them in my favorite shade of red: Bloody Valentine.

Seemed appropriate for a first date.

Diving back into the boy catalog with a little more gusto and higher standards had been the right move, just like moving on from Patrick was. He was sleeping back at his place, and now everything would go back to normal.

Nothing has changed. Nothing at all.

I was going to make dating my bitch. Good date today or bad, I was determined to keep going. As skeptical as I had been about finding a guy online, it was the perfect, low-impact way to ease myself back into the game.

I took a last look at myself in the mirror — skinny black jeans, ankle boots, leather jacket, big, shaggy hair. Lily said I intimidated guys, but I just figured it was an easy method for weeding out anyone who couldn't handle me. At least this way they knew what they were getting. Or at least I told myself that was why, and that it had nothing to do with me preferring loneliness to getting hurt again.

When I made my way into the living room, I found Ellie stretched out on the couch, red hair piled on her head. Her eyes were glued to the TV, which I figured had been on MTV since she'd turned it on, but what stopped me in my tracks was the fact that she was wrapped in Patrick's comforter.

I stopped behind the arm chair with my stomach in my throat, part of me convinced they'd had sex. Maybe on my couch. I thought I might puke. "Why do you have Tricky's blanket?"

Her face quirked as she looked over at me. "Hmm?"

"That blanket. It's Tricky's. Did you …"

Her brows shot up. "God, no." But her surprise slipped into a comical leer. "I mean, not like I wouldn't, if it weren't for the fact that you still want to bang him."

I scowled. "Do not."

"Yeah, right." She leaned forward and picked up a folded piece of paper off the coffee table. "The blanket was on the couch when I woke up. I found this note too."

I stuck out my hand to take it, but she unfolded it and began to read.

"Rose, I might take you up on your offer after all. Crashed on the couch, hope it's okay. Let me know. Tricky."

She handed it to me, and I smiled, only partly annoyed she'd snooped my note. Mostly, I was just relieved she hadn't slept with Patrick.

"So, he's going to be staying here after all?" she asked and wet her lips. "Tell me he sleeps naked."

I chuckled and rolled my eyes as I walked into the kitchen.

"You're impossible."

She waggled her eyebrows. "Is he tattooed *everywhere?*"

The pantry didn't have anything appetizing, so I decided on a lemon bar for breakfast. I salivated at the thought and reached for the bag on the counter, but it was empty. I pouted. "Only crazy people tattoo their dicks, Ellie. Fact of life."

She tilted her head. "But doesn't it look weird if he's tattooed everywhere *but* there?"

"Trust me, when it's in your face, that's the last thing you're thinking about. The piercing makes it look fierce enough."

Her eyes widened, and she giggled. "Oh, my God. Does he have any friends?"

"More than a few." I grabbed my bag and slung it on. "You'll meet them in a couple of days. Everyone's going to Habits for Tricky's birthday."

"Oh, goodie." She pulled his blanket up a little and stuck her nose in it, closing her eyes as she inhaled. "This smells good. Like boy and laundry."

I sighed and grabbed my keys, knowing all too well. "Yup."

"Where are you going, all dressed up?" she asked, confused.

"Meeting Music Mark at Roasted."

"I totally forgot. Want me to call you like fifteen minutes in? Give you an out?"

I chuckled. "After Stinky Steve, that might be a good idea, but I have hope."

"I should set an alarm or something. I can't be trusted to keep track of time on a normal day, never mind when Teen Mom is on." She picked up her phone.

"All right. I better get going. Wish me luck."

She waved enthusiastically. "Good luck!"

I laughed and grabbed my bag. "Thanks, El. Talk to you in a bit."

The walk to Roasted was a good one, with every step steady and full of decision. As if I could make my destiny just by willing it.

I wanted to move on, so I would. I wanted to date, so I'd do it, and God help anybody that got in my way, because I was on the warpath to getting past my past. Even though he'd come back to sleep in my apartment again after all.

I pulled open the door and stepped inside, scanning the coffee shop for Mark, but I didn't find him. Figured I may as well get my coffee while I waited, so I hopped in line.

It was nearly my turn when I heard my name. "Rose?"

I turned to find Mark smiling at me, and it was a great smile. He was a little taller than me, with a dark beard and hair long enough that it brushed the collar of his leather jacket.

"Mark, hey." I smiled back just as the person in front of me moved out of the way, and it was my turn. I stepped up to the register. "Hi, can I get a regular chai and a lemon bar, please?"

"Sure," the barista answered. "Anything else?"

Mark stepped up and pulled out his wallet. "Can I get a large drip?"

"Sure, name?"

"I'm Quincy, and this is Joan." He handed a twenty to her, and she gave him change.

I smiled as we moved out of the way to wait for our drinks, intrigued. "Quincy?" I asked, one brow raised.

He smiled and leaned in like we were scheming. "Jones. And you're Joan Jett."

I laughed. "I like it. How'd you know I was a fan?"

He shrugged. "You just put out that vibe, like you make the world your bitch on the regular."

"How can you kick the world in the face if you leave your badass at home?"

"My point exactly."

They called our names, and my optimism climbed a notch as we grabbed our drinks and sat down. I couldn't help but look him over, fooling with the cardboard sleeve as he settled in. Mark was cute, normal, bought me coffee, and called me Joan Jett.

First impressions, for the win. The guy was a charmer, that was for sure.

He sat back in his chair and manspread his legs. I tried not to form an opinion about that, figuring if his worst flaw was that he was a nightmare to sit next to on the subway, I was doing all right. Definitely a step up from a guy who hung out with dead animals for a living.

"So, you're a musician?" I asked.

"All my life."

"What kind of music?"

He made a face and shook his head, looking away. "I hate comparisons. No one said Nirvana sounded like anyone but Nirvana."

Oh, God. He was one of *those* musicians. Jack was one of *those* musicians. If I'd had to sit through another conversation with him defending Tom Waits, I would have broken up with him first.

I took a breath and smiled, sure I was just being too picky, like Lily always said. "Okay, how about a genre?"

He shook his head. "Labels are so confining. I just want to *create*, you know? Sometimes I'll sit for hours recording, just me, my keyboard, and my weed. I once laid down a fourteen hour atmospheric synth track." He looked so proud of himself.

My hopes were dashed. Mark may not have been the first musician I'd dated, but I decided then that he should probably be my last.

"Wow," was the only response I could muster, and I took a sip of my chai, glad Ellie would be calling any second.

"Thanks," he said graciously, thinking I'd been impressed. "I'm in between bands right now. Creative differences, you know how that is. Not everyone gets the vision. Like I have some instrumental tracks I recorded left-handed. Some critics say the sound is amateur. What they don't get is that it's a reflection of society's expectations."

A little piece of my faith in humanity slipped away.

He clearly wanted to talk about himself, so I kept the questions going as I slipped my hand into the pocket of my jacket to rest on my phone, waiting for the merciful buzzing that meant I'd have an excuse to leave. "Do you write your own lyrics?"

Mark scoffed. "Of course. Here, check it out." He pulled out a small leather notebook from his pocket and untied the leather strap, opening it in front of him. He cleared his throat and began to read. "Pain, it hurts. Aw, babe, it hurts. You left, and it hurt. The pain, it hurts. Aw, babe, come back, it hurts."

My mouth had slipped open just enough to show my bewilderment, and he shuffled, leaning forward when he realized I was confused. He just had the wrong idea why.

"It's better when I sing it." He closed his eyes and started singing. Sort of. Really, it sounded like this cat my mom had when I was a kid, Olive, who ate a Christmas ornament and shredded her vocal chords. Sort of a ragged grumble, like he'd been run through a cheese grater.

That was Misguided Mark to a T.

I shrank back in my chair, cheeks on fire as everyone in the coffee shop turned their faces toward the sound.

My phone rang, and I whipped it out of my pocket to answer it. Mark didn't stop singing.

"Hey, Ellie." I tried to sound cheery.

"Oh, my God. What the hell is that noise? Are you being assaulted? Should I call 911?" She seemed genuinely concerned.

"I'm fine, what's up?"

"He sounds like an animal. Like a drunk, *Pet Cemetery* zombie animal."

"Oh, you need me to come home? Water leak?"

Mark finally stopped singing.

"Maybe he's possessed," Ellie said. "Do you have any holy water?"

My eyes found his as I nodded, holding up a finger. "Sure, I can be home in just a minute. Thanks for letting me know."

"Glad I could help, Rose," she said. "Tell him to lose your number. You know, maybe online dating isn't the solution."

"You might be right. See you in a few." I hung up and put on my fake-ass smile. "God, I am *so* sorry, Mark, but I have to run. A pipe burst in my building, and it looks like my whole floor is flooded." I stood and backed away, bumping into the table next to us. I whirled around. "Oh, God. Excuse me."

"Man, that's crazy," he said as he stood too. "So, ah, can I call you?"

The plastic smile stretched wider as I course corrected and kept moving toward the door. "Sure. It's really nice to meet you."

He smiled. "Sure thing, Joan. Catch you later."

I bolted out of the coffee shop, realizing too late that I'd forgotten my coffee and lemon bar. Embarrassed and starving, I resorted to a dreaded group text situation to get the girls to meet me at Genie's.

All hands on deck. Only a cheeseburger and tots can save me.

took a huge bite of my burger and immediately felt better. I moaned.

"Hungry, Rose?" Lily said with a brow up while she watched me eat like a hog.

"Don't make fun of me," I said around a wad of food.

"It was really bad, Lily," Ellie said as she poked at her salad. "It was like somebody dumped a bucket of bolts into a garbage disposal."

Lily made a face.

I swallowed and took a sip of my Dr. Pepper. "It was probably one of my more awkward public moments in life. I really had my hopes up about him too."

Lily picked up her BLT. "Well, at least you made it out alive. Who's on deck next?" She took a rude bite and hummed her approval.

I looked at her like she was nuts. "There has to be a better way. I can't handle another shitty date with a weird-shit weirdo. I thought I could, but I can't."

"Aww, come on," Lily said with a frown. "Third time's a charm."

"I don't believe in luck." I popped a tater tot into my mouth.

"Come on. Give it one more shot. Let's up the standards, and no more guys with interesting jobs. The more boring, the better. And definitely message him some and get to know him before you agree to meet."

I grabbed my burger and took another bite, avoiding answering. Lily was tenacious, I knew. I wondered if she'd give it up before I gave in. I weighed it out. I could either hear it from Lily for the next week — at least — or I could go on one more date.

"I'll make you a deal," I said when I'd swallowed. "I'll go on one more date, but this is the last guy before I find another way to meet a guy, because this shit's ridiculous. I'm deleting the app if this one doesn't work out."

She pouted. "Forever?"

I bobbed my head, eyes on the ceiling. "For anywhere from two to six months."

That seemed to sate her. "Fair enough. Let's have a look." She held out a hand.

"You don't get to mention it for minimum of two months, either. Deal?" My voice was heavy with warning.

She sighed and rolled her eyes. "Fine, deal. Now get out your phone and get to swiping."

I chuckled as I took another bite and set my burger down, dusting off my hands before picking up my phone. I remembered *SkateTreason* again, and opened up his profile. "Hey, remember this guy?"

Ellie took my phone, and she and Lily bent their necks to look him over. "He's cute," Ellie said with a nod.

I snorted. "That's obviously not an indicator that he's actually interesting, if my other dates and like ninety percent of all profiles are any proof."

"Oh, yeah," Lily said as she looked over his profile. "You two have a lot in common. He's a barista, which is basically a coffee bartender. You both skate. His profile is funny." She passed the phone to me. "I approve. Message him."

"Fine, bossy." I typed out a message and set down my phone. "That's it. Last one. Now, we wait."

Lily raised a brow. "You sure you don't want to find a couple more, just in case he doesn't respond?"

"Yup." I tossed another tot into my mouth and smiled.

Bench Press

PATRICK

AC/DC *played over the speakers* in the gym as I rested between reps, watching West in the mirror with his jaw clenched. He pulled the barbell up to his shoulders, held it, and let it down as he exhaled. Then again, his neck straining before he set down the barbell and hung his hands on his hips, jerking his chin at me in the mirror.

"You're up."

I smirked and picked it up, standing in front of the mirror, watching my form as I pulled the barbell up and lowered it, then again, rep after rep.

A girl walked behind us, towel hanging around her neck, blond ponytail high and black shorts short. Her eyes were on me in the mirror, lip between her teeth. My smile climbed a little, though I looked back at myself before she made eye contact, watching my tattoos shift as my shoulders flexed.

West shook his head when she'd passed, smiling as he leaned against the mirror and retied his hair into a knot.

"That chick has walked by probably twelve times."

I lowered the bar. "Hadn't noticed." I pulled it up as I took a breath and held it.

"It's weird that you wouldn't notice. The minute we walked over here, no less than four girls materialized to half-ass use whatever they knew how to."

I did a rep. "I dunno, man. People look at me all the time." I lowered the weights. " I usually assume it's the ink," I said and pulled it up again, jaw flexing as the burn set in.

He folded his arms. "Yeah, they didn't look curious. They looked like they were starving."

I snorted and set the barbell down. "How do you know they're not looking at you?" We switched places, and he picked it up.

"Because I have eyes. Seriously, when you were doing dead lifts, one of them almost fell off the treadmill over there."

I laughed and picked up my water.

He lifted the bar and held it. "Lily's ready for your birthday, by the way."

"Oh, God."

He smirked as he lowered the weights. "Oh, yes. I know how much you're looking forward to it."

"Having everybody in the same place is rare. I just have to endure a little attention. At least there will be booze."

"Ha." He did another rep.

I took a drink, watching him. "Seth came by the shop the other day."

He glanced at me. "I heard."

"I figured," I said as I screwed the cap back on. "He's going to be at Habits."

"It's been a long time."

"Yeah."

"How are you feeling about seeing him?" He eased the barbell down and back up again.

"Not sure," I said, realizing he was the first person who asked me how I felt about Seth before offering their opinion. "Part of me really believes he's got it together. He's going to NarcAnon meetings, has a steady job … it's everything I ever wanted for him."

West nodded and did another upright row.

"It doesn't erase everything, but it's a start. I can't turn him away. He says he doesn't even drink anymore."

West huffed out a laugh. "Yeah, well, that's definitely good to hear. His drinking was the worst part. Almost more destructive than the drugs."

I shook my head and crossed my ankles. "I used to just plan on getting into a fight every time we went out. Like, I thought that was normal."

"You thought a lot was normal that wasn't."

"Sometimes, I'm still amazed at how different we all grew up."

West set down the weights, and we traded places again. "I know. I'm glad you met Joel when you did. I can't imagine what life would have been like otherwise."

I shook my head. "Me either." I took a deep breath before starting the reps quietly, trying not to think about it.

"Well," West said after a second, "I hope it's his time. It'll be good to see him sober."

I nodded, jaw tight. "Yeah. Me too."

I finished my set in silence and set down the barbell. West stepped over to the dumbbell rack. "Let's run the rack. Shrugs."

"One hundred to fifty?"

"Burn it out. I'll go first." He grabbed the hundred-pound

dumbbells, holding them by his side. He blew out a breath, brows drawn as he began to shrug, using just his shoulders to lift his arms and the weight until he strained, then set down the hundreds and moved to the nineties.

I was still cooling down from my last set, and as I waited, the girl with the blond ponytail walked by again. She smiled, and I shook my head, chuckling in West's direction.

"All right. I see what you mean."

He was too busy concentrating to answer, but his brows rose comically. I watched as he burned all the way down to the fifty-pound weights, setting them down on the rack with a clang.

His chest heaved, sweat dripping down his brow and shining on his skin. "You're up, Tricky."

I rolled my shoulders and shook out my arms before picking up the hundreds, blowing out a breath before grinding my teeth and hitting it hard, pushing until I couldn't push anymore, until my shoulders burned and a trickle of sweat rolled down the valleys of my back. My face was flushed as I set the fifties down, and I grabbed my towel to dry off.

West took a drink of his water and picked up his bag. "Tomorrow's leg day. No pussing out."

"I'll be here, will you?"

"Of course I will. I've got nothin' but time these days, Trick." He opened his arms in display.

I chuckled. "Seems like you're enjoying it."

"It's good. I usually hang out with Cooper during break. Luckily I have Lily this summer or I'd be awful lonesome."

I slung on my bag and took a drink of water, knowing he didn't realize that was where I was. Lonesome. "I'm happy for you, man."

He nodded down at his feet, smiling as we headed out of the gym. "Thanks. It's the strangest thing. Like everything in my life can be classified as before and after her. I don't know how I ever was me without her. Don't really care to ever know again." He glanced over at me. "I think she's it for me. Forever."

I smirked at him. "I know."

He met my eyes. "I'm going to marry that girl, Patrick."

My smile softened, heart warm in my chest. "That makes more sense than just about anything I've ever heard. I'm really am happy for you, West. For both of you."

His eyes held a shadow of sadness. "I want this for you. I want for you to feel like this."

I smiled and pushed open the door, and we turned to walk the blocks home. "I know. Wanting has only ever brought me sadness, but ignoring what I want with Rose is worse. So I'm trying to make the best of it for the last time with her."

"Rose doesn't do anything easy, does she?"

I sighed. "Neither do I. I want to want her. I want to hurt and pay for my mistakes. I want her to punish me just as much as I want her to forgive me, but that's only been killing the both of us. I can't pretend that I don't want all of her, and I'm not going to anymore."

He shook his head. "I'm glad you're going after her, but I wish it wasn't like this. I honest to God believe that if you just kissed her, she'd forget about all of it. She's hanging on to an idea that she believes is the truth, not the truth itself, and the second she lets that go, you're in the clear."

"I don't think it's that simple. Otherwise I would have already kissed her."

He chuckled.

"Look, it's like I said. I'm just trying to take this one step at a time, and I won't give up so easily. We're talking, hanging out again. She told me what she wanted, and I've respected that. I gave that to her because I owed her after how I handled things. Everything I've ever done is because I care about her, even when I hurt her. I just …" I shook my head. "I just want her to be happy. My happiness is secondary to that."

He let out a breath. "It's noble, I'll give you that. But you sacrifice what you want for everyone else."

"Because no one ever did for me."

His eyes went soft. "I guess that's fair."

"I'm not hurt about it, it's just a fact. That sacrifice is the most I can ever do for anyone, and I don't think twice about it. You don't, not when you love someone." I stuffed my hands in my pockets as we crossed the street. "But I have a feeling that what Rose and I want — *our* happiness — has the same answer: being together."

"There has to be a way to make her come around. I know she cares about you."

"I finally think you could be right. We just have to see. It's all going to come down to timing. I've got to wait for an opening, and to do that, I've got to be in her eye-line as much as possible." I sighed as we approached our building. "She met another guy today."

"I guess she's pretty serious about dating."

"Seems that way, but don't count me out yet. We'll see how it went. The worse they are, the better my chances."

"Well, let's forget about it tonight. We'll go drink scotch at Cooper's and play video games like the good old days."

"Deal," I said as we opened the door and climbed the stairs. "Let's shower and head over there. Is Lily home?"

"I think so. I don't know what the girls are doing tonight."

"Rose has to work. Maggie's probably leaving Cooper's for the night— I figured they were all getting together."

West opened the door, and Lily looked up from the couch where she lay reading.

"Hello, boys. Don't you look all sweaty and beefy." She waggled her brows.

West looked like he'd just found Shangri-La as he leaned over the back of the couch to kiss her sweetly. "Let me go get showered up and then I'll give you a proper kiss."

She closed her book, beaming, eyes roaming over his arms, across the sleeve I'd done for him. "Hmm. You know, I think I left something in the bathroom. Let me go check and see if it's there." It was like I wasn't even in the room.

She bounded off to the bathroom, and West looked over his shoulder with a shrug, dropping his bag and pulling off his shirt on the way to meet her.

"Guess I'll shower at Rose's," I said to myself, since no one was even in the room with me anymore.

I grabbed a towel and clothes from my room, leaving to the sound of the running shower and a string of giggles.

Rose's apartment was quiet and empty, and I made my way through, into her bathroom, turned the water on hot. When I pulled off my shirt, I saw her red lipstick on the counter, the dark hair ties and bobby pins, little signs of her everywhere. I undressed and stepped into the claw-foot tub and under the hot stream, thinking about those red lips of hers, wondering if they'd ever be mine again.

Ellie and I hauled ass up the stairs, plastic *Thank You* bag in hand full of feminine hygiene products, in preparation for my impending monthly. I was thirty seconds from peeing my pants and regretting not making a pit stop before leaving Genie's to run errands with Ellie. But whatever, at that point, it was every woman for herself.

Ellie cracked up as I ran down the hallway, face pinched as I hunched over, pressing on my bladder. "You run like a cow, Rose." She made mooing sounds, and I laughed, then moaned.

"Oh, my God. Don't make me laugh, you dick." I bounced as I slipped my key in the door and unlocked it, then dropped everything, keys and all, and bolted through the house unbuttoning my pants before throwing open the door to the bathroom.

And then I screamed. And maybe peed a little.

Patrick paused as he dried off his hair.

He was otherwise absolutely, completely, and blissfully naked.

It was probably only a full second, but I swear to God, my eyes combed every glistening, glorious square inch of him, every tattoo, the curve of his gorgeous ass, thighs, and then, the motherfucking Promised Land.

Not even ashamed. I one-hundred-percent stared straight at his dick. I had no will to stop. Tell me you wouldn't have done the same.

Time started in a burst of adrenaline and a sharp bladder pang.

"Jesus Motherfucking Christ, Tricky!" I screamed. "Get out! Get the fuck out!"

He wrapped the towel around his waist, looking at me like I'd lost my mind. I maybe kind of had. "Out of the bathroom, or—"

"Let's start there." I brushed past him, trying not to touch his soaking wet skin, attempting to not inhale the clean scent of him and failing horribly. I pushed him out of the room and slammed the door.

I rushed to the can and released the Kraken, sighing from relief, dropping my head into my hands, cursing the universe and Patrick alike.

After what was possibly the longest pee of my life, I washed my hands, grumbling at myself in the mirror. "Don't you fucking let that bastard off the hook. Not this time. It's too far. Too fucking far, and he almost made you piss yourself. Don't you forget that, Rose Fisher. You could have had piss all down the front of you while you stared at his dick like a fucking asshole." I turned off the water and wiped my hands on the towel, pointing at myself in the mirror again in warning.

When I opened the door, Patrick was just on the other side, leaning on the wall with a fucking smirk on his face, black hair dripping and hanging in his eyes, towel hanging around his hips, low enough that I could see that goddamn v, covered in tattoos, all the way down to his—

I snapped my eyes up to his and let loose. "What the fuck is the idea, Tricky? Nobody gave you permission to shower over here, not when you have a perfectly good shower right down the hall where you can get naked and wash your stupid muscles and, and, and *whatever the hell else* you need to wash. You," I poked him in the shoulder, "don't," poke, "live," poke, "here," extra hard poke.

But he was still smiling, that son of a bitch, and I realized he was enjoying this. "I'm sorry, Rose. Really. I thought you were gone, and West and Lily are … uh …" He rubbed the back of his neck, and I tried not to stare at his bicep.

My face screwed up. "Ugh. They are the fucking world's worst." I huffed and crossed my arms. "No excuse, man. You should have fucking put on headphones or something, gone for a run or a … I don't know. You should have *not come here*." I looked him over, fuming. "Why the fuck are you still standing here in a towel, anyway?"

He leaned to look behind me. "Because all of my stuff is right there." He pointed, and I saw his yellow gym bag, clothes folded neatly on top.

I huffed and stepped out of the way so he could pass, and he gave me a long look, still smirking as he closed the door.

Ellie was standing in the living room, mouth hanging open in a smile. And then, she busted out laughing.

I stormed past her and flopped on the couch, folding my arms. "Not funny."

She caught her breath. "No. You're right. That was a fucking riot."

"I'm glad you're amused." I scowled.

"Aww," she said, mock soothing me. "Don't be mad, Rosie. Let me make you a drink."

I was still scowling, but I felt a little better at the offer.

The door to the bathroom opened, and out walked Patrick, looking clean and fresh and not at all embarrassed that I'd walked in on him naked. No, he still looked amused, smiling crooked as he approached, gym bag in hand.

"Listen, I really am sorry, Rose. It won't happen again. Forgive me."

Those eyes of his begged me, and I couldn't say no. But I wouldn't let myself say yes, either. "At least text me a heads-up next time, dude. You've got to quit springing shit on me."

He nodded. "Deal. I'll get out of here. Hopefully West and Lily are … done in the shower. See you, Rose."

I sniffed and looked away. "Bye."

He shook his head, smiling as he made for the door. "Bye, Ellie."

Ellie waved, her eyes on our drinks as she poured. "See you later."

The door opened and closed behind me, and a few seconds later, Ellie sat down next to me and handed me a drink, turning so her back was against the arm of the couch.

"I mean, at least you got a peep show." She took a sip, watching me over the rim of her glass.

I glared at her, but I couldn't even hold it before we both started laughing. My cheeks were hot. "That was awful."

"Dude, you should have seen it. You were running like a leprechaun or something, your legs all bowed out. I thought you were going to faint when you opened that door."

"For a second, I thought I was going to, too." I took a sip of the sweet honey whiskey she'd poured. "And did you *see* that?"

Her brows were up, her smile wide as she nodded emphatically. "Uh, yeah I did. Way to go, Rose. You bagged a fucking winner."

I sighed. "Once upon a time. Feels like a million years ago. Or at least my vagina feels like it was a million years ago."

She laughed. "Yeah, well, I can see why your vagina misses him. I mean, *damn*."

"Yup." I took a drink.

"Like, he's tattooed almost everywhere. And I didn't realize how big his muscles were. He's fucking *cut*."

I shot her a look and changed the subject. "*Anyway*, I wonder if SkateTreason messaged me yet?"

Her eyes lit up. "Oooh, check your phone."

I pulled it out of my pocket and unlocked the screen.

"I still think you should hit up three or four hotties. Get a pool going. Better odds."

I had a message and I opened it up, feeling nervous and surprised. I was sort of banking on him not responding. "He messaged."

"What was your message to him?"

"I said, *'I couldn't help but notice on your profile that you're into hamburgers. I consider myself somewhat of an aficionado, so the question is, to bacon, or not to bacon?'*"

She made a face. "That's the weirdest pickup line I've ever heard."

I shrugged. "Maybe, but if he got it then he passes test number one."

When I didn't speak again, she asked, "Well, what did he say?"

"He said, *'Ah, the age old question. To burger without bacon is a sacrilege that can't be undone. Unless, of course, you're Jewish, in which case you should probably not bacon.'*"

Her eyes narrowed in thought. "Is that good?"

I smiled and settled into the couch. "Very good." *Tell me your thoughts on whiskey.*

The little messenger bubble said he was typing.

"He's online," I said.

Ellie bounced.

I took a drink just as his message came in.

I'm partial to scotch, but rye whiskey is an easy second. I wouldn't thumb my nose at bourbon. You can keep Irish whiskey wherever you found it, though. Also, is this a test?

I messaged him back. *Sorta.*

How am I doing?

So far, real good.

Well, that's a relief. So tell me, bacon and whiskey thoughts? Conversely, is there a way to combine those two things into one supermeal to rule them all?

I smiled even wider. "I think I may have found a winner."

Lucky Spot

ROSE

The next afternoon, i found myself sitting in Roasted once again, waiting on the guy who I'd *really* wanted to meet from the beginning — *SkateTreason*. Through our texts last night, I learned that his name was Greg, and he worked at a coffee shop, but more importantly, he loved my favorite things: bacon, skating, whiskey, and 90s movies.

He was basically my perfect match. Hence the nerves. I wiped my hands on my jeans again and picked up my phone to check the time. If this one was the disaster that the other ones were, I was deleting the app from my phone, end of story.

I hadn't seen much of Patrick that day, or the day before. I mean, besides his dick. I'd worked last night, and by the time I got home, which was extra late, he was already asleep on the couch, face soft in sleep. He looked like a boy, a beautiful boy covered in black ink, sleeping silently on my couch. But we hadn't hung out, which helped so much. Distance was key to keeping the lid on my feelings, and even just that little time away from him had me feeling more like myself than I had in a week.

The door opened, breaking me from my thoughts, and Greg walked in, longboard in hand, hat low, smile bright. He was tattooed, built but still slim, with a wide chest and narrow waist.

He was gorgeous.

"Rose?"

I smiled back, feeling like I'd hit the online dating jackpot. "Hey, Greg." I stood as he approached, and I hitched a thumb over my shoulder toward the counter. "Did you want coffee? The lemon bars here are amazing."

"Nah, I'm a little too nervous for coffee."

My smile stretched wider at his honesty. "Me too. This is actually hot chocolate."

He laughed, and we took seats at the table. "I'm glad you messaged me when you did. I was actually gearing up to delete my profile."

I watched him, amused. "That's funny, because this was my last date before I gave up."

He nodded knowingly. "How long have you been at it?"

"Not long enough for me to be as over it as I am."

"It's like Russian roulette, except with humans. Maybe less lethal."

I laughed. "Maybe. I wouldn't have been surprised if my first date tried to steal my kidney. He actually said — out loud, mind you — 'I'm really into dead things.'"

He sucked in a breath through his teeth. "Ouch. I mean, the last girl I met asked me to fertilize her eggs. Just like that, dead-faced from across the table. 'Fertilize my eggs.'"

"Oh, God," I said with a chuckle.

"Another one took me home to introduce me to her doll collection. She had hundreds of them, all lined up on shelves with porcelain faces. I'm pretty sure they were made with human hair."

I shook my head, smiling. "You win. That makes mine look like a cake walk. You're only my third date. One and two were a taxidermist who smelled like death and a musician who serenaded me at this very table."

"This table? Right here?" he joked and pointed at the surface. "This must be your lucky spot."

My cheeks heated up, smile stretching wider. "I'm telling you. I'm on a roll."

"Well, third time's a charm, right?"

"Looks like it just might be." I took a sip of my hot chocolate, trying to quiet my nerves. "So, you work at a coffee shop?"

His eyes were sort of blue and green, I noticed as I listened to him talk. "Yeah. It's not glamorous, but it pays the bills. And you're a bartender?"

"Sure am, going on six years."

"Did you do the whole college thing?"

I straightened a little in my seat, ready for it to fall apart with my answer. *Here it is. The real test.* "Nope. Just never interested me. You?"

"I tried, but I just wasn't motivated. So I took a tip from Ron Swanson: *Never half-ass two things. Whole-ass one thing.* So, I'm whole-assing my job at the coffee shop."

I laughed, relieved, and he shook his head.

"I'm not ready to decide what's next, you know? Everyone keeps asking me what I want to do with my life, and I just want to be like, 'If I knew, I'd be doing it.' Instead, I say 'Chippendales,' or 'Tilt-a-Whirl operator.'"

Seriously, *so* relieved.

"I totally get that," I said, cheeks flushed as I leaned on the table. "I'm a bartender, and everyone I know has this … *passion.* Passion for dance or literature or art. Charity. And I'm over here like, I read romance novels, watch a lot of TV, and drink a lot of whiskey. The things I love can't be monetized, so I bartend. I just want everyone to get off my dick about it, you know?"

"I do," he said with a nod. "One day, I guess I'll grow up. Maybe get some sweet desk job where I get a cubicle and have to wear polo shirts to work. Some place with an HR department and insurance."

I chuckled. "Insurance. That's funny. I hope to God I never get sick. Like, every time I get even a hint of tooth pain, I flip out. My dentist would be pleased though — I floss regularly. It's cheaper than fillings."

"I broke my wrist last year skating and it cost like two thousand bucks."

I winced. "Ouch."

"The worst pain was in my wallet. Trust me."

My phone rang, and I pulled it out of my pocket, smiling as I answered. "Hey, Ellie."

"How's it going? There's no screeching, so … better?"

I watched Greg from across the table with warm cheeks. "Yeah, you could say that."

"I can hear you smiling. Is he hot?"

Now my ears were warm too. "Mmhmm."

"Normal?"

"Yup."

"Good. Now hang up with me and go lick him like a lollipop."

I rolled my eyes. "Thanks, Ellie. See you tonight."

"Bye, Rosie."

Greg smirked at me as I hung up and put my phone back in my pocket. "Lifeline?"

I turned my coffee cup around in a circle. "She saved me from the serenade yesterday. What was left of me, at least. I'm surprised I had the nerve to show my face here again, but the lemon bars called me back."

"Well, they're only the best on the West Side." He smiled sideways at me, and I practically swooned.

"Obviously."

He glanced down at his hands before looking back up at me hopefully, but with a confident edge that made my insides flip around. "So, I guess it's a good sign that you don't have to leave to help your Aunt Edna after she dropped her wig and busted her hip trying to pick it up?"

"Yes, that's a good sign."

He leaned forward, still smiling. "Then tell me, Rose. Would you like to skate with me?"

I smiled right back. "I'd love to."

Patrick

I **stretched, recrossing my ankles on** Rose's coffee table late that afternoon. I hadn't seen her since the day before. I smiled to myself, picturing her face when she caught me in her bathroom. If I'd had any doubt that she wanted me, it would have been erased in that moment.

I'd denied my feelings for her for so long, now that I knew what I wanted, I'd been revived. Reborn. And all I wanted, all day long, was to see her again.

I thought about the time, wondering how her date had gone today. Ellie spilled the details when I'd gotten there after work, but I wasn't worried about it, figuring it was just as much of a disaster as the others had been. But I was anxious to see her all the same.

Ellie sat camped out on the couch next to me with Valentino asleep in her lap, eating Cheetos and watching MTV. Somehow, I'd gotten sucked in for two hours of *Teen Mom* and *Catfish,* and as the credits rolled on *Catfish*, Ellie sighed and reached into the foil bag for another handful of chips.

"This is my favorite episode," she said between bites. "I think I've seen it a million times. I mean, think about it. Alyx lied to Kya about being transgender. Can you imagine how scared he was to meet Kya? To think that this person you fell in love with doesn't know something that would end most relationships just on principle alone. But in the end, Kya accepted him just as he is. Like, that just makes me so happy. Any of us would be lucky to be loved that unconditionally." Her face was soft and dreamy as she ate another chip.

I sighed too and sank a little deeper into the couch. "Isn't that the truth?"

The television landed on the DVR screen, and Ellie turned to face me. Valentino gave her a look before stretching and hopping off the couch. "So, are you going to tell me what the deal is with you and Rose?"

I smirked. "Straight to it, huh?"

She shrugged and offered me the Cheetos bag. I took one and popped it in my mouth, buying myself a little time as I chewed.

"It's complicated," was the best answer I could come up with.

"But you like her, right?"

"For a long time, yeah." I watched her, wondering if she was angling to hit on me.

"Then what's in your way?"

"*We* are."

She dropped her chin and rested her forearms on her thighs. "Look, I've known Rose my entire life. She's practically a big sister to me. I *know* her, and she cares about you. Like, as in, more than a friend. As in, she's got it bad for you."

I smiled. "You say that like she's not on a date right now."

Ellie shrugged and ate another chip. "Trying to get over you. You're not making it easy, what with your naked shower shows and whatnot."

I chuckled. "That really was an accident."

"Oh, I'm sure it was, but it still happened." She laughed and shook her head. "Man, you should have seen her face when you were getting dressed. I think you should go after her." Ellie pointed a Cheeto at me.

"Well, you're in luck because I'm going to."

Her face screwed up in confusion. "Wait, what?"

I reached into her bag and grabbed a chip. "I said, I'm going after Rose."

She blinked. "Are you serious?"

I nodded and opened my mouth, tossing the Cheeto in.

"Wow, I thought that was going to take a lot more convincing. What's your plan?"

"No one gets anywhere with Rose by pushing, so I'm just waiting for the opportunity. My plan is to hang out here with her as much as possible until she caves. I get it now. I've seen it. I feel it. So I'm going to take a shot. Even if it's my last one."

She huffed, brows knitting together. "You can't just sit here on your ass and wait. She's out on a date right now, *literally right now*, and has been hanging out with this hot skater dude all day."

My smile slipped off my face. "Oh?"

"Yeah. So maybe don't push her, but definitely don't just wait like a good little soldier. You've got to take charge, before it's too late. Just *take* her. I don't think she has it in her to say no."

The door opened behind us to Rose's laughter, but before I turned to the sound, Ellie looked me dead in the eye and said, "You can't let her say no."

When I looked over my shoulder, I found Rose smiling a smile I hadn't seen in a very, very long time, legs long in cutoffs and Vans, flannel tied around her waist. Her head turned back to the guy following her in, and I couldn't help but check him out. Tall. Built. The vibe I got from him was that he was all right.

Naturally, I wanted to get up and deck him.

When Rose saw me on the couch next to Ellie, she might have said the same. Her eyes narrowed with suspicion.

She set her skateboard down next to the door and dropped her keys in the dish. "Ah, hey guys. This is Greg. Greg, this is my friend Patrick and my cousin Ellie."

Ellie smiled and waved, and I jerked my chin in lieu of a greeting, pulse thumping in my ears.

"What's up?" he said, smiling, and turned back to Rose. His voice dropped as he reached for her hand.

My eyes were stuck on their point of contact so hard, Ellie kicked me. I blinked and looked away, turning to stare at the television blankly as every molecule listened to them in the entry.

"I had a great time today, Rose," he said. "Thanks for hanging out, but I should probably head home."

"Are you sure you don't want to stay? Or we could go get a drink?"

I could hear her smiling — she didn't want him to leave. The knowledge made me feel sick. Maybe Ellie and Joel were right. Maybe I'd waited too long. Maybe I should have kissed her the second I had a chance and prayed West was right, that a kiss would be all it took.

"I feel like I should quit while I'm ahead. It was a great day." I think he was smiling too.

This is bad.

"Third time was most definitely a charm," she said as she walked him out the door and stepped into the hall.

I turned again, training my eyes on the door, trying not to think about what was happening on the other side of it.

Ellie smirked at me. "I've never seen somebody frosty and on fire at the same time before."

I sniffed and looked away. "What do you mean?"

She motioned to me, amused. "Look at you. You look like you

could explode, but you're cool as a cucumber too."

I turned back to the TV. "Yeah. Well, Rose does that to me."

The door opened again, and Rose walked in, blushing. Heat crept up my neck at the sight.

She shook her head at Ellie. "Have you moved at all today, Ellie?"

"Nope." She hopped off the couch and smiled at the two of us. "I got some bath bombs yesterday and we made a date for tonight. So I'm going to take a long bath in that gigantic tub of yours. Because I *take* what I *want* and tonight, that's a bath." She gave me a pointed look.

Rose chuckled as she made her way into the kitchen. "Uh, okay, Ellie."

Ellie twiddled her fingers and bounded off.

"Whiskey?" Rose asked from behind me.

I propped my feet on the coffee table, not sure how I felt, but absolutely certain that I needed alcohol. "Always."

I listened to her in the kitchen, the clink of glasses and ice, the low pop of the bottle's cork-top, trying to find meaning in what Ellie had said.

She brought in the drinks and sat next to me on the couch, passing mine over.

"Looks like your date went well," I said before taking a sip.

I tried to read her face, but it was blank. "It did," was all she said before changing the subject. "What have you and Ellie been up to?"

I shrugged, feeling salty. "MTV. I'm waiting on them to start a show about people addicted to their network."

"That sounds about right," Rose said with a laugh and took a drink. "Excited for your birthday party? One more day!"

I snorted and sank down into the couch, resting my head on the back with a sigh. "Yeah, you know how much I love being the center of attention."

"Aw, it'll be fun," she assured me. "It's just Habits. Although, I won't promise Lily didn't get a cake."

I chuckled. "Yeah, West told me."

She smiled. "I figured you'd like to know in advance. Pretty sure that's the only potentially embarrassing moment, though. Just sit through the fifteen seconds of Happy Birthday, and you're home free."

I groaned.

She looked down at her thigh and tugged at the fraying ends of her cutoffs, avoiding eye contact. "Hey, so Greg was going to come with me tomorrow night, if that's okay?"

"Why wouldn't it be?" I took a drink and looked away. *Lie, lie, lie.*

She twisted a long strand around her finger. "You know why. I just figured since there will be so many people there, and since we'd be at Habits …"

"It's fine, Rose. Really," I smiled, feeling like I was going to choke on the truth.

She smiled and bought it with a sigh. "Thanks, Tricky." She settled into the couch and took a drink. "So who all is going to be there?"

"Everyone from the shop. You guys. Seth."

Her face hardened.

"I know, I know. But it's a big deal that he's coming."

"Can't disagree with that," she muttered.

I frowned. "Come on, Rose."

"What?" she said defensively. "That guy's a vortex of drama, and I don't want you to get sucked in again. It's not fair to you when his shit blows up because you're the one that gets nailed with shrapnel. I just don't want you to get hurt again — you have to get that."

She didn't even realize that she killed me every single day. I took a drink to buy a second. "Look, what if Lily was sick? What if she needed you, but helping her hurt you. Would you do it?"

She gave me a flat look. "Lily would never be like Seth because she's Lily."

I gave her the look right back. "Humor me."

"If you're asking if I'd do anything for Lily, the answer is yes. But you know I have a line. There's only so much I can give, and if it got to the point where I'd said enough's enough, that would be it."

"Well, I guess we're different that way. I don't know how to walk away for good." I looked away and took a drink.

"Loyal to a fault?"

I shrugged. "I just like to call it loyal."

She sighed and changed the subject. "Anyway, tomorrow should be fun. I haven't seen Joel in forever."

"He doesn't really ever change. It'll be good to have everyone together."

"Plus, free drinks."

"And that," I said with a smile and took a drink.

So did Rose before resting the glass on her bare thigh. "Is Veronica coming?" Her voice was a little too controlled, her face a little too still.

My smile climbed on one side. "Yeah, she'll be there."

"Great. I'm sure that won't be weird."

"Ronnie said the same thing. Just don't make it weird and it won't be."

"Ha." She raised her glass. "Easy enough."

I gave her what I hoped was a comforting smile. "It'll be fine. Just as easy as Greg and I will have it."

"So, not at all?" she joked.

"It'll be fine, Rosie."

It wasn't something I called her much anymore, and it affected her, I could tell. She looked to the television, watching the logo of the cable company move across the screen so she wouldn't have to look at me.

She nodded toward it. "So, is this it for tonight?"

No reason why I couldn't keep the plan going where I could, so I made her an offer I knew she couldn't refuse. "It's looking that way. I was thinking about watching Better Off Dead."

She beamed. "Classic John Cusack, and the best Savage Steve Holland movie, hands down. *Two dollars!*" she said with a laugh.

I pointed at nothing. "*Go that way, really fast. If something gets in your way, turn.*"

"I live my life by that quote."

I chuckled. "So, you in?"

She turned to face the television and sank into the couch. "Definitely."

I started the movie as Rose grabbed my comforter and pulled it over her, slinging part of it over me too. Before long, she sank into the dip between cushions, finding her way closer to me as we laughed, reciting the lines we knew. And by the time the credits rolled and we started *Sixteen Candles*, Greg was a distant memory, and Rose was mine, even if only for a hundred and twenty minutes at a time.

Make a Wish

Ellie and I stood at the foot of my bed the night of Patrick's birthday party, staring at the pile of clothes on my bed. Valentino hopped on the mattress, climbed on the pile, and sat on it like the fashionable bastard he was.

I looked over the pile. "Who knew dressing up for a date for your ex-boyfriend's party would be so complicated?"

Ellie laughed. "Uh, pretty much everyone who ever thought about it." She hung her hand on her hip. "I vote that one." She pointed at a black dress that was far too short to be appropriate for a second date, or Patrick's birthday.

"Fuck it. I'm going with the classics." I picked up the cat, and he mewled lazily as I set him to the side so I could dig through the pile, slinging clothes over my shoulder. "Black jeans, white V-neck, leather jacket, hot pink heels. Bam. Done."

"So, the first thing you tried on?"

"Is there really another way to do this?"

She shrugged. "Not that I know of."

Valentino jumped down and rubbed against Ellie's leg, and she picked him up, nuzzling into his neck. "Nervous?" she asked me.

I chewed my lip. "Does it show?"

"Only if I look at you."

"Ugh. I don't know what it is."

"Well, you're about to go on your first *real* date with a guy you like, except your ex will be there."

My face fell. "Right. Probably not my best idea."

"Too late now," she sang, smiling.

"I mean, Greg is a good guy. He's straightforward, says exactly what he thinks, which means he's the opposite of Patrick. None of that unspoken words drama. Simple. Easy. That's what I need. Something easy."

She shrugged. "Sure, I guess. I mean, I like a little mystery sometimes, but that's just me." She kissed Valentino. "What time is it?"

I checked my phone and hissed a swear word. "Uh, late."

Ellie rubbed her nose against the cat's. "Come on, you sexy beast. Let's go get fancy."

I swear to God he winked at me over Ellie's shoulder as she left the room.

I threw on my clothes in a whirl and headed into the bathroom to get the rest of me in order. Luckily, I had a foolproof five-minute rush makeup system, one that had been forged over years and years of being perpetually late.

I blew through the motions, leaving everything laying on the counter — foundation, nude eyeshadow, cat-eyes with gel liner, applied off muscle memory alone. Then mascara and the pink lipstick that was the exact same shade as my shoes. I threw on my silver chains, all at varying lengths and textures, finishing just as the doorbell rang.

I fluffed my hair in the mirror, thankful I'd fixed it before the whole dump-out-my-closet fiasco, trying to remember if I'd applied deodorant as I hurried to the door.

Greg smiled and kissed me on the cheek, taking a moment to look me over. I assessed him right back, and I liked what I saw. Black jeans and oxfords, black and white gingham button-down cuffed just above his elbows. It made me just want to stare at his forearms, muscular and covered in tattoos.

He even had great hair, dark and combed neatly with a hard part. I was winning all over the place.

"You look amazing, Rose," he said as he touched my arm.

I felt my cheeks flush. "Thanks. You clean up pretty nice, yourself."

Ellie leaned out of the bathroom as she put in an earring. "Hey, Greg."

"Nice to see you, Ellie." He gave her a wave.

"I think we're just about ready to go." I picked up my clutch as Ellie walked in.

She looked like a disco ball again in a short, gold sequined dress and black heels. Her red hair was big, her lashes were long, and her lips soft pink. Her eyes were so huge, she didn't even need liner. I think she'd look like a Japanese cartoon if she put any on. I made a mental note to convince her to do it, just because.

"Bombshell," I sang in appreciation.

"Gotta use these hips for something." She bumped me with said hip, but she was so short, it hit me in the upper thigh.

Greg extended his elbow, and I slipped a hand in the bend of his arm just as Ellie took his other arm. His smile was sweet and snarky. "Today must be my lucky day. I get not one, but two lovely ladies on my arm."

Ellie looked around him, smiling. "And he's charming. Good one, Rose. Got any friends, Greg?"

"One or two."

I chuckled as we headed out the door. "I thought you were looking for one of the Tonic boys?"

She shrugged. "There's plenty of me to go around."

"What's Tonic?" Greg asked as we walked down the hall and to the stairs.

"The tattoo parlor where Patrick works," I answered.

"Ah. How do you know him?"

Ellie and I spoke at the same time.

"They used to date," she said, just as I said, "He lives down the hall."

I froze my face to give nothing away, even though I died a little inside. Ellie just kept talking, not even realizing I was mortified.

"They've lived down the hall from each other forever, but he's actually living with us now, sorta. On account of his roommate and Rose's roommate getting busy all the time."

Greg, being the goddamn gentleman he was, took it all in stride, smiling at me in a way that told me it was fine, and he knew I was embarrassed, and that he was sorry for that. "Well, that sounds simple enough."

Ellie laughed. "Yeah, right. Rose walked in on him getting out of the shower the other day and I thought she was going to have a stroke."

I laughed, or at least tried to make a noise that sounded like a laugh, though it came out more like a cough and a cackle, or something awkward like that.

Greg let us both go and pushed open the door to our building. Ellie passed first, then me, as I wished I could sink into the floor and disappear. But Greg touched my arm and smiled, saying, "Too bad for him that she's with me tonight."

My heart fluttered as I stepped out, and he followed, giving me his arm once more. Ellie was on her own and didn't seem to mind, just strutted down the sidewalk in that sparkly dress, nearly stopping traffic when we crossed the street. No less than four men and two chicks turned to get a good look at her walking away. She chatted the whole time, and I mercifully steered the conversation to LA, getting her going all the way to Habits.

Ellie was right. I picked a good one.

When we reached the bar, I was on top of the world, feeling hopeful. Very hopeful.

Until we stepped inside, and I saw Patrick. My very first thought, once I could think, was me wondering if I'd ever truly get over him.

Patrick stood in a pack of people, his friends — Joel, Shep, West, and Cooper — who were all laughing. But time stood still for a long moment as my eyes drank in every detail.

The line of his jaw was hard, yet somehow still smooth, his skin perfect, almost the only part of him that wasn't covered in tattoos — the ink on his neck licked at his jaw like black flames. His nose somehow made his face look boyish, his face always shaven, his hair always neatly combed, but that was all underscored by the chaos of the art that covered his body, the hardness of him at odds with the soft.

But his eyes were the most striking thing of all. They were eyes constantly burning, always on fire, eyes that told you exactly what he felt. And when they found mine, my knees almost buckled.

I held on to Greg's arm like a lifeline, looking away to search for Lily as I tried to regain some level of composure. It was my only defense against him — ignore, ignore, ignore.

Lily and Maggie sat at a high top, sipping their drinks. They waved as we stepped around the crowd there for Patrick, and I did my very best to pretend like he didn't exist. Not yet, at least. Not until my heart quit hammering.

Lily stood and hugged me, blond hair in soft waves, her dress made of pink lace and flared, lips red and smiling. I swear, the ballerina thing was coded into her genetics.

"Hey," she said, looking past me at Greg when she pulled away.

She extended a hand. "Greg, right? It's so nice to meet you. I'm Lily."

"It's a pleasure." He smiled amiably and gave her hand a squeeze.

Maggie waved, her short, curly hair bobbing. "And I'm Maggie," she said, her Mississippi drawl sweet and sugary.

"So," I said as I turned to Greg, "welcome to Habits, our home away from home."

Ellie stood at my side, blatantly shopping the guys, sizing them up. They didn't seem to mind in the slightest — in fact, I could practically see the testosterone wafting off them.

West and Cooper turned to us, and we said our hellos. As we all shifted to greet one another, I ended up next to Patrick. So I did what I was supposed to do. What I wanted to do just as much as I didn't.

I leaned in and gave him a hug, holding my breath so I wouldn't breathe him in. "Happy birthday, Tricky."

His hand slipped around my waist, bringing our bodies flush for a brief moment. "Thank you, Rose," he said near my ear, though I could barely hear over the sound of my heart, like it was calling to him.

I pulled away, overwhelmed, avoiding eye contact as I remembered myself and looked for Greg behind me. I slipped my arm around his as if to say I was his, pretending I was unaffected, though I could feel both men watching me. I smiled under the weight of it all.

I realized then that I wasn't as good at playing it cool as I thought I was. I also realized that bringing Greg here was a colossal mistake.

"Want a drink?" Greg asked, snapping me back to the moment.

I smiled my waitress smile that covered up my feelings like a mask, feeling like a fool. "Neat scotch, thanks."

He smiled back, and I had a feeling his smile was as fake as my own. "Be right back."

I stepped over to Lily again, keeping my back to Patrick. She nodded, smiling.

"He's super cute, Rosie."

Ellie set down her bag and took a seat next to Lily. "And nice, too."

"Yeah, but I shouldn't have brought him here. It's about a kabillion times more awkward than I thought it would be."

Maggie smirked. "It's the first time you've really been with a guy in front of Patrick, plus Greg is meeting all of your friends, all of whom are friends with Patrick too. It's a big deal."

"I mean, Tricky met him last night." It was the weakest defense ever. Ellie made a face. "Sort of. And he wasn't all smiles and handshakes."

I chuffed. "No, more like switchblade eyes and bro nods."

Maggie sighed and glanced behind me, presumably at Patrick. "It's like watching a panther circle its supper. I don't know how you don't cave."

"Sometimes I don't either."

Lily's face got a little more serious. "Oh, God. Rosie, don't look yet, but Veronica just walked in."

I'd nearly forgotten about her with everything else spinning around my head. I moved around the table like I was going to talk to Ellie so I could catch a glimpse and immediately wished I hadn't.

Veronica looked a lot like me, except with a badass supermodel upgrade. She was so gorgeous, she looked like she belonged in a comic book or something, all long legs and piercings, tattoos everywhere. She'd just approached Patrick — they were smiling, and she kissed him on the cheek.

I tried to swallow my feelings, but they stuck in my throat like a cork.

She was flanked by … Penny, I think was her name, with long hair the color of grass and bangs cut like a pinup girl. She was dressed like a pinup girl too, in high-waisted pants and a black, polka-dotted top with a sweetheart neckline and tiny buttons down the front. You'd think she'd look weird, having hair the color of a lime snow cone and all, but when coupled with her winged liner, piercings, tattoos, and deep red lips, she just looked like she belonged in a magazine too.

I felt about as fashionable as the K-Mart clearance rack.

Greg walked up with my drink, mercifully, giving me something to avert my eyes toward as well as eighty-proof liquor to calm my nerves. A large part of me was ready to bail. I looked up at him and smiled, trying to figure out the fastest way to get out of there. We could stay for a drink. Maybe go back to my place. Try to reset the weird.

I wondered if he felt it too. If I was reading his body language effectively, he definitely did.

West and Cooper pulled up next to their girls to chat with Greg, and I sipped my scotch, attempting to pay attention. I'd nearly finished my drink and was about to ask Greg if he wanted to get out of there when I felt a hand on my arm.

"Ah, Rose?"

Please, don't be Veronica, I thought as I turned, standing so straight, I could have had a two-by-four up my ass.

It was totally Veronica.

She glanced behind me at everyone and sort of waved at everyone. We'd all met her a few times before Patrick brought her into the bar after he dumped me. The group was still, faces frozen in smiles. Maggie waved back, a small motion, the only one.

"Um, I'm sorry to interrupt, but do you have a second?"

I looked up at Greg with apologetic eyes, then back at her. "Ah, sure."

I followed her away from the throng and toward the bar, feeling everyone's eyes on us, especially Patrick's. I swear, they burned hotter than everyone else's, and I exhausted a large supply of my concentration trying to focus on her.

"Can I buy you a drink?" she asked over her shoulder.

Mine was empty, and even if I could refuse the olive branch, I needed another stiff drink. And soon. "Thanks," I answered.

We stepped up to the bar, and Veronica leaned on the surface, waiting for Shelby to make her way down to us. I took the opportunity to look her over once more — her hair was black as midnight, lips a deep burgundy, dressed head to toe in black. She turned to me with those dark lips of hers smiling.

Fake-ass smile: activate.

"Listen," she started tentatively, "I just wanted to tell you that I'm really sorry. For what happened with Tricky, and all," she clarified. "I—"

Shelby walked up, and we shared a brief look before she asked, "Hello, ladies. What'll it be?"

"Makers and Coke, for me," Veronica answered.

"Glenlivet, neat. Thanks, Shelb."

"No problem."

Veronica laid a twenty and a few singles on the bar and turned back to me as Shelby poured our drinks. "Rose, I want you to know that I had no idea what was going on between the two of you when he asked me to come here with him that night. If I'd known, I wouldn't have agreed. In fact, I didn't understand what was up until we left."

Shelby brought our drinks by and picked up the cash.

"Keep the change," Veronica said with a wave, and Shelby smiled and walked away. She picked up her drink. "You know, we left here that night, and I thought he'd been a little weird, but I wasn't sure what was going on. Like, I knew you guys had dated, but I had no idea if it was serious or not, and I wasn't sure when you'd broken up. You know how he is … he's pretty private about … well, everything."

"Yeah, I do know." I picked up my scotch and took a sip.

"Anyway, when we left, he basically dumped me on the sidewalk. He told me a little about you two, apologized for bringing me into it. I could have punched him for the both of us, but instead, I bitched him out and left him standing outside the bar, hopefully feeling like a dick. I almost came back in here that night to talk to you, but you were here with your friends, and … I don't know. I was embarrassed. I should have come back then, and I'm sorry for that too."

I sighed, part of me wishing she was a bitch so I could hate her. But I couldn't hate her. She'd been taken for just as much of a ride as I had. Sorta.

She turned to face me. "You don't owe me anything, Rose. But I wanted to let you know."

"Thank you, Veronica. Really," I said, humbled. "You didn't have to come to me, and you didn't have to buy me this drink, but I appreciate it. All of it."

"It's the least I can do. Joel told me a little more about what kind of damage I caused, and I hate that I was a part of that."

"Don't let that get to you. I don't blame you. I blame him."

She chuckled. "I'm not gonna lie — I had a thing for him for a long, long time. But after that fiasco? You couldn't pay me."

I smirked. "Yeah, I know the feeling."

She glanced over at him and sighed. "No, what I mean is that I could never be with a man who was in love with someone else."

"Oh," I said quietly.

"Seeing you together makes it even more real. Like, everything makes a lot more sense." She looked down at her drink and smiled, shaking it to clink the ice together. "Anyway, thanks again. I'm glad we're cool."

"Cheers to that." I raised my glass.

She clinked her glass to mine. "Bottoms up."

We drank and headed back to the group. Greg caught my eye, and I smiled at him with barely enough time to be grateful that Cooper and West had kept him company, just before Seth stepped in front of me, effectively cutting me off.

I tried not to recoil and plastered that smile back on. "Hey, Seth. Good to see you again so soon. How's it going?"

"Can't complain," he said as I looked him over.

Seth had always been a good-looking guy, blond and fair,

gorgeous green eyes and a smile full of joy — the same he wore as he stood across from me in Habits, ginger ale in hand — however fabricated his joy typically was. He was fun, when the circumstances were right, witty, a charmer. But when he drank, when he was high, well, that was another story all together. It was his Mr. Hyde, the darkness brought out by addiction.

That part of him had all but disappeared. But I hadn't forgotten that it was still just under the surface, waiting for the moment it would boil back to life.

"You look good," I said. "Tricky said you've turned a corner. I'm really happy for you."

He stuffed his free hand into his pocket. "Aw, don't go getting sappy on me, Rosie. How many times did we come to Habits back in the day?"

I chuckled. "And how many times did I have you thrown out?"

He laughed and rubbed the back of his neck. "Not my best self, was it?"

"Not usually," I said with a smile.

He sighed. "Well, I'm just glad I made it out, you know? No more fighting to survive. Not everyone gets to say that."

"True." I didn't know what else to say, and my eyes darted to Greg, feeling the pressure to get back to him.

"Anyway, I'd love to catch up some time. Maybe we can get lunch or something. Dinner? Or maybe a movie?"

"Ah, sure," I said tentatively, wondering if he was trying to ask me out. By the look in his eyes, I thought the answer might be yes. I steered the conversation in the opposite direction. "Listen, I'm really glad you came through for Tricky tonight. He said you're not drinking anymore, so I know this wouldn't be your hangout of choice. It was a gift to him in itself, your being here."

"I hope so. I owe him everything," he said earnestly.

I smiled, genuinely, this time. "I'm going to get back to my date."

"Sure thing, Rose."

I stepped past him, catching Greg's eye again, trying to telepathically apologize to him as I walked through the people. And then, Joel grabbed me.

He laughed as he hugged me, picking me up easily with one arm around my waist, beer in his free hand. "Heya, Rosie."

I couldn't help but giggle in surprise and endearment as I held up my scotch, hoping I hadn't spilled on him. "Hey, Joel."

He set me back on the ground, though he held me close, looking down at me, smiling. "It's been too long. Much too long." He set his beer down with mischief in his eyes. "Have you met my friends *THIS*," he rested his right hand, tattooed with the word on my left cheek, "and *THAT*?" His left hand found the other cheek, and he squeezed, planting a kiss on my lips.

I laughed when he pulled away, cheeks on fire, wondering what the hell Greg could possibly be thinking about what he was seeing. "Only about a hundred times, Joel."

Patrick was just a few feet away, on the other side of Shep, watching us. *Mistakes for days,* I thought ruefully.

"What's going on?" I asked Joel as he let me go.

"Not much. I was just saying to Shep here that we should come by to see you. Cooper told us about your new business. A bookstore, huh?"

"Oh, he did, did he?" I said with a laugh and shot Cooper a look. Bastard raised his glass at me, and I rolled my eyes.

"I didn't know you were a reader."

I raised a brow. "Judging a book by its cover?"

He shrugged. "You probably wouldn't figure me for a reader, either, but I've read every Vonnegut book in print. Twice."

I laughed. "Well, how about that."

"Coop seemed pretty set on the endeavor. As an entrepreneur

myself, I have to say I wholeheartedly approve."

"We'll see, but I'm almost positive that me being someone's boss is a bad idea."

Joel chuckled.

I shook my head and took a sip of my drink. "I'll be back in a bit, gotta get back to my date."

Joel patted me on the shoulder as I turned, looking for Greg, but he'd disappeared. West caught my eye, looking apologetic as he nodded toward the back of the bar. Greg sat at a table alone, checking his phone, empty glass in front of him.

I steeled myself as I walked over to him, preparing myself to be chewed out. I deserved it. But I joked with him anyway, bumping him in the shoulder with a smile.

"What, are you already trolling the app for a better date? Bad form, Greg."

His smile was unable to mask his disappointment. "Sorry, Rose. Your friends are great, really, but I didn't realize what kind of party tonight was. I think I'm going to jet."

I was the worst kind of asshole. "No, it's me who's sorry. I should have known this wouldn't be like a regular old bar night. I'll come with you. We can get out of here together."

"No, you should stay. It's your friend's birthday, and you should be here," he said as he stood and touched my arm. "Really, it's fine, Rose."

I held my clutch in front of me, nibbling on my lip, feeling like an asshole. "I feel like I should apologize again, Greg."

But he touched my arm and smiled, though it didn't reach his eyes. "Don't worry about it." He leaned down to kiss my cheek. "Have a good time with your friends," he said before brushing past me, heading for the exit. I watched him wind his way through the people until I couldn't see him anymore.

"Well, this sucks." I slammed the end of my scotch and headed back to the bar to get another drink. This time, a double.

The night was long, a little bit easier with Greg gone, as shitty as that was. I'd wildly underestimated my ability to handle tonight with Greg, and I wondered just how permanent the damage was. But I relaxed after he left, making my way around to talk to everyone without needing to worry. I avoided Seth like Ebola, feeling like he wanted something more from me, probably something I was unwilling to give. The boys talked. The girls laughed. Joel and I sat down and ended up in a deep conversation about life and purpose, one of those conversations that leaves you feeling wiser, a little more in touch with yourself. He and I always did that when we saw each other — sometimes, he would drop this insight on you that would just hit you in some deep part of yourself.

Why he was single, I'd never know. By choice, I supposed. That was the only way it made sense.

Patrick and I found ways to be near each other, though I kept the wall in place and a few feet of air between us. I enjoyed it all the same, as much as I hated myself for it. We were friends. Only friends, just like we had been for years. I tried to let all the rest of it go and focus on that.

We stepped into the courtyard in the back of the bar and stood Patrick under the big tree, singing "Happy Birthday" as Lily brought out his cake, topped with twenty-eight candles. When she set it on a small table in front of him and it illuminated his face in shades of gold, my breath hitched, and I found myself unable to sing, or speak, or breathe. He smiled that rare smile of his as he looked around at us, the people who loved him most in the world, the planes and angles of his face glowing or shadowed, depending. And then his eyes found mine as the song ended, blanketing us in stillness.

"Make a wish," I said gently, and he closed his eyes for a moment before blowing them out, every one.

Fresh Pretzel

PATRICK

The cake had been eaten and the whiskey flowed once more as I stood in the bar with my friends, all pink-cheeked and laughing. Seth clapped me on the shoulder and said goodbye just after the cake, and I was thankful for him, thankful that the universe had released him from the hold it had on him.

It was a good birthday.

I'd asked for everyone's favorite books, anyone who'd questioned me as to what I wanted, at least, and I walked away with a haul. *Dune* from Joel, a Batman compendium from Cooper, *The Bell Jar* from Veronica, and *The Princess Bride* from Lily. Others gave me gifts they'd chosen, from a wooden crate packed with whiskey and drinking gifts from Shep — which came with a small crowbar that was necessary to open it — to a framed print by one of my favorite illustrators from West.

For much of my life, birthdays had been just another day, a day of no consequence. I didn't want for more, it was just another truth, a solid fact. It seemed the rules of life, of normalcy, had never applied to me. But I took it for what it was. Just woke up every day and kept going.

The first year West and I lived together, the notion that I'd never had a birthday party shocked him. He then made it his personal mission to show me the appeal. I'll admit, there wasn't much like the feeling. It's a day to pay tribute to someone you love, and the gratitude I felt with each passing year was more than I could express. I never expected it, yet it always came just the same, on warm wings.

The girls sat around a table behind us talking, though Ellie and Max, one of the guys from the shop, blew past us toward the door, holding hands. Joel was in the middle of a story —one that required a lot of hand waving and gesticulation — when I felt a hand on my arm.

I turned to find Rose.

She smiled softly and looked down at her hand, to the small box resting between her fingers. "I, ah … I wanted to give you this." She extended the gift and lifted her eyes to meet mine.

Rose was somehow a thousand miles away and just beyond my reach.

I took the box and touched her arm, turning us to an empty table nearby. The gift was in a black box, tied with a thin gold ribbon.

She leaned on the stool, hooking one hot pink heel on the bottom rung. "I wanted you to know that I'm glad we've been hanging out lately. I've … I've missed you a lot, your friendship," she said, eyes darting to mine briefly.

I nodded, looking back down at the box again. "Me too."

"Anyway, happy birthday, Patrick. Here's to another year." She raised her glass, and I touched the rim of mine to hers before we took a drink. She smiled at me. "Well, go ahead and open it."

I set down my glass and turned the box over in my hand before pulling the ribbon to untie it. When I lifted the lid, I found a worn old brown key, flat and utilitarian, strung on a chain that matched. The key was engraved with the word *Survive* in simple lettering.

Rose took a breath and began to speak. She was nervous. "I know it may seem strange, me giving you a necklace, but you don't have to wear it. I just saw it, and it made me think of you. No matter what life's thrown at you, no matter what happens, you always find a way to survive. You're indestructible."

My throat tightened. "No, I'm not."

"Oh, but you are. You just don't realize it, which is why I wanted you to have that key. So you can be reminded."

I took it out of the box and slipped it around my neck, inspecting it once more before dropping it into my shirt, where it hung just below my heart. "Thank you, Rose."

She smiled, the one that closed her off to me, and stood, stepping back to put more space between us. "You're welcome."

I watched her walk away, feeling the cold metal key against my chest as I gathered the box and ribbon.

I'd looked into her eyes and made my wish, and then she gave me a gift that made me wonder if there wasn't a way to have what I'd wished for. Because I wanted her. It was just another solid fact.

An hour or so later, we all made our way up Broadway toward our apartment, stopping for pizza at the counter on the way, snarfing it on the way home. Everyone was buzzed, and Patrick might have been drunk, though I wasn't sure. You never could tell with him, and it was rare to see him well and truly blazed. It was because of the drugs, he'd told me once. He was always afraid he'd slip, if his inhibitions were low enough. But he drank almost exclusively with us. It was where he felt safe, I knew.

Ellie had disappeared just before we left, flying by me in a sparkling whirl to tell me not to worry, that she'd call me, so Lily, West, Patrick and I walked back to the apartment, laughing and eating, just like the old days.

We parted ways with Lily and West in the hall just outside my door with the exchange of a few last minute jokes and a few hugs. And for one fleeting moment as they walked to West's apartment, Lily tucked into his side, all I could think of was just how different everything was.

I slipped my key in the door, very aware of Patrick behind me as I unlocked it and pushed it open.

A shoe hit the back of the door, and I jumped, my heart stopping from the shock.

Ellie's naked leg popped over the back of the couch, followed by a burst of giggling just before a man's boot flew toward me. I ducked just in time, and Patrick held up his hand to bat it away.

"Oh, my God," I said to myself.

Patrick sighed as he set down his bag of gifts. "That's my bed."

More giggling. The disco dress flew up in the air.

I closed the door and ran a hand through my hair. "You'll have to sleep in Lily's room, I guess."

Max sat up and pulled off his shirt, tossing it over his shoulder, grinning as he disappeared behind the back of the couch. No one had acknowledged our entrance.

Patrick shook his head. "I know Max. This isn't going to be over any time soon, and I don't know if I can deal with them moving *that* into the bedroom." He gestured to the couch.

I gave him a flat look. "So you're going home?"

His eyebrow climbed, and he smirked. "You really think West and Lily are going to go to sleep tonight? I have to work in the morning."

I blinked, not getting what he was after. "So, then, what?"

He shrugged and started pulling off his boots. "I'm sleeping in your bed."

All the blood in my body rushed to my face. "The hell you are," I sputtered.

One boot hit the ground and he reached for the other, smiling at me over his shoulder. "I'll sleep on top of the covers, if you want. Swear I won't make a move. I just want to sleep." The other boot hit the ground.

I pictured him stretched out in my bed, eyes closed, his naked back, covered in tattoos, rising and falling as he —

"No." I threw the word at him like Thor's hammer.

The Patrick who usually stood back and followed my lead was MIA, replaced with a rogue bearing a crooked smile and a devil-may-care attitude. I decided then that he must definitely be drunk.

"Rose," he said as Max growled and Ellie giggled in answer, "it's my birthday, and all I want is a good night's sleep. You're really going to say no?"

I folded my arms. "Yup."

He chuckled, dark eyes twinkling at me as he turned. "It's happening. You want to take a chance in Lily's room?"

I gnawed on my lip as I watched him walk through my apartment, stripping off his jacket, the muscles under his shirt bulging. He glanced at the couch and made a face before looking back at me.

"I'm telling you, Rose. You don't want to be subjected to that fuckery."

I clenched my teeth and huffed. Having him in my bed was beyond dangerous, but no, I didn't want to witness my cousin getting nailed into next week, and I didn't want him to have to either. And he had to play the fucking birthday card.

"Fine," I said, the word flat, though it still held an edge. "No funny business, Tricky. I've got a baseball bat under my bed, and I'm not afraid to brain you if you get grabby."

His back was to me, but I swear he was smiling.

I walked past the couch, risking a look at Ellie and Max, which was a mistake. They were a writhing flesh pretzel, right there in my living room, and there were zero fucks to be given by either of them. They'd spent all their fucks on each other.

Thank God I'd left the light off.

I sped up to try to leave that visual behind me, though it didn't work. What *did* work was what I saw when I turned into my room.

It was nearly dark, with just the small lamp next to my bed lit, and Patrick stood on the far side of my bed, reaching over his shoulder to grab his shirt between his shoulder blades. He pulled it over his head, exposing his tattoos. The centerpiece was a replication of The Hermit, a tarot card, with the roman numeral nine just above. He wore a gray hooded robe and a white beard, head bowed, staff in one hand and a lantern in the other, extended in front of him to light the night. The only variation was that the hermit's hands were tattooed just like Patrick's.

It was a symbol of loneliness and of enlightenment, one of searching and introspection. The surrounding art was all line and dot work, giving it the feeling of movement, almost like the illustration was reverberating.

I realized I'd stopped walking and hurried over to my dresser to dig for a pair of shorty shorts and a T-shirt. When I glanced over, he was stepping out of his pants, his sculpted ass in tight, short boxer briefs right there, right in front of me.

Pretty sure fire sprinklers went off in my panties.

I turned — it was the only way I could force myself to look

away — and went into the bathroom to change, talking myself down all the way. I washed my face. Tried not to freak out when I saw his toothbrush next to mine and brushed my teeth with a little more vigor than was entirely necessary. And then, I made my way back to my room, feeling like there was a bomb in my bed. I guess in a way, there was.

Patrick lay on his back, arm hooked over his forehead, eyes closed and chest rising and falling slowly. He was almost asleep, if he wasn't already.

I hoped to God he was as I slipped in next to him and turned off the light.

He sighed and rolled over to face me. "Thanks, Rose. Really. For everything."

"You're welcome." I settled into my pillow, willing him to stay right where he was. I wasn't sure I had the power to stop him if didn't.

"It was a good birthday," he said softly.

"I'm glad," I whispered back. And then, he was asleep, although I didn't know if there was enough whiskey in the world to knock me out with him that close to me. So I stared in his direction, wondering how I'd gotten to where I was, lying across from the boy who I couldn't escape but couldn't have.

Deal

PATRICK

didn't know what time it was when I woke — the room was pitch dark, her fan whirring — but it was day, I knew. Though as my brain shook off the dust of sleep, I realized my wish had come true, in part, at least.

Rose and I were wrapped in each other — her body pressed against mine, my arms around her as she slept. Her face was buried in my chest, her breath hot and steady against my skin. We'd always slept like that, found each other even in sleep, needing to touch.

It can't be real.

I didn't move, couldn't move, worried she'd wake and the moment would pass. Because in that moment, the wall would slide between us again, closing me off. But for now, it was gone, and she was in my arms.

I'd dreamed of it a hundred times.

But I only had a taste, a glimpse before she sighed, and as quickly as I'd gotten it, it was gone.

When she realized what was happening, she jolted back, rolling over to get away just like she had on the couch. I grabbed her arm as she swore, keeping her from toppling onto the floor.

"Whoa, there," I said with a laugh.

The light clicked on, and she blinked at me. "I … I'm sorry."

I propped my head up with my arm and smirked. "What for?"

She made a face and hit me with a pillow.

I chuckled and smoothed my hair that had fallen in my face. "I don't think either of us needs to apologize. But I'll tell you one thing."

She hugged the pillow to her chest. "What's that?"

I tried not to look at the curve of her hip and naked thigh, even though they were in my periphery, mocking me. "I'm not sleeping on the couch anymore. This is the best night's sleep I've had in forever."

She laughed and shook her head. "No way. That was your birthday treat. One night of sleep, hand delivered. You're on your own, mister."

"Come on, Rose. Do you want me to beg?"

She eyed me.

"All right." I flipped off the covers and climbed over her, making a show of it as she giggled. I got down on my knees next to her bed and clasped my hands, face in a solemn pout and eyes as puppy-dogged as I could get them. "Rose Fisher, I'm the scum of the earth and don't even deserve to breathe your air, but if you'd only let me crash in your bed, I'd give life and limb."

Doubt flickered across her brow as she rolled over to face me. "I don't know, Tricky."

I took her warm hands, smiling past the thundering of my heart. It was a window I could climb in. A small one, only open a crack, but it was there. I told her the truth. "It's temporary. I swear, I'll behave. I know where you stand, and I'm not asking you for more." *Yet.*

She snickered. "So you're just using me for sleep."

"Is it so wrong?"

She laughed, and hope bloomed in my chest.

"You'd do the same."

"True," she conceded and watched me for a beat. "Let me think about it."

"Come on, Rose. It's not a big deal. Do you have any idea how uncomfortable that couch is?"

"No, tell me about it, you big baby."

"Oh, you're gonna play it like that. All right, well, then you asked for it." I grabbed her by the arm and thigh, flipping her over as her face stretched in surprise.

"Oh, my God!" she squealed. "Don't you fucking do it, Tricky!"

I pinned her down, grinning. "Nuh-uh. You asked for it." I held her arms behind her back and squeezed the back of her thigh, just above her knee.

She screamed, laughing and thrashing, her voice muffled by the pillow.

"Come on, Rosie. Let me stay."

I squeezed again, and her hair flipped, whipping me in the face as she laughed hysterically. She couldn't speak.

I wiggled my fingers, digging them into her thigh. "Say yes and I'll stop."

She gasped. "Oh, my God, I'm gonna pee."

I laughed and squeezed again, and her feet thumped against the mattress.

"*Fine!*" she said, half laughing, half gasping for breath. "Fuck, stop it!" She broke out in a fit of giggles again. "*You win!*"

My smile widened as I climbed off her. "See? That was easy."

She rolled over, still laughing, wiping tears from her face. "You fucking dick," she said and pointed a finger at me, trying for stern, but I found all the permission I needed behind the facade, something in her eyes, the corners of her lips. "Don't make me regret it, Tricky."

STACI HART

"Never," I said as I stood.

I made my way to my clothes and sorted through them, pulling on my pants first, buttoning the fly. When I looked up, Rose's eyes were on my hands, bottom lip between her teeth. I tried to suppress the smile, looking back down to grab my shirt and pretend like I hadn't just seen it. But I had.

Something about her lying in bed, watching me, chest still heaving as she caught her breath … I had a shot, all right. I had a damn good shot.

"See you around, Rose," I said as I picked up my leather jacket and headed for the door, looking back at her once more as she turned off the light again and settled back into bed.

"Later, Tricky."

I closed the door and quit trying to play it cool, walking through the apartment and down the hall to my place, practically whistling Dixie.

Hope. I had real hope for the first time in a very long time.

Lily and West were still asleep, and I got ready for work, showered, shaved, and dressed, smiling all the while. The feeling of Rose in my arms was still fresh, the smell of her. That taste I'd gotten wasn't enough. I needed more.

If ever a woman was a drug, it was her.

The spring in my step hadn't left me as I headed to work, feeling like a fucking baller. And it was apparent enough that Joel looked at me like I had an extra leg when I walked through the door to the shop.

"You have a good night, Tricky?"

I smirked and walked up to the counter. "You could say that."

He eyed me, smiling from the other side. "You didn't."

"I didn't. But I'm back in the game."

A laugh burst out of him. "Well, how about that. You kiss her?"

"Nope."

He snorted. "Doesn't sound like you're all *that* deep back in the game."

I snapped my fingers and pointed at him. "But that's the thing, Joel. When it comes to Rose, slow and steady is the only way."

"Well," he said as he laid his palms on the surface and a know-it-all tone to his words, "if you didn't even kiss her, then how, pray tell, are you back in her good graces?"

"I have Max to thank for that. If he hadn't been nailing Ellie on Rose's couch, I couldn't have insisted that I slept in her bed."

Joel laughed, a big, full sound. "She did not agree to that."

"Oh, she did. And when I woke this morning …" I sighed. "We were wound up in each other, and somehow I convinced her to let me sleep in her bed for the short-term future."

He shook his head, amused. "Of all the things. You sneaky fuck."

I put up my hands in defense. "Hey, I didn't say a thing that wasn't true. In part, I really, really don't want to sleep on her couch again. I also really don't want to sleep in my apartment. I just didn't mention that I really *do* want to sleep with her."

He snickered.

"I told her I'd keep my hands to myself though, and I will. For now. She's going to have to make the move. I might nudge her into it, but I think she'll do it. I really do."

"Working your way in like a goddamn emotional ninja."

I shrugged. "Hidden talents."

He held out a hand, and I slapped it. "Well, good for you, man. I hope it works."

And I smiled, imagining that day. "I do too."

So Much Nope

ROSE

I **woke slowly to the sound** of those goddamn cats as my dreams slipped away. I hit snooze and buried myself for nine more minutes, chasing the dreams, trying to hang on to them, which was about as effective as trying to fish with my bare hands. I remembered something about a wheelbarrow full of saltwater taffy, then Patrick was there, undressing. Oh, I smiled to myself thinking about that part where he was holding me, his arms around me like a cage of warm, safe, awesome.

My eyes flew open.

That wasn't a dream.

Everything came back to me, dreams disappearing in a poof as what actually happened crystalized in my mind.

I'd agreed to let him sleep in my bed again.

I rubbed my face. *Way to fucking go, Rose. Grade-A fuck up.*

It was the mother of bad ideas. A terrible mistake. My tired brain scrambled for a way out, to call it off because there was no way that would end well. Him being in my apartment was bad enough, never mind him being nearly naked in my bed. Nightly.

I groaned.

"Idiot. You dumb, stupid idiot."

I remembered how much scotch I had, and the thought made me feel a little better. I'd been drunk. That was all. I was just drunk, and it was his birthday. And this morning when I agreed he could stay, I was probably still drunk. That was the only reasonable explanation.

But I didn't have to keep letting him sleep there, even if I'd agreed. It was my bed, after all, and I didn't think he'd push back if I put my foot down.

And so, it was settled. I'd get my ass up, get through my mid-shift, and then tell Patrick to shove off. Or at least shove out of my room.

It was then that I remembered Greg.

I picked up my phone and checked my texts, but I'd gotten nothing, which sparked a lot of weird feelings — anxiety as to why, relief that he wasn't bugging me, hurt at the radio silence, shame because my ex had slept in my bed, even if we did nothing other than some apparently epic subconscious cuddling. My solution was to text him, try to be charming, and hope I got the chance to talk to him soon.

I lay in bed in the dark, staring at my messages, touching the screen again every minute or so to keep it from falling asleep as I tried to come up with clever. It was maybe the fourth or fifth time before I'd figured out something decent to say.

So, was it just me, or was it way too crowded last night?

I read it over again, chewing my lip before I hit send. I really hope he picked up on the sarcasm and didn't just think I was being weird. Then I spent a few minutes regretting sending the text, wishing I'd gone with something normal, like *Hey*, or *What's up*, or *Sorry I dragged you to my ex boyfriend's birthday party.*

I blew out a breath that made my lips flap, feeling flat as a pancake. But when I sat up, pain shot through my brain, just behind my eyes. I pressed my hand into my eye socket, and two things dawned on me.

1) I had definitely still been drunk this morning when I'd agreed to let Patrick stay, and

2) I'd had far more scotch than I'd realized.

Fortunately, I'd reached Drinking Level: Expert years ago. I'd survive.

As I peeled myself out of bed, I took a body assessment. Stomach was okay, a little rumbly, but nothing a little Pepto couldn't fix. Head was definitely a problem, but an Excedrin would put that to bed. Mostly, I just felt thick and grumpy, which wasn't entirely new, and likely also fueled by my PMS.

I grumbled my way into the bathroom to wash my face, then back into my room to get dressed for work. I checked my phone to see if Greg had messaged back, but he hadn't. I couldn't even blame him, not after the weird-shit message I'd sent him.

I grumbled a little more.

A little bit later, the five-minute makeup was applied, hair was brushed and dry shampooed, still fluffy from last night, and Greg still hadn't texted me. So I stuffed my phone in my back pocket and tried not to worry about it as I grabbed my bag and headed into the too-bright day.

Everything felt sideways as I walked the block to Habits. My sunglasses weren't dark enough. People were smiling a little too much. People named Greg weren't texting me back. I stopped by the small coffee shop on the corner to grab coffee and immediately burned my tongue so bad, it fried my tastebuds and scalded the roof of my mouth. My scone was stale, who knew if it even tasted good, after what the coffee had done. And the coup de grace — when I reached into my bag for my favorite lipstick, I realized there was a hole in the lining and that expensive tube was lost somewhere in between. I didn't even have the heart to fish it out.

When I walked into Habits, the owner, Sheila, smiled at me apologetically from a table in the back where she sat across from a girl I'd never seen before, a small girl with gigantic brown eyes and long, pretty blond hair. I'm sure she was perfectly nice, a lovely girl, but my patience level at that point was somewhere around rabid dog, and when Sheila told me she was a new trainee, it took literally every ounce of willpower I had not to absolutely lose my shit.

Instead, I tried to smile, though it was about as tight as a nun's asshole. I introduced myself to Bayleigh — she made it a point to spell it out for me — and walked back to the office, doing my very best to calm the fuck down and failing pretty epically.

I was in the process of shoving my bag in one of the small lockers when Sheila came in, looking apologetic. "Hey, Rosie. I'm sorry to spring this on you, but Brent hired Bayleigh yesterday and told her she'd start today."

"Your brother's not a bad-looking guy, can't he get laid without hiring the girl he wants to nail?"

Sheila chuckled. "She seems nice enough. Maybe it won't be so bad."

I gave her a look. "Like Farrah, or whatever her name was?"

"Phaedra. Or Gina?"

"Ugh, Gina. Day two and she came in hungover and puked in the fucking ice well. I had to burn it right in the middle of the rush."

Sheila laughed as a shudder rolled through her.

"I mean, most of them don't even last three days."

"I know," she said with an understanding nod. "Just humor me today."

"Sheila, I don't know if I've got any humor left in me today, and it's only noon."

She smiled reassuringly. "Well, I'll be here all day with you until Shelby gets here at five. Then it's all her, okay?"

It was a fair deal in which I got to leave several hours earlier than usual, so I sighed again and tried to smile. "Okay."

She smiled back. "Thanks. So, what's got you sour?"

I raised a brow. "Aside from being up too early?"

"Hey," she joked, "it's only like twice a month that you have to work a mid, and it's the only time we get to work together."

"True. Last night was Tricky's birthday."

Her eyes widened — she knew all about, well, all of it. "Oh, yeah. That's what Shelby said."

"Yeah, and it was a mess because I brought a date like an idiot."

"Oh, God."

"And then I let Tricky sleep in my bed."

Her eyes bugged. "*Oh, God.*"

"Yup. Dumbassery all around. And now I'm hungover and tired and not really in the mood to teach *Bayleigh* how to make Harvey Wallbangers."

"Well, I'll get you out of here as soon as I can, and I'll owe you one. Cool?"

I waved a hand. "Yeah, it's fine. Let's just do this."

And thus started the longest day ever.

Sheila was right — Bayleigh was nice enough and enthusiastic, but she'd never even waited tables before, which ultimately meant me telling her to just watch for the day so I could power through. But then, we got busy, and not with the easy beer drinkers. Oh, no.

First was a group of nine chicks about my age who filed in for happy hour at two in expensive clothes and humorless lips. I walked up to the table knowing full well what to expect, and they didn't disappoint.

I heard them refer to themselves as 'young professionals' as I took their drink order which consisted strictly of bullshit like cosmos and martinis — one of them specifically and pointedly requested I chill her martini glass. Like there was another way to make a martini. Every single one of them ordered a drink in a martini glass that required a shaker to make, except for one. She ordered a frozen margarita.

So I put on my fake ass smile and walk behind the bar, planning out the order in which I'd need to make the drinks to get it done as quickly as possible — first the martinis, then the cosmos. The margarita could just fucking hold its horses. — just as three more people walked in and sat at the bar. I sent Bayleigh to get their drink orders, and she came back to bear the bad news that they'd ordered an Old Fashioned, a Tequila Sunrise, and a Kentucky Mule.

I asked the universe where the fuck the gin and tonics were.

I took a deep breath and buckled down, placing the first four drinks for the bitch brigade on a beverage tray for Bayleigh. She smiled at me sweetly as she picked it up, swearing she had it, and I watched the alcohol in those glasses splash and sway as she walked away.

The second she took her eyes off the tray to look at the table, it tipped over, and four martinis hit the floor with a crash. The entire table glared at me. One of them looked at her watch with an eyebrow raised.

Bayleigh turned to me with sheer panic on her face. Mine I'm sure was as flat and cold as a marble wall.

"Go get Sheila," I ordered, and got back to work.

And so my day continued as such. At least Sheila stayed on the floor to help me, keeping me behind the bar making drinks and away from people, which was wise. Very wise.

The rush finally ebbed right about when Shelby came in, and Sheila released me from perdition with a hug and a shot of tequila. My head hadn't stopped throbbing, that low, dull ache behind my eyes and nape of my neck, and if I thought I'd felt flat as a pancake before, I was now somewhere closer to a crepe.

I slammed that shot of tequila like it was medicine, and Bayleigh watched me before extending a lime. I waved her off.

"That was badass."

A short, quiet laugh huffed out of me. "No, that was desperate. Nice to meet you, Bayleigh. Sorry I was a horrible bitch today. I'd like to tell you this isn't usual, but that could prove to be a lie."

She laughed. "You're fine, I get it. I'll see you later."

I smiled, though it was tired and sagging, then headed to the back to grab my things. I'd been so busy, I realized on my way out that I'd forgotten about Greg again. I grabbed my phone and checked it for messages.

Nothing.

I frowned. And then I decided, probably unwisely, to go to his coffee shop to talk to him. Because putting people on the spot always works out. I rolled my eyes at myself.

The truth of it was that I needed a resolution, and I wanted to apologize to him again. I needed to.

I was nervous and not optimistic as I pulled open the door of the coffee shop where he worked. He stood behind the counter, and I smiled at the sight of him, feeling better for a split second until he smiled back. Something was definitely off, but I approached him anyway, because what else could I do at that point?

I did my best to keep it breezy and cool, which was legitimately the opposite of how I felt. I leaned on the counter. "So, I was in the neighborhood and wanted to swing by. How's your day been?"

His face told me nothing. "Good," he answered. "Want a drink?"

"Will you judge me if I get hot chocolate again?"

He smiled. "Never. Nervous?"

"A little," I admitted. "I wanted to talk, if you have a second?"

"Sure. Have a seat, I'll bring it over."

I pulled a ten out of my pocket and tried to hand it over, but he wouldn't take it, so I stuffed it in the tip jar and took a seat at a small table near the back.

Greg sat down across from me a few minutes later and slid the paper cup across the table.

"Thanks," I said and wrapped my hands around it.

He watched me for a second. "I'm sorry for bailing last night. But I have to say I felt a little out of place."

I nodded, feeling like a jerk. "I'm sorry too. I can't say it enough."

"I mean, between you getting hauled all over the bar and the vibe between you and your ex, it was a little much for a second date. I really like you, Rose. I had a great time the other day. But it seems like you might have some …" he rubbed the back of his neck, "… baggage to deal with. I mean, don't get me wrong. Everybody's got baggage. But yours hangs out at your house and stares at you from across the room in a way that makes me uncomfortable."

I let out a breath. "I really am sorry, Greg. My situation is more complicated than I guess I realized. I hate that I made you feel like that."

But he smiled. "Don't feel bad. I get it. I just don't want to be caught up in the middle of whatever's going on between you two."

I nodded, my mouth so dry that my lips stuck together. I took a hopeful sip of the hot chocolate, but it coated my mouth like paste. I didn't know what to even say. "I feel like a real asshole. I wanted to come talk to you because I really like you too."

He smiled, but it was sad. "After all the shit dates I'd been on, you were a breath of fresh air. I'm not mad, Rose. It's just that I'm not trying to get into something complicated."

"Yeah, me neither, but it just sort of keeps finding me."

"Well, if you ever shake it, give me a call."

I tried to smile. "Thanks."

"Thank you for restoring my faith in the dating game." He stood, and so did I.

I gripped my paper cup. "I'll see you around, Greg."

"Take it easy, Rose."

I kept my chin up and walked out of the coffee shop, embarrassed and annoyed, trying not to hurry away but wanting to leave my regrets behind me.

I shouldn't have asked him to come to Habits. It was too soon to subject him to that.

I should have known better.

I spiked the hot chocolate into the first trash bin I came across as my embarrassment simmered and bubbled until it was hot and steamy and ready to blow.

Deal 2.0

ROSE

I **walked toward the subway with** one word on my mind.

Patrick.

Seven months had passed since we'd broken up, and he was still somehow so present in my life that I couldn't even date without it blowing up in my face. No, *somehow* he was living in my apartment. Sleeping in my bed.

I flew down the stairs and through the turnstile, trying to retrace my steps through the choices that led me to where I was as I stepped onto the train.

Except it all started with a choice I *hadn't* made — him sneaking in to sleep in my place. Honestly, it had started even before, when he *chose* to break up with me, and he *chose* to wave another girl in my face. It was *his* choices that led us here, which was exactly why he wouldn't be staying with me anymore.

Deep down, I knew he hadn't been trying to manipulate me by sneaking in like a thieving bastard. I knew where his intentions lie. I knew it was more complicated than I was making it out, but as I stood on the packed train during rush hour, it didn't matter.

As far as I was concerned, everything was his fault.

If he would only let me go. If he would just stop looking at me like he did. Why couldn't he just date? Find someone new? I mean, how many times did I have to say I didn't want to be with him before he'd leave me alone? Because the once should have been enough.

I told him we were through, and I meant it. But he just wouldn't listen, couldn't get the hint. And because of that, because of the position he put me in every goddamn day by making it so painfully clear that he wanted me, I lost a shot with a guy who could have been perfect.

Frustration rolled through me like a rumbling storm as I blew off the train and up the stairs, walking up Broadway and into our building.

I unlocked my door, scowling deeper when I found Patrick sitting on my couch. Again.

I closed the door a little harder than I should have, and he looked over his shoulder at me with an eyebrow up.

"Hey. How was your day?" he asked innocently. I could have punched him in the larynx.

"Fine." I clipped and set my bag down on the kitchen table. A bowl was in the sink and a pot on the stove, both with noodles stuck to the edges. "Is this yours?"

"Yeah, sorry. I was going to clean that up."

I turned around, knowing my eyes were like death rays. They zeroed in on his boots on my coffee table. "Get your feet off my coffee table."

He moved them slowly, his eyes still on mine. "Sorry. Let me wash those dishes," he said as he stood.

My cheeks were hot. "You don't fucking live here, Tricky. I told you from the start that I didn't want this to happen, you hanging out here all the time, leaving your shit in my sink, putting your dirty boots on my furniture and your toothbrush in my bathroom."

His eyes narrowed. "Right, but then you told me I *could* hang out. You understand better than anyone why I don't want to go home."

"Yeah, well, I take it back. I can't deal with this, you being here, you sleeping in my bed. I can't do this, Tricky."

"What happened?" he asked, his voice low.

I fumed. "You mean besides you scaring off my date last night? Or bringing Seth around? I think he might have been asking me out, as more than friends, or at least that's the vibe I got."

His body tightened.

"Yeah. And Veronica came and talked to me, too. I can't deal with the drama, Tricky. I just can't. You've got to go home."

He took a step toward me, shoulders square, eyes burning.

I threw my hands up. "Ugh, stop looking at me like that, Patrick."

He took another step, his eyes smoldering deeper still. "Like what?"

"Like you want to eat me."

Another step. "I'll stop when you do." The words were a quiet promise. One more step. He was just inches from me, stealing my breath.

"I don't know what you're talking about," I whispered, my eyes still locked on his.

He slipped a hand into my hair. "I think you do."

"No, I don't."

"Then tell me to leave. Look me in the eye and tell me to go."

I searched his eyes and opened my mouth to speak as thoughts screamed through my brain like sleet. But instead of saying the word I should have said, I closed my eyes and pressed my lips to his.

It was relief I felt the moment we touched, frantic relief as I sucked in a breath through my nose, eyes closed, breathing him in, not knowing where it came from, not caring enough to stop. My arms were around his neck. His tongue passed my lips and tangled with mine. His hands slipped down my waist, hips pressing me against the counter as I pulled him as close as I could, and we bumped into the cabinets with a thump.

It didn't faze us.

My legs wound around his waist, and he spun around, pinning me against the wall with his hips, one hand on my thigh, the other braced against the wall as he kissed me so deeply I couldn't get enough oxygen. My back was flush against the wall, hands scrambling blindly for the hem of his shirt, not wanting to stop, not wanting to think. Just wanting his skin, wanting him so badly that my body ached.

Months of wanting him. Months of needing him.

Every reason I had for staying away dissipated and disappeared.

He was the last person to touch me like this, and he hadn't forgotten a single thing. The way his lips moved, his tongue against mine, his fingers. Maybe it was instinctive, like our bodies were tuned to each other, because I hadn't forgotten either. But reasons didn't matter, not in that fevered moment as I pulled his shirt off, and not in any of the moments after.

Patrick broke away for the briefest moment as the shirt slipped over his head, mouth hung open, lids heavy, but his lips were against mine again before it hit the ground.

He spun me again, and I shifted to hang on, knocking him off balance and into the hall table. The lamp fell over with a crash that left us in near darkness, but I barely noticed — every thought was focused on his hand as it slipped up my waist. He pushed off the wall, our lips still connected as he carried me toward the bedroom until he ran into my closed door, pushing me against it. His skin was so hot, so soft, fingers digging into my thigh, hard length pressing against me as he flexed his hips. I moaned into his mouth just as his free hand found the doorknob and turned.

I tightened my arms around his neck, bringing us as close as we could get, our lips a hard seam. He kicked the door closed, and in three steps, he was lowering me onto my bed. My hands found the hem of his jeans, heart hammering so hard it hurt as I felt him shift to kick off his boots. I did the same when he pulled off my shirt and threw it, and our eyes were down, drinking each other in. I looked down his chest at the tattoos running across his skin, my fingers trailing down to his waist and to the buttons, and I looked up and into his eyes just as I slipped my hand inside and wrapped my fingers around him.

His eyelids fluttered, a heavy sigh passing his lips as he flexed, pressing himself into my palm. He took a breath, then took my mouth, hot and wet, lips swollen.

I'd missed him so much. Too much.

He made quick work of the rest of my clothes, first slipping a hand under my back to unclasp my bra faster than I could have, then did the same with the button of my jeans as my free hand pulled his pants over the curve of his ass.

I watched him back away, his eyes dark and deep, locked on mine as he dropped his pants. And just like that, he was naked, right there in front of me like I'd imagined a hundred times. He pulled off my pants in a split second, and then I reached for him, begging him to hurry, before reason found me and I could say no.

There was nothing I wanted in that moment more than him. Only him.

My hands found his length again, my thumb skimming across his crown, down his shaft and the barbell there, remembering what it would feel like to have him inside of me. My body clenched at the thought. His fingers trailed up my thigh, hooked my panties and pulled them out of the way as he licked his lips and dragged the pad of his warm finger up the wet line.

I gasped.

"Yes," I whispered up at him, and he kissed my bottom lip, biting gently as he slipped that finger inside of me.

My hips flexed against him. Another finger slipped in, curling as he palmed me.

I couldn't keep my eyes open, couldn't think, couldn't breathe, not with him stroking my body like it was his.

My body squeezed his fingers, hips rolling hard. I was close — so close. And then they were gone.

"Not yet," he whispered, reaching for my nightstand while I panted, pinned underneath him. I could feel the tip of him just against me, and I moaned, rolling my hips to force him in. He kissed my parted lips as he tore open the condom. "Not yet."

My eyes wouldn't open, but I wanted to see him, so I pried my lids apart to catch a glimpse of the top of his head, the lines of his shoulders and biceps, his hand gripping his shaft as he rolled the condom on and angled himself to press against me. And then, he looked at me, looked through me as his hand cupped my neck, and mine found his jaw, and our lips came together once more at the exact moment that he flexed until he filled me completely.

Forget all of the moments before or after. In that moment, we were perfect and whole.

His hand squeezed my hip, holding me still as he pulled out slow and slammed in. Then again. And again and again. His hands were on my breasts, in my hair, pinning my arms over my head. I couldn't move. I didn't want to.

"Harder."

His hand clamped around my wrists tightened, his fingers on my hip squeezing as he gave me what I wanted, rolling his body, knowing exactly what I needed. And when I opened my eyes and saw him above me — his dark eyes, the swell of his lips, the cut of his jaw — I lost the hold I had on my body, neck snapping into an arch as I sucked in a breath and held it. My heart stopped, starting again with a bang, and I pulsed around him as I let go, squeezing him, holding him.

He was right behind me, kissing me once, deep and possessive, before he took what he needed. A deep thrust, his muscles tight as a soft cry passed his lips, and he rocked his body, filling me as much as he could, as if through the motion he could claim me. As if I was anyone else's.

As he slowed, he collapsed on top of me, face buried in my neck as he let my hands go. I cradled him in my arms, still too drunk off of him to think. It was a glorious limbo, those few minutes before our minds caught up with our bodies. But when they did, I felt the shift, the wall between us, creeping taller, sprouting barbed wire and broken glass.

He propped himself on his forearms and looked down at me, hands in my hair.

My voice was rough. "That was …"

"I know," he said as his thumb shifted against my cheek.

"This doesn't change anything," I said, willing it to be true.

His eyes were on my lips. "I know."

And then, I said the thing that would be the final nail in my coffin, pushing my fears aside with false bravado because I needed him. That much, at least, I knew. And I could have him, for a moment maybe. And I'd make that moment last as long as I could.

"Can we do it again?"

He smiled and met my eyes. "Absolutely."

Go With It

PATRICK

Two days in a row, Rose was in my arms when I woke.

Whatever magic fueled my luck, I only hoped it didn't run out.

My eyes were closed as we lay in the dark, her back pressed against my chest, my arm nestled between her breasts and forearm. Our fingers were clasped, shifting slowly as she breathed in, breathed out.

It was early — my alarm hadn't gone off yet — but I knew there would be no going back to sleep. The difference between that morning and the morning before mirrored in my mind. From my fears and hopes yesterday to today — to the moment that I knew when she woke up that she wouldn't pull away. She wouldn't say no. For now, at least.

The night before rolled through my thoughts, and I smiled, savoring the sweet burn of the memory like the first sip of whiskey after a long, lonely day.

The kiss — that first kiss, when she closed her eyes and gave herself to me — was everything I knew it would be. I stepped into her knowing the risk, but I saw it in her eyes. She didn't want me to stop any more than I wanted to, and instead of telling me to leave, she gave me that kiss, the one that opened that cracked window enough that I could climb in.

Part of me wondered how long it would last. The rest of me told that part to shut up and go with it.

A good while later, when I finally convinced myself to leave, I kissed the curve of Rose's neck in parting. She shifted against me and hummed.

"See you later, Rosie," I whispered, and she kissed my fingers before letting me go and settled back into sleep.

I climbed out of her warm bed and pulled on my clothes, grabbing my phone on the way out of her room, trying to keep the smile on my face in check. The broken lamp was still on the floor, the only thing really intact being the shade. I swept it all up and threw it away with Valentino watching me, tail curled around his back paws as he licked his front paw like a prince, then set up her coffee machine for her, leaving a sticky note on the start button.

Have a good day, Rosie. -Patrick

Her apartment was quiet as I left — Lily's door open and Ellie absent — as was the hall, though my thoughts screamed Rose's name.

I unlocked my apartment to find West stretched out on the couch, reading. "Hey."

"Hey," I said as I closed the door.

That one word was all it took. He looked me over with shock on his face. "What happened?"

My smile somehow stretched wider. "Rose."

More shock. "Rose?"

I smiled.

West blinked. "How the hell?"

I didn't want to sit down, didn't want to stop moving, so I made coffee. The energy working through me was so different from yesterday. Rather than being amped up from wondering what it all meant, I felt certain. Quiet. Now the only question was when I would see her again.

I poured out the old coffee and filled up the pot. "She came home from work yesterday pissed. I mean, really pissed. She was spitting nails at me from the second she walked in the door, told me I couldn't stay anymore." I poured the water into the tank as I spoke and reloaded the filter and grounds, hitting the start button.

"And then?" He sat up and laid his book on the coffee table.

The machine began to sputter as I walked through the kitchen and sat in the armchair. "And then, I went for it. I was just about to kiss her, but she beat me to it." I shook my head, smirking as I rubbed my jaw. "Then she was taking off my shirt, and then we were in her bed. I swear, I thought she was going to stop me at any moment, but she didn't."

He scratched at his beard. "What does it mean?"

I shrugged, shaking my head again. "She says nothing. I'm not sure I believe her. I'm not even sure she believes herself."

"And for you?" he asked.

"I'll take what I can get. I don't know what it means, and I don't need to know. Not yet. So I'm just going to take it one day at a time."

West smiled. "I knew if one of you made a move, you'd end up back together."

"Hey, man. No one says we're together. I'm not counting on that, not this soon, at least. Who knows. Rose could spend the day freaking out and trip on me again tonight."

He sat back in his chair and threaded his fingers behind his head. "She won't."

I chuckled. "Says you."

"Yeah, says me. We've been watching the two of you for months. Rose can say all she wants that she's not interested, but that's a bold-faced lie."

"Because she doesn't *want* to be interested in me. That's the problem, and that's exactly why I'm not getting my hopes up, but I feel better than I have in a long, long time. Even if it's just temporary, I'm riding the wave until the surge is over."

"Well, if you ask me, it's been a long time coming. I hope it's not temporary, this time. I hope this is it for you two."

I sighed, smiling, imagining it were true for only a moment before I brought myself back down to reality. "It could be sweet."

woke before my alarm went off, rolling over in the dark, though I nestled back into my comforter, not quite ready for the cold world outside my bed just yet. I was more relaxed, more sated than I had been in forever.

My mind groaned into gear and the night came back to me, piece by piece, kiss by kiss. A smile found its way onto my lips.

What are you doing, Rose?

I wasn't even sure how it had happened. One minute I could have set him on fire, but he'd set me on fire instead.

It had been coming for months, I supposed, an inevitable explosion after being in a pressure cooker with him for all that time. It was exactly what I'd been afraid of when he started staying with me. Now the lines had been crossed, and there was probably no going back.

The only thing that surprised me was how little I regretted it.

I'd been fighting my feelings for him since we'd broken up, and now I was free of it all. Like I'd been drowning, kicking and clawing to get to the surface, but it wasn't until I let go and sank into his dark arms that I found peace. And that's exactly how I felt. Peaceful. Like everything was going to be just fine.

I felt more whole than I had since before he'd ended things.

The pain of that memory stirred deep in my chest, reminding me that he was dangerous. Reminding me to keep him away.

When I told him nothing had changed, he said he knew, thus agreeing to keeping things the way they were — I wasn't his, and we weren't back together. Outside of the comfort of my room and bed, at least. Those boundaries would keep me safe, the knowledge that it was temporary. That I had some modicum of control.

We'd have to figure things out eventually, but for now, I didn't want answers. Expectations were what had killed us last time, so maybe the trick was to just not talk about it. Ever, as far as I was concerned, however unrealistic that might have been.

If we kept things simple, maybe he wouldn't get scared, wouldn't run. He wouldn't leave.

I turned on my light and climbed out of bed, heading into the living room in search of caffeine.

Ellie leered at me from the kitchen table with her hair in a red knot on top of her head. "Well, hello there, Rosie. How'd you sleep?" She shoveled a spoon of Froot Loops into her mouth.

She knew. I sighed. "Fine."

She snorted. "Ha. I bet you did."

When I reached the coffee pot, I smiled, pulling off the note he'd left for me in neat, uppercase letters, my eyes lingering on his name. *Patrick.* I'd barely called him that since before we broke up. Calling him Tricky was an easy way to make a concrete distinction from the man I wanted and the one I hated. I hit the brew button and sighed. "Go ahead. Get it out of your system."

She giggled. "I cannot believe you hooked up with him, Rose!"

"How do you know we hooked up?" I folded my arms across my chest and raised a brow.

Ellie rolled her eyes. "Oh, please. Look at you. You're freshly fucked if I ever saw it. Anyway, it's not like we all didn't see that coming from a mile away."

Lily burst through the front door with rosy cheeks and twinkling eyes. "Spill it, Rose."

I shot a look at Ellie, who shrugged. "I texted her."

"I see that." I took a seat at the table. "All right. Come on. Let's talk about it."

Lily sat down and leaned on the table, absolutely rapt. "Tell me everything."

I took a deep breath and said, simply, "I slept with Tricky, and it was awesome."

She blinked at me. "What does it mean? How did you …"

"Well, see, he put his penis in my va—"

Her lips were flat. "I know how it works, Rose. I mean how did you go from barely speaking to having sex?"

I shrugged. "I yelled at him, and he shut me up with his dick."

Ellie burst out laughing.

Lily rolled her eyes, but she laughed too. "You're awfully flippant about this, considering."

"Considering what?"

She shook her head, looking me over. I think she approved, even if she was confused. "Seriously, what has gotten into you?"

Ellie snickered and pulled her knees up to her chest. "I think I know. A little Tricky dicky."

I snorted. "I wouldn't call it little, but yeah."

Lily watched me. "I'm a little concerned about you not taking this seriously. I have to admit, I thought you'd be more freaked out after having sex with *Patrick*. I mean, Rose. It's *Patrick*."

"Yeah, well." My smile fell. "I don't really know what else to do." I got up and poured my coffee so I didn't have to look at Lily, pouring her a cup too. "I just had kind of a shitty reentry to dating. I haven't had sex in a very long time, and I can only resist Tricky for so long, you know? With him staying here …" I spooned sugar in and stirred it around. "I caved, I guess. I was tired of fighting it. And now, well, I can't really take it back, can I?" I sat back down and passed hers over before warming my hands on the mug. "So I'm accepting the inevitable. I'll clean up the mess later."

"Well, I approve," Lily said with a small nod of her head and picked up her coffee.

"Really?" I asked, bewildered.

"Maybe this is how you two patch things up."

I raised an eyebrow. "By not patching it up at all? Ride on the flat tire until the rim is bent? Even I know that's a bad idea."

But Lily shrugged. "Maybe. Or maybe you just rode over a bumpy patch and the tire's fine."

"Ha. Not fucking likely, but that's a nice thought." I took a sip of my coffee.

"Seriously. If the two of you would just get out of your own way, you'd be fine."

I frowned. "That's not really fair, Lily. You guys love to talk about it like we're being irrational, but we have reasons for every decision we've made. It's not as simple as you like to pretend it is."

Her face softened. "No, I know. We just want you two to get back together and be okay. You're miserable without each other, and it's not easy to watch. So I'm glad you got naked."

Ellie nodded as she chewed and swallowed. "I always approve of getting naked."

I chuckled and took a sip of my coffee. "Tell me something I don't know."

She waggled her copper eyebrows.

"So what's up with Max?" I asked.

She beamed. "He's just amazing, that's all." She lowered her spoon into her bowl and moved it around absently. "A total freak in bed, but sweet and funny too. Plus, Valentino loves him, and he thinks he's better than *everyone*."

The gigantic black cat jumped on the kitchen counter at the mention of his name and pranced across it, one white paw in front of the other, head high like he was telling us exactly what he thought of any rules we might have of him doing otherwise.

"Anyway," Ellie continued, "I'm going up to see him at the shop today. You guys should come with me." She took a bite of cereal.

"Are you just going for lunch or what?" I asked.

She shook her head as she swallowed. "No, to get my nipples pierced."

Lily choked on her coffee, then burst out laughing along with me.

"Oh, my God, El."

"I don't get what the big deal is," she said with a shrug and took another bite.

"It's not at all," Lily replied. "It's just funny that you care so little what other people think."

"Whatever. Life's too short to try to meet someone else's expectations. I have zero secrets, and I like it that way. Take it or leave it, bitches!" she crowed to the universe. "Anyway, you should seriously come with."

Lily took a sip of her coffee. "I can't. West and I are going to the library."

Ellie laughed. "Oooh, hot date. Bang in the erotica aisle for me, would you?"

I chuckled and rolled my eyes. "Don't dare her. She'll do it. Besides, they've been banging everywhere else, anyway."

"Hey," Lily said, mock-hurt. "Not everywhere, just all the time. It's different."

"Tell Patrick that."

Her cheeks flushed when she smiled. "Seems like he's got his hands full now anyway."

"Seems that way." I took a drink coyly and turned to Ellie. "I'll go with you, El. I have to work at six, though."

She lit up. "Ooh, you should get yours done too."

I held up a hand. "Pass."

"Max said it doesn't hurt all that bad."

"I'll take his word for it."

Ellie chuckled and picked up her phone. "I'll let Max know we're coming. Maybe we can all go get lunch afterward."

"Sure, if you're not passed out," I joked. "If nothing else, we can go get a drink. You might need that more."

She giggled. "Probably." Her phone buzzed, and she glanced at the screen. "Max said Tricky looks like he won the lottery."

"I bet he does," Lily said.

I smiled. "I can't deny I'm a catch. Let's just see if he can hang on to me, this time."

Pins & Needles

ROSE

glanced over ellie as we walked toward Tonic that afternoon in the glorious summer sun. "Nervous?"

She shrugged and pushed her red hair over her shoulder. "Not really. I feel a little … I don't know, intense?"

We stepped off the curb and crossed the street with a stream of pedestrians. "Adrenaline. I get that before I get a tattoo. But nipple piercing? That's next level. I'd be crawling out of my skin."

"I *really* think you should get yours done too." She waggled her eyebrows.

"Nah, I'm good."

"I bet Tricky would love it," she coaxed hopefully.

I smiled, imagining his reaction if I told him I wanted to do it. "Maybe he would, but I'm admittedly way too much of a pussy to let anyone near my nipples with a fourteen-gauge."

"But you have tattoos. That's got to be worse, right?"

I shrugged. "I dunno. It's different. Like, it just stings. You don't get stabbed with a gigantic needle, just grazed by a tiny one."

"Max said just hurts for a second. I bet it's a long ass second, but still." She perked up. "Are Tricky's nipples pierced?"

I wet my lips and pursed them. "Mmhmm."

"Anything else?"

I smiled down at my shoes as I stepped back onto the sidewalk. "Mmmhmm."

She giggled. "Tell me it's his dick, please."

"It's his dick, please."

Ellie squealed. "Oh, my God. I forgot. I've always wondered what that's like."

"Uh, awesome. Duh." I rolled my eyes, joking.

She was excited, eyes big and smiling. "He doesn't have anything crazy though, right? Like a Jacob's Ladder? I can't imagine getting one piercing there, never mind like eight. And not just because I don't have a dick."

"It's called a dolphin. Like a Prince Albert but with a longer bar, so it goes from that part under his crown down his shaft like two inches."

"Fuck." She shuddered, whether from imagining the pain or thinking about how hot it was, I didn't know. Maybe both. "Ugh, but I can totally imagine he has that. Does he have a pretty dick?"

I laughed. "God, Ellie."

"What? I couldn't see it when you walked in on him in the shower. Trust me, I tried. Anyway, cousins don't let cousins get down on ugly dick, pierced or not."

I sighed. "No, it's basically the supermodel of dicks, just like the rest of him."

"Does the piercing make it more fun to go down on him?"

"For sure. Like there's all this stuff to *do* with it."

She laughed. "I never got girls who bitch about blow jobs. If you hate giving blow jobs, you're doing it wrong."

I raised the roof. "Preach."

"I mean, I'd figure most guys don't want to just fuck your bored mouth. Think about it — it'd be the equivalent of a guy who goes down on you and gives it some half-assed, obligatory lick or two before he jams his rod in. The worst! That's an instant dump situation. You gotta get in there and get weird on it. I mean, not too weird, but you know what I mean. If it feels good for you, it feels good for them."

"Blow jobs: 101."

She nodded seriously. "I should teach a class."

I snickered. "I mean, it's bad if there's a hygiene problem. Like, wash your balls, bro. And if you have four-inch pubes, I'm not going to want to go downtown and tour the Chrysler Building. Do a little manscaping. Not too much, because bald dicks are weird too. But a little trim goes a long way."

"I'm sure it's the same for guys, though. And our junk is way more offensive than theirs. Sometimes, I even offend myself."

"It really isn't fair, is it?"

"Fuck you, nature!" she shouted, and the lady in front of us shot a dirty look at us over her shoulder.

We busted out laughing.

I pulled open the door to Tonic, and we were greeted by the heavy guitar licks of Death From Above 1979. The guy's voice sounded like sex. On ice cream. Drowning in chocolate.

I'd always loved the shop — it looked dark and old while still modern, with a hint of creep about it. The mirrors were all old and spotted around the edges. There were things like a shadow box displaying small animal skulls, and what looked to be a very old Ouija board hanging on the wall. The waiting area was filled with furniture from the 1800s that had been painted with skulls and butterflies that looked like old wood cuttings. And it always smelled faintly of spices — cardamom and anise, maybe a hint of orange. I don't know what kind of witchy brew Joel had going on, but he should have bottled and sold it.

Max stood from his booth toward the back, and Ellie giggled and took off, leapt into his arms, and wrapped her legs around his waist. Some serious tongue action ensued, and I shook my head, smiling as I looked to Joel, who was laughing.

"Hey, Rosie." He stepped out from behind the counter and gave me a hug. "Twice in one week. What'd I do to get so lucky?"

I chuckled and gave him a squeeze. Or at least I tried. He was like a gigantic lumberjack, barrel chest and all. "Hey, Joel."

Patrick stood, smiling at me as he approached. "Hey." He stopped close to me, and I looked up at him, momentarily stunned, waiting for him to kiss me.

His eyes darted to my lips, and he wet his own with a small slip of his tongue, looking back at my eyes as he shifted away from me. But he smiled, and that smile told me plenty.

Pretty sure mine matched.

"Hey," I said.

"Here for Ellie's piercing?"

"I couldn't let her do that without some solid moral support. She tried to convince me to do it too, but I draw the line at piercing needles."

He chuckled.

"How's your day?"

"Better now."

I smiled and looked away, not sure how to respond. I was overwhelmed, feeling like I shouldn't have come, but also like I wanted touch him, kiss him, do something to tell him I'd meant what I said. That I wasn't going to throw on the brakes just yet.

Ellie's feet finally hit the ground again, and she adjusted her shirt, smiling at me. "Did you want to come back with me?"

"Do you want me to come back?"

She wrinkled her nose. "Kinda."

"Then I'm there." I smiled at Patrick. "Wish me luck."

"Luck," he said with a smirk.

I followed Ellie and Max back to one of the rooms in the back and closed the door behind me. The rooms looked like a Victorian torture parlor — purple velvet damask walls, all the hardware black, even the tray, which was covered in plastic covered tools that stood just next to the padded blood-red leather inclined table.

"All right, babe. Hop up here and take your shirt off." Max patted the seat, and Ellie did as she was told with rosy cheeks and doe eyes as she pulled her shirt off and lost her bra, tossing them on the chair in the corner without hesitating. He washed his hands, put on black rubber gloves, and grabbed a Sharpie, looking very serious as he examined her nipples and marked her where he'd pierce her.

The room was silent, and I stared at the pattern on the wall to keep me from *also* examining her nipples.

Max turned and looked at the mirrored wall. "How's that look?"

Ellie tilted her head, shifting her shoulders to get a good look. "Uh, I don't know. I guess that looks fine."

He smiled. "It's gonna look great. Lie down."

Her cheeks flushed, and she reached for my hand. I kept my eyes on hers as best I could.

What? Ellie has great tits. Plus, when boobs are out, there's no way *not* to look. It's just a fact.

Max came back with a huge clamp. "Okay, now, this is almost going to be worse than the needle. You ready?"

She gripped my hand, the first flicker of worry passing across her face. She nodded.

He opened the monstrous clamps and lined the markings up in

the holes. "Take a breath, El."

She did, but her face blanched when he closed the clamps, squashing her nipple until it looked almost nothing like a nipple.

"Good girl. You okay?"

"Mmhmm," was all she could eek out.

"Rose, could you hold this?" He motioned to the clamp handles as he removed his fingers.

"Uh …"

"Just for a second. Here."

I slipped my fingers in just as he let go. And there I was, holding my cousin's nipple clamp in the back room of a tattoo parlor.

I felt a little lightheaded myself when he turned around with the gigantic hollow needle.

There was a reason why I didn't have piercings.

Max got eye level with the clamp, checking it one more time to make sure it was straight before he commandeered it from me.

"Okay. Take two or three deep breaths, and keep your eyes on the ceiling. You ready?"

"No, but do it anyway," she said.

He smiled. "That's my girl. Okay. One … two … three."

Her hand squeezed, and I looked down, which was a mistake. My eyelids were glued open as I watched him push that big ass needle through her nipple. Blood dripped down the side of her breast.

I was hot, so hot. Sweat rolled down my back, and my face tingled. "I don't feel so good," I mumbled, the room going dim.

"Oh, shit. *Tricky!*" I heard Max yell as my vision faded, and a strong set of arms caught me before I hit the ground like a sack of bricks.

When I woke a few minutes later, Patrick's face was the first thing I saw, dark brows bent in worry, blue eyes burning with concern. I lay stretched out on his chair, feeling dizzy. Something cold pressed against the nape of my neck, and it felt amazing.

"Hey," Patrick said softly, smiling down at me. "Don't sit up yet."

"I fainted."

"You did."

I sighed, closing my eyes again as I shifted. "I am officially the coolest."

He chuckled. "You aren't the first person to hit the deck in here. It happens every day."

I cracked a lid and raised a brow. "Have you ever passed out getting modded?"

He smirked. "I like to watch."

"You're really sick, you know that?"

He handed me a tiny box of apple juice. "Here. Drink this. It'll make you feel better."

I took it and drank a little just as Ellie materialized next to me, eyes wide. She touched my arm and peered at me. "Oh, my God, Rosie. Are you okay?"

I smiled. "I'm fine" I nodded to her chest. "Are you?"

"Hell yeah. But thank God Max took the clamp away from you before you fainted, because I never would have forgiven you if you'd ripped my nipple off."

I chuckled and sipped my apple juice. "So are you all finished?"

She lit up. "Uh-huh! Check it out!" She lifted up her shirt to display her naked boobs. We were about ten feet from the street window, where I noticed one guy do a double take before skidding to a stop.

A laugh shot out of me. "Uh, they look great, El, but maybe you should put them away."

She lowered her shirt, still beaming. "That was fucking awesome. It hurt like a bitch though."

"I can only imagine. Actually, I did imagine, and it made me faint, so you just got serious badass points in my book." I looked over at Patrick. "I feel a little better. Can I sit now?"

"Sure." He grabbed my arm as I sat, and I used his weight to pull myself up.

I closed my eyes and ran a hand through my hair with a sigh.

When I opened them, Patrick was watching me. "Are you sure you still want to get lunch?"

I did the classic body assessment, checking all my parts — including my stomach — and found them intact. "Yeah. I should probably eat something, anyway. What are we thinking?"

"Tacos," Ellie said definitively.

I almost moaned, and my mouth watered. "Tacos. How about El Corazon? They make their own tortillas, which is the equivalent of taco unicorns in New York. If they'd only stay open twenty-four hours, my life would be made."

Patrick leaned against his desk. "I'm in."

"Good," I said as I lifted myself off the chair, but the second my feet hit the ground, my knees went out from under me, and I was falling again, straight into Patrick.

"Whoa," he muttered and stood to catch me, pulling me into his chest. I looked up at him, and he looked down — our noses were inches from each other. My breath froze as I waited for him to kiss me, my eyes on his lips, but instead of meeting mine, they smiled, and he hugged me tighter, lowering his face to my ear. "I'll give you that later, Rosie."

If he hadn't been holding me up, I would have hit the ground again because my knees were no longer functioning joints.

But then again, Patrick always did have that effect on me.

Patrick

'd been back at the shop for a few hours after lunch as I hunched over my desk, sketching as I waited for my last client. I smiled down at the paper, thinking about the feeling of her hand in mine as we walked to El Corazon, her thigh against mine at the table, the sound of her laugh.

That sound made me more happy than I could find words to describe. Especially knowing I was the reason for it.

I smiled down at the page, shading the shadows of a woman's face. It wasn't Rose, not exactly at least — she'd been a muse since the first time I laid eyes on her. I'd always been drawn to the female form in art, the delicate features of a woman's face, the soft curves of her body, but Rose was the standard to which I held all features. Sometimes it would be her eyes that I'd start with, though the rest of her face would be different. Sometimes it was her lips. Or an expression she wore. But there was a small piece of Rose in everything I drew. I supposed there was a piece of Rose in me, too. There always would be.

I looked up from my work when the bell on the door rang.

Seth smiled, and I stood, surprised to see him but glad all the same.

"What's up, man?" I said as he approached. We clapped each other's shoulders.

"Not much. Just got off work and wanted to say hi." He took a seat in my chair, and I leaned against my desk. There was a hint of worry in his face, and the familiar dread of responsibility for Seth crept in.

"Everything okay?" I asked.

"Yeah. Or it will be."

"What's up?" I didn't know if I was ready for the answer.

He sighed. "That's not why I came here. Don't worry about it, Tricky. What's up with you?"

I folded my arms. "Come on, man. What's going on? Are you clean? I mean, you didn't—"

He shook his head. "No, no. Nothing like that. It's just that my roommate bailed a couple of months ago. I'd been doing okay, but my savings are almost gone, and I've been looking for a roommate, but it hasn't been easy. I'm recovering, you know? Living with a stranger could be dangerous for me — I don't even know if I can have liquor in the house, you know? And almost everyone else I know is a junkie."

"Yeah, I know." I knew then what was coming, and the war in my thoughts began. "How can I help?"

"It's not your problem."

"I know it's not, but I still want to help."

He smirked, trying to make light of it. "Well, if you know anybody who needs a roommate, you could give them my number."

There was only person who I knew who fit the bill. Me. My living situation was nowhere near stable or permanent. I knew I didn't want to go back to West's, and I'd need to find somewhere to go sooner than later.

"I may need a roommate soon."

His brow quirked. "Yeah?"

I nodded. "You know I've been sleeping on Rose's couch, but I don't know how long that will last, and West and Lily should stay in our old place. I just don't know when I'll need to decide. How long do you have?"

"A couple of weeks."

"I can handle that. Let me think about it, and if you find somebody else, just let me know."

He smiled and shook his head. "Man. It'd be just like old times."

I laughed. "Except better."

Seth rubbed the back of his neck. "Maybe a little less drama. Anyway, I'm starving, thought I'd see if you wanted to get something to eat?"

"Can't. Still have another client, but I'll take you up on that soon. Hit me up."

"All right." He stood, still smiling. "I'd better get something to eat. Take it easy, Tricky."

We embraced again, and he headed out as I sat back down at my desk.

Living with Seth again after all this time? If you'd have told me a few weeks ago I'd be considering it, I would have said you were crazy. But I was in limbo, even if it was a happy limbo. Even if I looked at it solely from an objective point of view, it made sense. I'd have to figure something out eventually. Did the timing matter?

My first thought was that yes, it did. Staying with Rose might have been the only thing keeping us together. At least right now. After a few weeks, maybe things would be different, but right now? I had a tenuous grip on the situation, and I wasn't ready to risk letting it slip away. But that didn't change the fact that I had no place to call my own. Clothes at one place. Toothbrush at another. Never sleeping in my own bed.

I sighed, setting down my pencil as Joel approached.

I eyed him. "Are you about to lecture me?"

He put up his hands in surrender. "Nope. Promise. What'd he want?"

"He wanted to eat, but I also found out he needs a roommate. And, technically, I need somewhere to stay."

His eyes were hard, though the rest of him relaxed as he tried to hold back what he really wanted to say. I'd known him too long to let that get past me. "Mmm," he said noncommittally. "What are you going to do?"

"I'm not sure yet."

He didn't seem satisfied with that answer, but he nodded anyway.

"It's been a while since you've been by for a beer. You busy tonight?"

"Not until later."

"Good. We'll walk up after your next job." He smirked at me as he walked away.

It was that simple, that easy. Being friends with Joel always was. When I moved in with him after he hired me, when I got clean, I was amazed at just how simple it was. My first real friend — Seth — had been anything but simple. My relationship with my father was strained, and I barely remembered my mother. And that was just about the extent of the people who were a part of my life for more than twelve months at a time, before Joel.

It wasn't until I met him then that I began to realize my view on the world was far more hopeless than life really was. The reality was that the people in my life had sucked me dry, and that if I could find people who gave as much as they took, it would change everything. And it did.

I closed my notebook and setup my station, finishing just as my next client walked in. I had drawn up a memorial piece for the man's wife, who had recently passed away. He was a quiet, solemn man and sat in my chair as still as stone as I worked, hands clasped in his lap, eyes locked on the window, blank.

At one point, I asked how he was holding up, but he shook his head, eyes still on the window.

"I want it to hurt. The pain reminds me that I'm still alive."

I nodded. I'd been there more than I cared to think about, and every drop of ink on my skin was a display of that pain in one way or another. My body was a canvas, an exposition that required no words. Just a reminder that I was alive. That I would remember my faults and my mistakes, never to make them again.

They were a reminder that life would always go on.

I inked the lines, shaded and filled, the machine vibrating in my hand, up my arm until the familiar feeling became a part of me. Neither of us spoke.

I shook his hand when he left, felt his sadness. Felt the connection of being a part of something that meant so much to him, something that would exist on his body to remind him. But I knew that the mark was only a symbol. It was for others even more than it was for him. Because he would never forget. Neither would I.

I cleaned up my station and grabbed my bag, heading to the back where Joel waited so we could walk up to his place together. He and Shep lived in the apartment above the shop, the same place I'd lived while Joel put me back on my feet. As we walked through the door, the familiar smell of the apartment settled into me, clinging to me like a part of me never really left.

It was home.

It was my first Christmases and Thanksgiving that felt like the family you saw in movies. Times when I felt loved unconditionally. It was the first time I knew what it was like to have someone in your life who'd always have your back, who had your best interest at heart. Someone who loved you.

Moving to New York opened my eyes. Moving in with Joel changed the course of my life.

I took a seat on the couch, and Joel walked into the kitchen and grabbed us beers. He handed me one by the neck as he took a seat in an armchair, propping his boots on the coffee table before twisting the cap off with a hiss.

He took a sip and inspected the bottle as if the liquid inside hadn't been what he thought it'd be. "Man, that's good."

I took a drink and settled into the couch. "Now are you going to lecture me?"

He shrugged and brought the bottle close to his lips. "Maybe."

I looked away, trying not to smile as I took another drink.

"I'll start small. What happened today with Rose?"

"We just went to lunch, but it was good. Normal. Two days ago, I didn't know if I'd ever kiss her again. Today, I held her hand. Tonight, I'll go home to her." I sighed deeply and shook my head. "I don't know. It feels good, but I'm just hoping it's not too good to be true."

He nodded nostalgically. "You never know with the old fight and fuck. I know the dance well. My entire relationship with Liz revolved around it, but I don't suspect you and Rose will end up that bad. Liz and I were just gonna keep going until there was nothing left of either of us." He took a drink. "So, are you two back together?"

"We haven't talked about it. It feels like we're together, but with an asterisk next to it. As in, together until we *do* talk about it, and then it's likely to implode. So I'm not trying to talk about it."

Joel chuffed. "Well, that sounds foolproof."

"It's all I've got, for now. She feels good. Being with her feels good. I've waited for this since the moment I fucked it up, and if I play my cards right, I might end up keeping her for good. I'll play it however I have to. I'm not going to waste the opportunity."

"Well, I can't say I wouldn't do the same if I were you. Just be careful. The longer it goes on without figuring it out, the farther you have to fall when it falls apart. Because if you don't talk about it, it'll definitely fall apart."

"Noted." I took a drink.

"All right. See? That didn't hurt so bad. So now I'll ask what's up with Seth."

"Nothing. His roommate bailed on him and he needs a replacement."

His brow dropped. "Tricky, if you need a place to stay, you can always stay here."

"I know. Technically, I don't need a place to stay. But I don't want to stay at West's anymore, you know? Like, it doesn't feel like my home, not that it's his fault. I just feel him and Lily starting a life, or something. I don't fit there anymore."

"I get that." He brought the bottle to his lips.

"And at Rose's, I have Rose, but everything is up in the air. The situation could break down tomorrow. Tonight. A week from now. Never. But Seth has a room now, and he needs a roommate. At some point, I'm going to have to find a place to stay if I'm not staying with West and if Rose and I don't last." My stomach turned at the thought. I did my best to ignore it.

His brow was still low, though he wasn't judging me. He was worried. "Why do you always feel like you've gotta save him?"

I wiped the sweat from the cold bottle with my thumb. "He was the first friend I'd ever had, Joel. I was sixteen and alone in New York with nothing but the money my dad gave me when I left."

"Fuck The Sergeant." He raised his bottle.

I did the same. "Hear, hear."

We both took drinks.

I recrossed my feet in front of me, staring at the laces of my boots. "Seth was … I don't know. He was free and wild. Being with him made me feel like I was invincible. I was closed off to the world when I met him, and he showed me what the other side looked like."

"And got you hooked on drugs. Heroin, at that. He couldn't have just smoked weed like a normal person."

I shook my head. "He just doesn't know when to quit. Like his self-preservation gene is dysfunctional."

Joel pointed the mouth of his bottle at me. "He's weak, and he preys on you."

I gave him a flat look. "I'm not stupid, Joel. My eyes are wide open when it comes to him. The last time we lived together and I came home and found him sprawled out in his bed, barely conscious with a needle in his arm? I called it, man. I pulled the trigger the second he was coherent, and I kicked him out. That was it. I'm not a sucker, man."

"No, but you've got a soft spot for him. It's no wonder he's around. He needs something."

"Maybe. But he didn't ask me for anything."

"Yet."

I dragged in a breath and let it out slow. "I don't know. Maybe you're right. I'm not jumping to move in with him, not with so much to figure out with Rose. But Seth is clean, or says he is, and he seems to be. I've never seen him like this before, and I want to believe this is it. I'm not going to turn him out. It's been a long time, and if he has his shit together, I'm willing to entertain the idea."

Joe's eyes were heavy with knowledge and warning. "You miss the good old days, but here's the thing, Patrick. Those good old days weren't real. It was a mirage, an idea that you had of him that wasn't the truth because you were thirsty for a friend. The truth is that he's too weak to quit. Not everyone has what you have, the spit, the scrote, you know? They're not warriors."

I felt the key Rose gave me, hanging against my heart. *Survive.* And then I looked into his eyes and told him the real reason, the one I usually kept guarded, hidden. "I have to believe that anyone can change, Joel. I have to believe that if you want something bad enough, you can make your own destiny. I have to believe there's a choice."

"There is a choice, and anyone *can* change, but it's harder for some than others. Look, I know Seth *wants* to change. But what we want and what we do aren't always the same thing." He sighed. "I'm gonna be honest. I don't like him hanging around, and I certainly don't like the idea of you living with him."

"You don't say," I said with a smirk.

"Smartass," he muttered and took a sip.

"I hear you, man. I really do. I'll watch my back, okay? Just trust me to handle it. I've earned that, right?"

"Yeah, you've earned it," he said begrudgingly. "I just worry, you know."

"I know. But you're not responsible for my actions any more than I am for Seth's."

But he shrugged, smiling at me. "What can I say? I'm invested."

Nice & Slow

PATRICK

left joel's to head to Habits to meet West and Lily, but mostly to see Rose. She stood behind the bar, dark hair down and red lips smiling.

That smile was mine.

The night was mostly inconsequential, just the four of us hanging out as Max and Ellie canoodled a few seats away. Lily and West seemed to be watching me and Rose. I couldn't take my eyes of her, and instead of her looking away or avoiding me all together, she met my gaze through the night, touched my arm, slipped her fingers into mine.

Seth was on my mind, and I thought about telling her. But it had to wait. We had to figure *us* out first.

By the time Lily leaned over the bar to kiss Rose goodbye, Ellie and Max's make-out session had grown progressively heavier, and with more visible tongue.

Ellie broke away, lips swollen and lids heavy as she smiled at Rose.

"We're heading to Max's, so you two have the place to yourselves. Don't break any more lamps, okay?" She winked as she grabbed her bag and slipped off the stool, grabbing Max by the front of the shirt to snap him out of it. He grinned at me and followed her out of the bar like a puppy dog.

And then, Rose and I were alone. Or as alone as we could be in Habits. The bar was almost empty other than a couple in the back, Shelby, the other bartender, and Bob, who was awake by only a degree as he nursed something neat and amber at a booth in the back corner.

Rose sighed, smiling as she cleared away the glasses and cocktail napkins and talked about her days. Everything about the night was familiar, the same thing we'd done a hundred times, but somehow, everything was different too. She was different. Excitement buzzed through me at the prospect of this lasting. I tried to push the thought away, telling myself the shoe would drop at some point, but I wasn't strong enough to bury the feeling all together.

As much as I wanted to know how she felt, I didn't want to ruin the moments between us with the business of what would come. I read her expression, her body language, and I knew — she was happy too. So I wouldn't ask questions I didn't want the answer to. Not until I needed the answer.

Right now, there was only one thing I needed, and it didn't require a single word.

Shelby made her way over smiling, eyes bouncing between us. "Head home, Rose. I'll shut it down."

"You sure?" she asked hopefully.

"Yup. I can handle Bob, and Craig will be here in a few, so I've got muscle to walk me home."

"Thank goodness for beefy boyfriends," she said with a laugh.

"Thanks, Shelby. Let me restock and finish cleaning up at least."

She raised her hands. "If you insist. Have fun, you two."

Rose moved a little faster, blowing to the stock room and coming back with bottles in her arms, and I watched her, the line of her neck, the curve of her waist, her fingers as she lined the bottles up. And then she was smiling up at me as she walked around the bar and took my arm.

I felt like I was high, caught between everything we had been when we were together and everything I'd wanted when we were apart. Memories, wishing, all of it had amalgamated into whatever we were now.

We were shoulder to shoulder as we walked the blocks to our building, chatting easily, and when she leaned into me, I tucked her under my arm, reveling in the feeling. We walked up the stairs, through her front door. When I closed it behind me, I watched her back for a moment as she set down her purse and bent to pull off her boots.

She stood again, and I stepped behind her, turned her around, slipped my hand into the curve of her neck. Searched her face, her dark eyes full of questions and answers. But instead of asking for them, I kissed her.

Last night we needed each other. Tonight, I would take my time.

Her arms wound around my neck slowly, hands slipping up my nape and into my hair as I closed my mouth over her bottom lip and sucked.

Her arms tightened, bringing her flush against me.

I picked her up, carried her through the apartment and into her room, standing her up at the foot of her bed. She looked up at me, eyes burning.

I stripped off my leather jacket, my eyes on her lips, hers on my hands as I unbuttoned my shirt. Her fingers slipped under the fabric, tracing the lines of my tattoos down my abs as I pulled off my shirt. Her fingertips ran across the tattoo low on my hip, one she must not have noticed before.

She looked up at me, eyes big and open, still touching the rose inked into my skin, surrounded by thorns. "Patrick …" she whispered, the word heavy with sadness.

But I smiled. "A reminder of my regrets. I won't make the same mistake twice."

I covered her mouth with mine before she could speak, not needing words. Not wanting them yet. I could feel her heart through her touch, the bittersweet ache of yes and no warring through her.

One hand found her face, fingers splayed across her cheek, her chin in my hand, and I gripped, angling her just how I wanted as my other hand crossed her back, pulling her close, as close as I could. I felt her let go, give me control, as if she'd given me permission to do with her what I wished. So that's exactly what I did.

I broke away and stepped back, watching her pant, barely able to open her eyes.

"Take off your clothes." The command was gravelly and low, my voice partially lost to her.

Her lips were swollen, parted, eyes locked on mine as she crossed her arms, reaching for the hem of her shirt to lift it over her head, hair spilling out of the neck and down her bare back. I unzipped my pants as she unbuttoned hers, slipping my hand in to grip myself, thumb stroking slowly as I watched her fingers pop the button of her pants. With her eyes on my hand, she pushed them down her thighs, stepped out of them and turned, looking back at me over her shoulder to meet my eyes once more as she unlatched her bra and slid the straps down her arms and to the floor. And when she hooked her thumbs in her black panties and pushed them over the swell of her ass, I wouldn't wait any longer.

I reached for her.

She pressed her ass against me as I kissed her neck, hand gripping her hip. Her back arched, arm curling behind her to cup the back of my head where she slipped her fingers into my hair and squeezed, urging me on. My free hand found her soft breast, the curve resting in my palm, and I squeezed once, gently, before trailing lower, stopping between her legs.

She took a breath when I dragged my finger up the length of her, wet and warm, circling when I reached the top, then back down again and up, circling again as her hips rocked slowly.

"Lie down." I let her go, and she crawled onto the bed and rolled over onto her back, watching me. Waiting.

It seemed like one of us always was.

I climbed onto the bed, reaching for her leg, kissing her thigh as I hooked it over my shoulder with my eyes on hers. I made my way higher, feeling her thigh tremble against my hand, my lips. And when I reached the top, I ran my tongue across her gently, closed my lips over her and sucked. She gasped — her fingers found my hair and twisted.

I knew what she wanted.

I rolled my neck as my tongue traced unrecognizable shapes against the sensitive spot, and my fingers ran up the line, spreading her open before slipping inside slowly. She moaned.

If my lips hadn't been busy, I would have smiled.

I knew her body like it was mine — the months apart had erased nothing. She gasped again as I pressed deeper, and when she clenched once around my fingers, hard, I let her go, kissed up her stomach. Her fingers were still in my hair, and she pulled, urging me, sitting to meet me and take my lips. I cupped her neck, kissing her deep as her hands fumbled with my pants, slipping them in to grip me the second she was able.

I grabbed her around the waist and rolled us. She moved down my body licking a trail, her hand stroking me slowly until she was between my legs, looking up at me as she licked up my shaft, over the metal ball of my piercing, across the thin, sensitive layer of skin over the bar, then the second ball, rolling her tongue before closing her mouth over my crown. She sucked.

My mouth hung open as I watched her and she watched me. I ran my tongue along my bottom lip, and she hummed, lids fluttering closed as she dropped down.

I watched myself disappear into her mouth, reappear, disappear, her tongue flicking against my piercing, sending a shock deep into me. She knew exactly what she was doing to me. I gripped the back of her head, urging her down as her arm wrapped under my thigh, hand gripping my waist as she moved faster. My ass flexed to get as deep as I could without hurting her.

"Come here," I growled when I couldn't take it anymore, and as she climbed up my body, I grabbed her, flipping us over again. I settled in between her legs and reached for her knee, spreading her thighs. She sucked in a breath, rolling her hips, cradling my shaft with her wet length. The bottom ball of my piercing circled her with every wave of her hips, and her lids closed, dark hair fanned out around her.

I needed her.

I thrust hard enough to make her gasp before reaching over to her nightstand.

"No," she muttered.

"Rose …"

She rolled her hips again, circled the piercing. "I haven't been with anyone else since you. Have you?"

I brushed her hair from her face and traced her jaw. "No."

"Then no. It's safe. IUD," she breathed, dragging her nails across my ass as she slipped herself up my shaft until my tip rested just at the edge of her. "Now fuck me."

My tongue slipped across my lip as I flexed, slipping into her, pushing until I hit the end. She moaned, head rolling, and I pulled out, eyes down as I flexed again until our bodies met in a seam.

I bent to kiss her neck stretched out before me like an invitation, licked a trail up to her ear where I breathed, humming soft. She brought up her other knee, her calves pressed against my ribs, opening herself up so I could get deeper.

"Fuck," she breathed and reached over her head, bracing herself against the headboard as I pulled out and slammed back in. Her eyes were closed, lips swollen, breasts jostling with every thrust. Her neck arched. Her brow furrowed. Her lips parted with a gasp, stretching wider with a silent cry when I flexed once more, and she exploded around me in a burst, squeezing, pulsing, body tight as she let go.

I slowed as she did, bending to kiss her breast, closing my eyes as I traced a circle around her nipple before closing my lips, pulling it gently into my mouth. Her fingers slipped into my hair, and I spent a long moment there, cradled in her arms, her breast in my hand, against my tongue.

When I pulled away, I kissed her sternum and sat, gripping her hip.

"Roll over." The words were thick.

Her lids were heavy as she did what I asked, raising her ass, shoulders pressed to the bed. She looked back at me again, and I ran a hand down her spine, to her hips, grabbing to lift her higher. My hand gripped my base, angling myself until my crown pressed against her.

I took a breath and pulled her onto me.

Her lids fluttered closed again with a sigh. Both hands found her hips, heart hammering as I pushed and pulled, my eyes taking everything in. Faster. She moaned. Harder. My heart ached. Deeper. I came with a cry, breath coming in long drags, and I bent over, slipping my arms under her, my chest against her back as I waited for my body to relax.

She rocked her hips in tiny waves, just enough to send shocks through me, down my thighs.

I kissed her shoulder blade and ran the tip of my nose across her skin.

It was more than just sex. I knew from the way she wound her fingers though mine and kissed them with tender lips. I knew from the way those lips curled into the smallest smile. I knew from the way she breathed, from the beat of her heart — I could feel it through her ribs, through my ribs and into my own heart.

And more than ever before, I was afraid I'd lose her again.

Crimson Ed

ROSE

The second i woke up, I knew the day was going to suck. It didn't matter that Patrick's arms were around me, as confusingly comforting as that was. It didn't matter that I had the day off, because I'd spend it in the worst way possible.

I felt that tiny ovarian tweak, the one that turned into a dull ache, then into a cramp that doubled me over as my stupid uterus punished me for not giving it a baby.

I groaned and hauled ass to the bathroom, dropping my head into my hands as I peed. Because once every month, that dirty redheaded demon who I called Crimson Edwina showed her face and ruined my life for five to seven days.

See, I was one of those lucky uterus owners who had horribly hellish periods. Periods that no IUD or high-powered birth control could tame. I guess I shouldn't complain — since getting the IUD years ago, I didn't have to take muscle relaxers or drink myself stupid for several days to survive Ed's wrath. So I guess the tradeoff for a solid twenty four hours of hell was better than crying on the couch for a week. Because that first day was always a nightmare.

Win some, lose some. I was counting it as a win.

Still didn't make it fun.

One Super-Extra-Plus tampon, a pad that bordered on diaper status, and a handful of Advil later, I limped back to my room and climbed into bed, trying not to whimper.

Patrick pulled me into his chest. "Is it Ed?"

"That stupid bitch," I muttered.

He chuckled. "Hungry?"

"No. I want to die."

"That's exactly what she wants. Don't let her win, Rosie."

I couldn't find it in my heart to laugh, but I smiled.

"Think you can go back to sleep?" he asked.

"Maybe for a bit."

"Give it a try. Get some rest, okay?" He started to pull away, but I grabbed his arm and tugged him back to me.

"Don't go yet. I need a hug."

He smiled and squeezed me tighter. "Want me to wait until you fall asleep?"

I nodded, and he stroked my hair. Even Crimson Ed couldn't withstand that, and within minutes I'd drifted off to sleep.

I woke when I heard him come back in a few hours later, kicking off his boots before climbing back into bed with me.

"I thought you were going to work," I croaked and nestled into him.

"I'm off today. How are you feeling?"

"Like a donkey kicked me in the vagina."

He kissed my hair. "Hungry yet?"

I groaned.

"I went to Cake," he cajoled.

I perked up at that. "Did you get butterscotch cupcakes?"

"Yup, and chocolate peppermint."

I groaned again, but for entirely different reasons. "Oh, my God."

"I picked up coffee too. Feel like getting up for that?"

"Fuck yes." I crawled out of bed, pulling the comforter with me. I wrapped it around my shoulders as I shuffled into the living room behind him. A heating pad sat waiting on the couch, already hooked up to an extension cord and warming up.

I paused in the middle of the room, feeling overwhelmed. He'd done all of this for me — I watched his back as he plated cupcakes.

I felt lucky. Very lucky. I also felt a very large dose of fear.

Ed carved her name into my guts with a razor, and I hunched over, collapsing onto the couch with a grunt. I pulled the heating pad into my lap, thanking the heavens that such a magical thing existed in the universe. I almost immediately began to feel better.

Patrick handed me a small plate with the most beautiful cupcake on it before setting my paper cup on the coffee table. I licked my lips as I peeled the paper off, and Patrick walked back to the table for his own, coming back to sit at the other end of the couch.

He picked up the remote as I took a bite.

I closed my eyes and moaned when the sweet, soft cake hit my tongue. "Humugah, thish ish sho goo," I said with my mouth full.

He smiled. "Feel better?"

"Mmhmm," I answered as I took another obscene bite.

"Good." He clicked on the television. "So I locked and loaded some movies for you. *She's All That, The Craft, Mall Rats,* and *Empire Records.*"

I swallowed. "I can't say no to Sexy Rexy. Plus, slutty teen Renee Zellweger? Score."

"*Empire Records* it is." He hit play and settled back into the couch as "Video Killed the Radio Star" through the opening credits.

I watched him unwrap his cupcake, my eyes on his tattooed fingers as he pulled off the paper, then on his jaw as he opened his mouth to take a huge bite. This felt together. Very together. Except that things weren't supposed to change. I wasn't supposed to be with him. I'd made my peace with that, for the most part. Kind of. Except here he was, bringing me cupcakes and cuddling with me and acting like he was my boyfriend.

I felt very still, very quiet as I set my cupcake on the plate and rested it in my lap. "What are we doing, Patrick?"

He glanced at me and swallowed hard. "I don't know, Rose. I don't know that I need to know. Not yet, at least."

"I don't know if I can handle this again."

He set down his plate and turned to me, his face stoic as he reached for my hand. He watched his fingers as they played with mine. "I'm not looking for any answers. I don't need a definition. Not yet. I just know that this feels good, really good. So can we let it ride until we figure out what we want to do about it?"

"We tried that last time, and look how that turned out."

"Do you really think that this time would be the same?"

I considered it and said, plainly, "No. It could be worse."

He shrugged, still watching his fingers. "Or not. I'm not asking you to take a chance on me. I'm suggesting that we don't talk about it just yet, until we've had a little more time."

"So you want to play house? Ignore it until we can't anymore?"

Patrick met my eyes and smirked. "Maybe not that long, but at least until we've had a minute to think about it, about what it all means."

I pursed my lips, glancing at the screen where the staff of Empire Records danced around the record store.

"Do you want me to go?" he asked.

"No."

"Do you want whatever this is to end?"

"No," I answered quietly. *But I'm afraid it will.*

He took my plate away and set it on the coffee table, leaning over to touch my face. "We don't have to decide what's next yet, Rose. One day at a time. I'm not asking for anything more than that."

I couldn't say no, not with him looking at me like that, not when I wanted it to magically work itself out, just like he did. "All right." I cupped his cheek, and he leaned in to kiss me softly, sweetly. And it was then that I knew that one of us would end up brokenhearted.

Step One

PATRICK

A **lmost a week had passed** easily, simply. Happily. One day at a time.

It was the mantra that kept us going. It was about each minute, every second, and being in it, together. It was as if the months apart had never happened, even though the unspoken hurt still waited under the rug,

I hoped it would stay put indefinitely.

When I wasn't with work, I was with Rose, sleeping in her bed, spending days with her, nights at Habits. We were *together* again. It wasn't just about sex like she'd said in the start — for most of the last week we didn't have sex at all, thanks to Ed. But I didn't mind. It meant more to me to sleep with her curled into my chest than sex ever could.

Everything felt right.

With every day that passed, my confidence about the next step grew to the point that I was less afraid, less apprehensive. I didn't feel certain — I'd presumed to know what Rose felt once, and I paid for that. But I felt like the odds were good. Real good.

That morning, I'd left Rose asleep in bed with a kiss and a sigh to meet Seth for lunch at Genie's, which was where I sat, digging into a burger across from my old friend.

Seth moaned as he chewed. "Jesus. I haven't had one of Genie's burgers in forever."

"Shame." I took another bite.

He adjusted he burger, angling it for a bite. "How's it going with Rose?"

I smiled. "It's good. Really good."

"What's the deal with you two? Like, how did that go down? Because I've got to be honest — I always thought if either of us had a chance, it would be me." He chuckled and bit into his burger.

I shrugged off a territorial flash as I set down my burger and dusted off my hands. "So this one night, we were at Rose's place. Lily was already asleep, and Rose and I were watching a movie. I'd felt something … I don't know, *change,* a couple of weeks before. I didn't really know what to do about it until that night. She just looked at me. That was all she had to do. I knew right then I was a goner, and I knew she felt it too. So I proposed a deal."

"A deal?"

"I didn't want to lose what we had, our friendship, so I thought if we just sort of didn't talk about it, didn't label it, we could slip out of it as easily as we slipped into it."

"How'd that turn out?"

I chuffed. "It could have worked out, but I fucked it up. Anyway, I told her that if either of us stopped feeling it and wanted out, all we had to do was say the word. We'd call it off, no questions."

"Why'd she call it off?"

"She didn't. I did."

He looked at me blankly for a split-second. "Man, that's an exceptional level of stupid, Tricky."

"Yeah, you're telling me. I was scared, Seth. You know I don't do a lot of long term, and I didn't know how to handle how I felt."

"I get that. You've been alone enough of your life, either abandoned or betrayed by dicks like me, right?"

I shook my head. "Come on. I know you did the best you could, but I couldn't be around what you were caught up in, and you knew that. Not while I was trying to get clean. Stay clean. You said you'd quit."

"I know. I haven't been reliable. I haven't been a good friend."

"You couldn't help it," I said, knowing it was the truth.

"Stop making excuses for me, Tricky," he answered quietly.

I sighed. "I always felt like I abandoned you too, you know."

"Can't help somebody who won't help themselves. It's not your fault." He turned the conversation away from our past. "So, *you* dumped Rose Fisher?"

I adjusted the top bun of my burger, avoiding his eyes. "I just … I don't know, man. It was just before the holidays, and everyone was with their families. That time of year is always weird for me, and that year I was also in a relationship, one that had gotten serious. And I wanted that, you know? Like, I wanted her so much that I couldn't imagine what would happen if she left me. Then I realized she probably would. So I bailed first."

"Damn."

I nodded. "We didn't really talk after that, not until recently. She shut the door hard, locked it tight. It's been hell, man. I see her almost every day, and most of the time, she wouldn't even look at me. But now …" I picked up my burger again. "She's mine again. I just don't want to lose her."

Seth wiped his mouth with his paper napkin. "Yeah, I get that."

I took a bite and thought about it. "Part of me believes that if the circumstance is right, everything will be fine. Another part of me is afraid we're doomed, but that part of me gets quieter every day." I sighed and took a drink to wash the fear away. "Anyway, tell me what's up with you. Find a roommate yet?"

Seth sat back in the booth with a sigh. "Not yet. It's scary, man. As hard as I've worked to start a new life, it's still new. I don't know how to live 'normal,' whatever that is. Like, without partying. I mean, how is it that I don't even drink anymore? How is that a thing?" He shook his head. "I don't even get what people do for fun, otherwise."

I knew how he felt. I was lucky I had Joel when I left Seth and the rest of our friends. He knew what I needed and helped me get clean. I tried to pass that on to Seth and failed. "You can always call me."

He nodded, smiling his easy. "Thanks. I'll probably take you up on that." He picked up a fry and popped it into his mouth.

"Well, I've been thinking a lot about moving. I'm just ready to have my own space again."

"Really?" he asked, the word thick with hope. "I figured since you and Rose were together, it wasn't even a question."

I shook my head. "I want to be with her every minute that I can, but …" I rubbed my face. "I don't know, man. I don't want to fuck it up. I don't want to burn her out, and I need my own place. I can't live with her yet — it's too soon to put that kind of pressure on her, or us. And as much as I'd like to wait and see what happens with her, you need help now. It makes sense. I just need to talk to her first."

"You didn't mention it to her?"

"No. I didn't know how she'd react, and I wasn't even sure it was happening. So now I've just got to find a way to talk to her about it."

"Well, I hope it works out."

I smiled. "Me too."

"And … thank you. I didn't expect this, not after everything you've done for me and everything I've done to you. You're the best friend I've ever had, Tricky."

"I'm just glad I can help, man."

With him sitting across from me in the diner, smiling like I'd saved him again, I was overcome by the rightness of it all. Like everything was finally falling into place.

woke the next morning when Patrick did, ate with him before he left for work. He kissing me goodbye in my doorway, a long kiss, a hot kiss that promised me there was more where that came from.

The last week had been all I'd ever wanted.

I wasn't afraid he'd leave. I wasn't afraid it would end. I was just blissed out on him, taking every second for what it was.

We were together — so together that I knew this was it for us. The relief of having after wanting for so long was a tangible thing. I just wanted to be with him.

Every once in a while, the reminder that we hadn't talked about anything, hadn't defined anything, would send a rush of fear through me. I hoped we were strong enough to deal with it when we couldn't avoid it anymore, but mostly I hoped we wouldn't have to deal with it at all.

I glanced at the clock as I closed the door, noticing only then how early it was. I took a look around the apartment, wondering what to do with myself. Getting up early meant I had way more time on my hands, and I'd been getting up early with him more and more, going to sleep at normal hours when I could, just so I could fall asleep with him.

I caught myself smiling as I picked up my book, a re-read of one of my favorites — *Outlander*. It was the book that made me realize I had a thing for redheads in skirts, and I curled up on the couch. Valentino strutted out of Lily's old room, tail flicking, and hopped up next to me, curling into my legs. Ellie had been at Max's almost every night, and I think her cat was missing her. I scratched his head, and he looked at me like I'd do.

A couple of hours later, a knock rapped on the door once before it opened and Cooper peeked his head in, smiling when he saw me on the couch.

"Oh, good. You're up."

I quirked my head and closed my book. "Hey, Coop. What's up?"

He stepped into the apartment and closed the door, somehow still looking rich as fuck in khaki shorts and a Henley, sleeves pushed up his forearms.

"Sorry to bug you on a Saturday."

I shrugged and set my book down, standing to greet him. "Saturdays are like my Thursdays. What are you doing here? Patrick is at work ... were you on your way to see West?"

"Gee, don't act so happy to see me, Rosie."

I rolled my eyes, smiling. "It's not like that, asshole."

He took off his bag and set it on the table, opening it to retrieve a portfolio. "I just wanted to talk about Wasted Words."

"What?" I said with a disbelieving laugh.

He looked at me like I was a dum-dum as he took a seat at the table. "The bookstore?" he joked.

"Uh, yeah, I remember, but you can't be serious about that."

"Why wouldn't I be?" He opened the portfolio and looked up at me expectantly. When I didn't move, he gestured to the chair across from him.

I took a seat reluctantly. "I don't know, Cooper. Because it's crazy?"

"How so? We have a mutual interest. I have the funds to back the business, and you have the means to run it. Do you have the want to run it?"

I leaned on the table with my mind spinning. "I … I don't know. I hadn't seriously considered it."

Cooper smiled. "Well, now's the time." He began pulling papers out of the portfolio, pushing them across the table toward me. "I've talked to some of my real estate advisors, and it seems that the Upper West Side has a big market for this kind of thing, especially around the Columbia campus." He pointed to the spots circled on the map. "I've found a handful of locations that would be great, larger, two story lofts. My favorite is this one." He tapped one of the locations. "We'd have to buy two spaces and rip out the wall, but it would be perfect. We're going to need to install the plumbing for the bar, but check this out."

I reeled in my seat as he placed some photos on the table.

"This is the interior. I'm thinking in the loft we can have some party rooms for book clubs or meetings. On this side, we can have all the comics and graphic novels, even rare finds, maybe even an untranslated Manga section" His eyes sparkled. "Like, a dream comic shop, all stops pulled. The other side would be the fiction. Equal in size, whatever proportion of genres you'd like. Think about it. We can line up bookshelves like this," he said as he traced lines on one of the photos, "then put couches and coffee tables between. Oh, I also had the thought that one side of the bar could be a coffee bar, and the other side liquor."

"You're serious." Disbelief. That was all I could muster.

"Dead serious. This could work, Rosie. I can't help run it, but I can help you plan and I can give you all the cash you need to make it work. I already spoke to my financial advisor, and she's worked up some numbers on cost and profits. I have advisors, accountants, bookkeepers, all ready to work on this. All I ask is to help pick out the stock for the comic side. Past that, you have free reign."

I stared at all the papers spread out on my kitchen table. "I don't know what to say to this, Coop."

"Say you're in. Honestly, if I didn't have a job I loved that required all of my energy, I'd do it myself and hire you to manage it. But I just can't, not now. You should do this with me. I built into the budget your first year of pay."

He pushed another piece of paper toward me with a bunch of numbers. My salary was highlighted.

I took a deep breath and held it until my lungs burned. Then I pushed the paper back at him.

"I can't accept that."

"Sure, you can. You just say, 'Wow, that looks great, Coop. Let's do this.' It's simple, really."

"That's more than I make in like two years, Cooper."

"Good. Then it should be an easy choice. And that salary will stick for the duration of your tenure — more once we get out of the red and into the black."

But I shook my head. "I can't take your money."

"You're not. This is a business offer. Trust me, that money isn't going to seem like all that much when you see how much work it's going to be to get off the ground. But that's what I'm here for. I've got the means to make this happen, and I want to do it. You're smart — you know how to run a bar, and you know how to handle people. Once you've hired people, you'll be able to choose a manager to run all the day to day grind. You'll have freedom. I want you to accept my proposal, Rose. Let's be business partners."

I chewed my lip, thinking it over, but I couldn't form a coherent thought. "Can I think it over?"

"Of course. Keep all of this stuff," he said as he collected the papers and stacked them up, slipping them back in the portfolio. "Everything we've talked about in terms of our roles will be outlined in the contract. Really, I just want to be a part of something like this. A passion project. An investment. And it gives you something to pour yourself into, something you're passionate about. Something you'd be good at — I believe that. I believe in you, Rose. So, think it over. If it's something you want to do, let's make it happen. We can start as soon as you're ready."

My throat was tight, and I swallowed, feeling overwhelmed. "Thank you, Cooper. Thank you for asking me to be a part of this and for your faith and trust in me. I just need some time to process all of this as an actual possibility."

His smile was crooked and easy. "Take all the time you need — there's no pressure from me. The offer stands indefinitely." He leaned back in his chair. "What are you up to today?"

"Staring at these papers until I have to go to work tonight. Are you guys coming in?"

"We'll be there." He pushed back from the table and stood. "I'm heading over to West's for a bit, if you want to hang out. Otherwise, I'll leave you to it."

I stood too and stepped over to give him a hug. "Thanks, Coop. Really."

He gave me a squeeze. "You got it, Rosie. I'll catch you later," he said before leaving me alone with my thoughts.

My own bookstore. My own bar. I sat back down at the table and pulled out the papers again, touching them all, imagining what it would be like. Could I do it? Could I really do it and run it well? I knew a lot from working at Habits, enough that I could handle the bar easily. If Cooper had advisors that could help with the rest … did I want to do it?

In a perfect world, the answer was hell yes. In our imperfect world, the question was *could* I do it.

The answer to that was, of course, that I wouldn't know until I tried. I just had to be brave enough to take the leap.

Ass Bust

ROSE

It was late that afternoon when Patrick and I walked through the park, holding hands with longboards under our arms for his first lesson. I was giddy, so giddy I could barely even play it cool, and not just because he'd finally agreed to let me teach him how to skate.

"So, Cooper came by today," I started.

He glanced over at me, smirking. "Oh?"

"Mmhmm." I took a breath. "He really wants to do Wasted Words. Like, he had a portfolio and charts and spreadsheets and …" I took another breath to stop my rambling. "He really wants to do it, Patrick. And he wants me run it."

"That's … that's amazing." His face was soft, full of wonder, and his fingers squeezed mine. "So, are you going to do it?"

"I don't know," I said. "I really want to, but I also think it's crazy and ridiculous. I mean, I don't know the first thing about running a business, but Coop has people lined up to advise me on it. I just … I don't know. What do you think about it? Do you think I should do it? Or am I just insane for thinking it could maybe work?"

We came to a stop on one of the less crowded, flatter paths, and Patrick turned to me, letting my hand go so he could cup my cheek. "I don't think you're insane or crazy or ridiculous." He stepped closer, until our bodies touched, looking down at me with eyes full of adoration. "I think you can do anything, Rose. I think you should do it."

I smiled, overwhelmed, and he kissed me, thumb stroking my cheek, lips giving me all the confidence I'd ever need.

When he broke away, I leaned into him, not wanting the kiss to end. His lips brushed my temple, and he stepped back to set down his board. I set mine down too and looked around. Golden sunshine poured through the trees as the sun began its descent, though we probably had a couple more hours before it would be gone for good. It was days like this that reminded me of home. My favorite kinds of days.

"All right, this looks good. Are you ready for this?" I found myself grinning like a teenager as I watched him put my spare board on the path and scratch the line of his jaw.

"I think so."

"I can't believe you're finally going to let me teach you how to skate."

He smirked. "Just promise you won't judge me too hard when I look like a clown."

"Okay, well, keep in mind that people falling happens to be one of my weaknesses, so I can't make any guarantees. I *will* promise that I'll feel really bad about laughing, if that helps?"

He laughed. "I guess I'll take what I can get."

"Probably wise."

He was still smirking at me, and when he put one foot on the board and stuffed his hands into the pocket of his dark jeans, my heart did a flip flop in my chest.

I jumped into my teaching role, because if I kept standing there staring, I'd end up kissing him, which would lead to him kissing me, which would lead to me dragging him home so I could rip his clothes off.

I cleared my throat. "All right. So the good thing about longboards is that they're easier to learn on and cruise, so you shouldn't fall as much."

"As much?" he asked as a brow climbed.

"Yeah, because you're going to fall. Just get ready for that."

He chuckled.

I shoved him hard in the shoulders, and he took a step back to catch himself, giving me a look.

But I smiled. "You'll probably ride regular, since you caught yourself with your left foot."

"There's no other test for that?"

"There are, but that one was the most fun. For me, at least." I put my right foot on the board near the back. "So your dominant leg will stay on the board closer to the back, and you'll balance over your left leg. Rest it closer to the front, a little farther than shoulder width from your back foot, between the trucks."

"The wheels?"

"The axles, yeah, where the bolts are on the deck," I said as I pointed at the board. "Okay, go ahead and get on."

"Where should I put my feet?" he asked.

"Don't worry about it besides putting your right foot in the back."

He got on, feet perpendicular to the board and looked to me for instruction as I got on mine, facing him. "All right. Now just get the feel for it. Crouch down and stand back up to feel where your balance is. Bounce a little so you can feel the give."

He did as he was told, then shifted his hips, moving the board back and forth under him.

I smiled. "Good. Okay, now try moving your feet up and down the board a little without stepping off."

He looked a little stiff as he tried to move around the board without falling.

"Bend your knees a little more, that'll help. Think about which way you're leaning and try to be aware of it. I used to lean back when I first started.

He bent a little. "Oh, yeah. That's easier."

"How's it feel?"

He nodded. "Good."

"Okay, so now, you push." I took the stance. "Put your weight on your left foot, and push with your right. Just do one for now." I pushed and cruised as he watched on.

He nodded and pushed once, looking pretty solid. I smiled wider as he cruised toward me.

"Think about where your center of balance is. The lower you are, the more comfortable you'll be, so if shit gets real, get low to try to regain control of your balance, but watch out — you'll go faster too."

"Get low. Got it."

"Push a couple of times this time and then cruise."

He did, and I kept up with him, cruising beside him, riding goofy so I could face him. "What do you think?"

He smiled at me. "I like it."

My heart fluttered again, like a skipping idiot in my chest, and I looked ahead of us as we pushed again. "Okay, so see that little slope coming up? Don't push again, just coast down it and bend your knees as you pick up speed."

He looked determined. "All right."

I watched as he handled the slope like a boss, smirking at me once he'd slowed down.

"So, stopping?" he asked.

"That's a little harder. We shouldn't be going fast enough today for you to need anything more than foot braking. Basically, just drag your foot on the ground to slow you down. Or you could just ride out the speed. But if you lose control, just point yourself toward the grass and bail."

"Like, jump off?"

"Tuck and roll, Tricky. Tuck and roll."

He chuckled.

"Just kidding. Usually you just hit the ground running, but if you're going faster than you can run, definitely roll. You can slide to stop too, but that takes practice. Okay, come on. Let's cruise again." I kicked, and we got a good easy speed going. "So to turn, you carve — lean in whatever direction you go. That'll also slow you down."

He stared down at his Converse as he cruised.

"Try to keep your eyes up. Your feet know what to do, even though it feels weird."

He nodded and looked up.

"Hanging in there?"

He smiled. "Feels good."

"Then let's ride." I pushed our pace a little faster, and he kept up, finally getting to the point where he could talk instead of strictly concentrate. He looked good on a board, like he belonged there.

We rounded a bend a bit later to be met with oncoming traffic, two people riding bikes next to each other with a dog on a leash. Patrick had been comfortable enough that we were moving fast, for him, and his eyes went wide.

I braked, dragging my foot against the asphalt to put him in front of me. "Tricky, carve! Toward the grass."

He leaned and headed for the grass, but he forgot to jump and the force threw him off the board just as the pack passed us.

"Assholes!" I called after them, giving them the bitchiest look

I could muster, which meant I wasn't paying attention. My board crashed into his, and I flew off. "Whoamagod!"

I hit the ground with an *oof*, landing on my stomach right next to Patrick, who lay on his back with his hand on his chest, laughing at me.

I couldn't help but laugh too, dropping my head to my forearms as I tried to catch my breath, since it had been knocked out of me. I rolled over onto my back, our arms touching, and he threaded his fingers through mine. We turned and looked at each other, and his fingers grazed my cheek, my lips.

He wanted to tell me something — there was something behind his eyes that scared me. I didn't know what it was. I didn't think I wanted to know. So I kissed him instead, hoping to wipe away the thought, for a moment at least.

In that, I was right. When we opened our eyes again, it was gone along with my dread.

We skated a bit more, then went home, ordered in, and spent another evening blissfully alone — Ellie had been staying with Max almost every night. I lay with my feet in his lap on the couch, reading a book as he sketched. We brushed our teeth next to each other in the bathroom as if it were the most normal thing in the world.

Over the last week, I'd forgotten the bad. I'd remembered how good we were together.

But I felt our past, always there with us, the subtext in each kiss, each word. As much as I hoped we'd just wake up one day with the whole mess behind us, I knew better than anyone that it would bubble up in every argument, every fight, every bad day. It wouldn't leave us alone. It was the one lesson I'd learned from being a chronic avoider. The one thing I could count on.

Lying there with him, I realized our situation was about as stable as nitroglycerin, and I knew the explosion would be quiet and destructive, all at once. Because that was how he and I worked. And here we were, living together, pretending it was all just fine when really the gas just kept leaking and leaking into the room. I only wondered who would strike the match.

tick tock

PATRICK

felt good as I climbed the stairs of our building the next night. I'd decided to sleep on it, and this morning I woke up still feeling like moving in with Seth was the right thing to do, and what I wanted. I'd tell Rose tonight.

I smiled to myself. It was going to work out. Everything would work out.

I slipped my key into the lock of my apartment, opening the door to find Cooper and West sitting at the table with a bottle of scotch between them.

Cooper stood to grab me a glass as we said our hellos. "Have a drink with us before Habits."

I settled into the chair as Cooper poured. "I've been waiting for one of these all day."

"Well, I'm happy to oblige." He took a seat and picked up his glass. "How's it going, Trick?"

I shrugged, not sure if I wanted to talk about it. "Fine, I guess."

West chuckled. "That was convincing."

I smiled. "It's complicated."

"Isn't everything?" Cooper asked and took a drink.

"Where are the girls?"

West leaned on the table. "At Habits with Rose."

I relaxed a little, knowing Lily wasn't within earshot. I rubbed my jaw. "Listen, West. We've got to talk about my place here."

Smiles fell as we slipped into seriousness, and I took a pull of my drink.

"I think it's time I moved out."

West's face was solemn, and he looked down at his drink. "This was your place first, Patrick. It's still your place. Lily and I could move. Or we could relocate to her place."

I shook my head and smiled reassuringly. "No. You belong here, together. And whatever Rose and I are, we're not ready to move in together, not officially. I just need to take a step, because living in limbo is getting to be too hard."

"Where will you go?" West asked.

"Seth needs a roommate. It's close by, and he's in a bind."

Reproachful eyes met me from both sides of the table.

"You sure that's a good idea, Tricky?" West's dark brows were low, eyes a darker shade of blue than usual.

"No. But what I *am* sure of is that I can handle it. I trust him, but I'm not blind. It could be a chance to be an example for him. Be a friend to him now that he's alone, sober. I think it would be good for him, but I'm not going into this with any delusions. Just hope."

Cooper sipped his drink, and West rubbed his beard. "I'm not gonna lecture you, 'cause I'm not your mother. If you think you've got a handle on it, and it's what you want, I can't tell you not to. Just know you've got a place here. We don't want you to go, and I know Rose doesn't either."

"I know. But I'm ready to have a place of my own again."

West shook his head. "I didn't think it would turn out this way."

I frowned. "What way?"

"I mean, I was glad you were staying over there, but I didn't think Lily and I would lead to you leaving."

The glass was cool in my hand as I took a drink. "It's not just about that, West. I'm happy for you guys, and I'm happy with Rose. But this is the smart thing for me, and I can help a friend in the process. There's nothing to fix. I just wanted you to know that it was happening."

He sighed, his eyes sad. "Well, it's been a good run, friend."

West raised his glass, and Cooper did too, and I touched the rim of mine to theirs, smiling. "That it has."

A few hours later, we all sat around the bar at Habits, just like always, watching Rose, feeling the shift again. Before, it was happening around me, and I was still, watching it all move farther away. But now I felt myself caught in the current, felt the change pull me, moving me whether I wanted to go or not.

I drank the tail end of my whiskey just as Rose passed me another. We shared a smile, the kind that can only exist between two people who've known and loved and hurt each other. And then I said a little prayer that everything would be all right.

Kamikaze

ROSE

Patrick stayed until *we closed* down the bar, long after everyone had waved and smiled their goodbyes, and all the lights had gone down. We held hands as we walked home in content silence, both of us seeming to be lost in thought.

The apartment was quiet and dark, and we walked to my room in silence, not bothering to turn on the lights, just undressing before slipping into bed together. And then I was in his arms. His heart beat against my cheek, his legs entwined with mine. After a moment, I tilted my chin, leaning back to cup his jaw, and I kissed him.

It was simple, the easy way our hands moved, our lips, our bodies, the slow way we came together that night, when everything was exactly what it was for those moments. Connecting. Reconnecting after what happened. It all seemed so silly now, meaningless. Like the things you did when you were young that left a mark on you, but you couldn't remember the details, only the result. And I could still feel the tear in my heart, the sting of the wound, even though it had healed so much.

I was beginning to convince myself that he wouldn't hurt me, which was of course the moment when he did.

We were wrapped in each other, hearts finally slowed, his fingers in my hair as we lay there together, just breathing. And then he spoke.

"Thank you for letting me stay, Rose."

I smiled. "You're welcome."

"I've been thinking a lot about us. About how much I've missed you."

"Me too," I said softly. "So much."

He took a breath, and I felt his heart beat faster under my cheek. "I had dinner with Seth the other night. He … well, he needs a roommate."

I chuckled. "Tell him to get on Craigslist."

"It's not that simple. He can't have a regular roommate who drinks and smokes weed and has liquor in the house, not when he's trying to stay clean. And I'm in a position to help. I don't really have a home anymore, and as much as I love being here with you, I can't keep staying here like this."

My entire body tensed. "You're not seriously considering it, are you?"

"I already told him I would. I need a place of my own, and he needs the help."

I sat up, pulling the sheets with me. "Seth always needs help."

He clicked on the light and sat too, propped against pillows. "Yeah, well he's sober and trying. It's different this time, Rose."

"You can't be sure that's true."

"I have to believe that it is."

My heart pounded. "You can't live with Seth. I mean, what if he steals from you? It wouldn't be the first time. Or what if he gets you caught up in something and you end up arrested again? He could have drugs in the house. You can't put yourself in that position, Patrick."

His brow dropped. "Being here is just as scary, just in a different way."

I felt like I'd been slapped. "Did you just compare me to Seth?"

"I'm putting myself at a risk here just as much as I am with Seth. We haven't even talked about … anything, really. Nothing about what happened before or what will happen next. Not a word about how we feel right now."

"Because *you* said we should just ignore it."

"That's not what I said, Rose. I said one day at a time, which is what we've been doing. But I'm caught between here and my place like a quarter in a coin toss. I have no home, and I can't keep staying here."

"So, you're going to live with *Seth* instead?" I shook my head, my cheeks hot and tingling. "That can only go up in flames."

His eyes narrowed, jaw hard. "How am I supposed to know that this — whatever this is between you and me — won't end in flames too?" He waited for an answer for a brief second. "I don't. I don't know any better than I know about Seth. But I have faith in both of you."

I breathed deep, trying to keep up with what was happening. "I don't understand. After everything Seth has done to you, I can't believe you would have any faith in him. He hurt you."

"And I hurt him. And you hurt me, and I hurt you. It's all a risk, no matter what I do."

"I hurt *you*?" My hands trembled as I held the sheet under my arm. "I hurt you. *You destroyed me.*"

His jaw clenched. "Do you think this has been easy for me? Seven months I've been trying to move on. Seven months of punishing myself, of wanting you to punish me. Seven months of regret. You weren't the only one who was hurt, Rose."

"Well, *you* fucked up." Tears burned my eyes. "You left me with no explanation. You left me here wondering what I'd done, if I wasn't enough for you, and then you brought someone else in just to drive the point home. I thought you were it. I thought you were everything, but you didn't even respect me enough to tell me why you were leaving."

His voice cut through me with every word. "And you didn't respect me enough to give me a chance to explain. You didn't care enough to put your pride down and forgive me. You let me suffer all that time. Did it feel good? Did it make you feel better to know that I'd spend the rest of my life knowing I'd never get a chance to make it right? You knew how much it hurt, and you let it happen."

My body was ice cold. "Just because I pretended not to care doesn't mean this has been easy for me."

He shook his head. "You couldn't fight for me then because you were scared, and you're still scared."

"I'm not scared. You're the one who ran away, Patrick."

"The difference is that I came back." He flipped back the sheet with a snap and stood, striding across the room to his clothes. He grabbed his pants, pulling them on as I gaped, heart slamming against my ribs.

"This is what you do. You leave. We can't solve anything because you won't talk to me."

He spun around, his face bent in pain. "No. We can't solve anything because we're too broken for this to work. You can't let me in any more than I can because we're fucked up. I want you. I want to be with you. But you can't ask me to stay. You can't stand up and tell me you'll fight for me. It's too big and hard and scary, and you'll run away forever. And I can't keep chasing you, Rose. I can't—" His voice broke, and he turned again, bending to pick up his shirt. "I can't, Rose. I just can't anymore."

I got out of bed, dragging the sheet with me, reaching for his arm as tears slipped down my cheeks. "Patrick, I …"

He turned to me, his face full of fear and hurt and hope as he waited for me to say the words, words that piled up in my throat like a train wreck. I couldn't speak, my aching heart stunned silent, and the hope left his face, slipping away like a dream.

"After all of this, you still don't trust me. I've done everything I can, everything I know to do. So there's nothing left to do but go." He turned and walked away, disappearing into the dark. "See you around, Rose," he said, and then he was gone.

Fault & Blame

PATRICK

I **hauled another box of art** supplies up the stairs of Seth's building the next day and kicked open the door, adjusting my grip as I walked through the apartment and into my new room. It was a good size, good light. So far, all I'd moved were art supplies and a duffle bag full of clothes, which I set down on the air mattress Seth had set up for me.

I hung my hands on my hips as I looked out the window, heart thumping just a little hard, breath just a little heavier than it should be with my eyes on the street below.

It hadn't been easy. Nothing had ever been easy. But every choice I'd made brought me to where I was standing. Maybe if my life had been different, I'd be different. Maybe not. Maybe I wouldn't be afraid. Maybe I would.

When nothing in your life is certain — not your family, not even your friends — you push everyone out. No, not push them out. Hold them away from you. Stop them from getting in. Because once they get in, you have something to lose.

It was why I left her the first time, but this time was different. This time, I was just tired.

I couldn't drag her, hold her hand and pull her to keep up. She couldn't say the words. She couldn't tell me she wanted me, after everything, after all this time. That moment marked the end of it. I needed to hear that I was important to her. That I meant something. But her silence told me everything I needed to know.

There was only one way to move on, and it was to stay as far away from Rose as I could. And to stay away from Rose meant to stay away from all of them. I loved them — they were my family. But everyone was moving on, and I had to follow suit.

It was the only way I could salvage what was left of my heart.

Seth knocked gently on the doorframe, and I turned to find him looking somber. "Hey, man."

"Hey." I reached into a box of paints, shuffling them around with no purpose other than to occupy my hands.

"You okay?"

"I will be."

"You always are." He glanced at the boxes. "Have anything else?"

"Just this, for now."

He walked to one and peered inside. "Bring anything besides paint and clothes?"

"What else do I need?"

He chuckled. "So, what's your plan? With Rose, I mean."

I picked up my easel case and began to assemble it, avoiding his eyes as I tried to sound unaffected. "Nothing. Lay low, I guess. Work. Paint."

"No chasing her down? No grand gesture planned? You're just

letting her go?"

"When you squeeze Rose, you bleed for it. There's no going back, not now. I just …" I ran a hand through my hair. "I don't know, man. I don't even know if I want to try anymore. As much as I want her, as much as I *need* her, I just can't keep killing myself. One of us will fuck it up, so why hang around waiting for it any longer than I have been? Because I'm tired of waiting. So I'm cashing in my chips."

"That's pretty bleak, even for you."

I chuckled down at my feet. "Yeah, well. I'll be okay, and so will she. We'll both be happier this way, in the long run."

"How are you going to do that and still hang around her all the time?"

"I can't. But things aren't what they used to be. Everyone's busy and pairing off and … growing up, I guess. Moving on. The only way past Rose is to just remove myself from the equation."

He sighed and pushed a hand through his blond hair. "I'm sorry, Patrick."

"Don't be."

He nodded. "I'm glad you're here. Really glad."

I smiled gently, wishing for a hundred things I couldn't have, but thankful for what I did have all the same. "Me too."

I woke that afternoon cold. Maybe it was the sheets around my waist, exposing my naked arms to the whirring fan. Or maybe it was because I was alone.

I grabbed my comforter and pulled it up, wrapping myself in it like a burrito.

It's your fault he's gone.

I closed my eyes against the pain.

He was right, I knew. About all of it. I couldn't ask him to stay. I couldn't tell him I wanted him, even when he asked. I couldn't give him what he wanted. I couldn't even give him what I wanted.

I *was* afraid. And once again, I let him walk away.

It seemed we were doomed to keep repeating ourselves, on and on, ad infinitum.

My door creaked open as a tear slipped down my cheek. "Rosie?" Lily called from my doorway.

"Hey," I answered, the sound muffled, and I bent my neck to wipe my tear away against the comforter.

The fan clicked off, my lamp clicked on, and the mattress dipped as Lily climbed in with me. She tugged gently at the edge of the blanket. "You in there?"

"No."

"Come on. Give up some blanket. It's cold in here."

I peeked out and found her familiar, smiling face, eyes big and soft, and fresh tears burned the backs of my eyes. I blinked to ease them and shuffled to relinquish a hearty portion of my shelter.

We turned to face each other.

"Patrick told me what happened."

I raised an eyebrow.

"Well, sort of. You know, in that Tricky way — one sentence at a time and with very broad strokes."

I chuckled.

"You okay?"

"Not really."

"Want to talk about it?"

"Not really."

She smiled, and the gesture she made told me she thought I was full of shit.

I sighed. "I don't even know what to say. He was here, and it was good. And then Seth came poking around, and now he's gone."

She gave me a look. "Are you really trying to blame this on Seth?"

"Well, sort of. If he hadn't shown up jingling the keys to his apartment, we wouldn't have had the fight."

"Fair enough, but that isn't really what the fight was about, was it?" she asked like she already knew the answer.

I dodged the question with one of my own. "What did Tricky say?"

"He said he was moving in with Seth and didn't give up all that much about the actual fight. Just something about him being convenient and you not being ready."

I resisted the urge to burrow into my covers so she couldn't see me. "I don't know, Lil. It started off about Seth, but it wasn't really about Seth at all. It was about us. It was the truth about how we saw everything, and it didn't feel good to hear. It didn't feel good to say."

"Well, that doesn't sound irreparable. Maybe you just need some time to cool off."

"I don't think so. I think …" I swallowed hard. "I think this is it. He wanted me to ask him to stay, and I didn't. I couldn't. I let him down, but it wasn't fair either, to demand that I just say what he wanted on the spot."

She rolled her eyes. "Don't be dramatic, Rose."

"Ha. That's funny coming from you."

"Ha, ha." She pinched my arm, and I snickered. "I mean, I get it. You don't do well under pressure or when you're put on the spot."

"No, being backed into a corner does that to me." I sighed.

She shook her head. "No, you're right. That wasn't very fair."

"But then … I don't know." I shuffled under the blanket, feeling uncomfortable. "We hurt each other. I don't think there's any way for us to get past it. I don't think either of us can get over what we feel to see the other one's side."

"So it's snowballed into this dirty old mess."

"No, the dirty old mess had been brewing. Probably since the first time I ever laid eyes on him."

She gave me a look. "Seriously, who are you, dramawhore?" she joked.

"I don't know," I said with a hint of desperation. "I feel like I'm devolving. Next thing you know, I'll be crying into a tub of ice cream watching The Notebook."

"I thought your period was over."

My face pinched. "I don't need an excuse to have feelings, Lilith!"

She laughed. "I mean, I can get some Ben & Jerry's and make this happen. In fact, I've got some Boom Chocolatta in West's freezer, if you want me to get it."

I chewed my lip. "Maybe."

"Just say the word."

I looked into her eyes, and sadness overcame me. "Everything has changed."

"I know," she said softly.

"I don't know where I fit in. Neither does Patrick. That's why he was here, really, and I get it. And at some point, probably soon, you and West are going to really move in together. And then what happens?"

She sighed and picked at the blanket. "Honestly, we haven't really even talked about it. I don't mind Tricky being around, and neither does West, but he seems to mind being around us, beyond the whole sex thing. Don't get me wrong, he hasn't made me feel unwelcome or anything, but I can tell that something bothers him about it, something bigger than how he feels about West and me."

"You're a reminder that we're alone."

She didn't respond, though her eyes went even softer.

I reached for her hand. My best friend. "For all that time, we were alone *together*. It's just different now. You and West are like a unit. It's not like we don't see you alone, but part of you is always with the other one. It's beautiful and brilliant, and we *want* that for you, but it underscores the things we lack. For a second, I thought … " I sighed again. "I guess I thought Patrick and I had found something together again. I should have known we'd never work out. We're doomed."

"You two just need to talk to each other," she said, matter-of-factly.

"We don't talk, Lily."

"Ugh, that's so annoying."

"What? Not everyone's like you."

She huffed. "I know, but still. Ninety percent of your problems would be solved if you just talked about it."

"But this is our thing. This is how we work, Lil. When we're fine, we're fine. And when we aren't, we walk away and shut down. The issue is that we're *both* like that, so a grand total of zero problems get solved."

"So break the cycle. Go talk to him." She gave the advice like it was just that simple.

"And say what? I swear to God, I walk into conversations with him with every intention of being honest and open, but in the moment it's like my dum-dum switch gets flipped, and I lock up. Like my mouth just goes on the fritz and all I can say is stuff like 'Whatever,' and 'Fine.' That's not a conversation. We just don't know anything else."

"What about writing him a letter? That way you can think about everything you want to say."

"I don't even know what I *want* to say."

"Well, obviously you need to figure that out first."

I thought about it, about what I'd say, but the second the ache in my chest peaked, I pushed it all away again. "I'm not ready."

Lily smiled and pulled me into a hug. "Well, that's step one. And there's no rush." She squeezed me tighter. "It's all gonna be okay, Rosie."

The tears found their way back, hot and burning at the back of my eyes, emotion climbing up my constricted throat. I couldn't find it in me to be so optimistic.

Prince Solves Everything

PATRICK

I walked with West toward Habits that night full of dread, feeling no better about any of it after a long conversation he and I had in his apartment, rehashing it all. My only comfort was the resolve I found, strengthened with every conversation I had about it.

Rose and I were bad for each other. There was no repairing what we'd shredded — we'd done enough damage for a lifetime.

Everyone would be meeting tonight because Maggie had been accepted as a full-time, salaried employee at the homeless shelter, and I'd never refuse to be there to congratulate her just because of Rose and me. I'd been making it work without her for all these months. Now was no different.

The minute we walked through the door and I saw her behind the bar, I realized how much of a lie that was.

I almost stopped walking but caught myself and pressed on, averting my eyes from hers to scan for everyone else. The group stood gathered at the end of the bar, laughing and smiling as always, the happy couples, plus me and Rose.

They greeted us as we approached.

I made my way around to say my hellos, congratulating Maggie with a kiss on her cheek, trying to put as much physical distance as I could between me and Rose, to match the chasm between us. But it was no use. Somehow I found a way to step to the bar and order a drink from her, standing in silence watching her pour in silence. I couldn't look away. She seemed happy enough, shoulders back and chin high. But I knew it was for show. I could feel her pain just as much as if it were my own.

She avoided my eyes, handed over my drink as I passed her cash and found a place to stand where I was far enough away, at an angle where we wouldn't make eye contact. Every minute was torture, and soon after finishing my drink, I said goodbye.

The evening was chilly for June, the wind blowing just enough to push the cold through you, into your bones. But I didn't want to take a cab. I wanted to feel the cold, feel the ground under my feet. I wanted to remember why this was the right thing to do, the only thing to do. But I found myself searching for answers, repeating the reasons over and over in my head, like a prayer.

B *eing in the same room* with him was hell.

I felt him when he walked in, my eyes finding him, his finding mine before snapping away like he didn't know me. The only words we spoke were when he ordered his drink, his gaze on me so heavy as I poured, I could barely breathe. But when he left a few minutes later, it was without a glance.

The chill crept into my heart.

The second he was gone, our friends looked at me like my grandma had died. I rolled my eyes, playing it off like I didn't feel like I'd been shot.

"Cut it out, guys."

Everyone tentatively looked away, and Cooper took the lead, sparking a new conversation with the group. Lily leaned on the bar with her brow furrowed.

"You okay?" she asked quietly.

"I'm fine."

Her eyes were on her drink, but her brows were up. "You can't lie to me, Rose Fisher."

I took a breath, dropping my chin as my eyes narrowed and emotion climbed up my throat. "What do you want from me, Lil? That fucking sucked. That was terrible, and I want to crawl under this bar and drink a bottle of whiskey alone." My voice trembled. "There. Do you feel better? Was that honest enough for you?"

She eyed me. "Karaoke."

I huffed and threw my hands up. "That's not an answer, goddammit."

Lily shrugged. "Of course it is. You want world peace? Get the whole world together to karaoke The Humpty Dance." She turned around on her stool to face Ellie and Maggie. "Karaoke is happening. You in?"

Cooper opened his mouth to speak, but Lily waved her finger at him.

"Nope. Girls only. Whaddaya say, ladies? I think a little karaoke therapy in the form of "When Doves Cry" is just what the doctor ordered for Rosie here."

I rolled my eyes again, swallowing my tears, joking past the pain. "Please. Prince is way out of my range."

The girls nodded and laughed, and Lily turned to me, looking smug. "See? It's happening."

I shook my head. "I can't. I'm going to be here until like three in the morning."

Lily flagged Shelby. "Shelbs — can we steal mopey Rosie tonight before closing? We need to get her liquored up and singing eighties songs, stat."

"Yeah, you do." She smiled. "As soon as this rush dies, get out of here."

I tried not to scowl at the adorable traitor, though I narrowed my eyes at Lily. "All right. You win."

She laughed, clearly gloating. "What's new?"

A few hours later, the four of us sat at a high bar table as a man in a cowboy hat with a thick grey mustache sang a Roy Orbison song, eyes closed and face full of conviction.

"Karaoke rules." I raised my glass and whooped along with the rest of the crowd when he finished. Once I'd gotten a solid howl in, I slammed the end of my whiskey and picked up the fresh glass our waitress had just dropped by.

We were all undeniably drunk. And I was numb enough that I could pretend like the last few days hadn't happened. It all seemed far away, like a story of something that happened to a girl named Rose and not like it was my actual life.

Five or six or eight whiskeys did that to me.

The DJ came on the PA and called Ellie's name. She hopped off the stool and bounded over to the stage, giggling into the microphone.

"Hi, everybody."

The men whistled and cheered, and she grinned, smoothing her short dress over her hips just as "Like a Virgin" began, and we witnessed the most hilarious, Betty Boop rendition of the song I've ever heard in person. It was all wagging hips and puckered lips, her cleavage banging and red hair spilling over her shoulders. I swear to God, every man in the place had his eyes glued to her. I could practically hear a collective *aooga* when she ran her free hand down her body during the chorus.

We could not stop laughing.

"I'm gonna pee," Lily squeaked.

"Oh, my God, if you pee, I'm Instagramming it." I breathed.

Maggie couldn't even make noise. She dropped her head to the table, shoulders shuddering with laughter.

Ellie waggled her fingers at us and winked, giggling again at us in the microphone as she strutted across the stage, stroking the mic like a giant dick.

By the time she finished, we'd caught our breaths enough to scream for her as she hung up the mic.

"Marry me," some random guy screamed from the crowd.

Ellie smiled in his direction. "Show me your bank statements, and you're in, honey." She twiddled her fingers to whistles and screams as she stepped off the stage.

We clapped and cheered as she approached.

"That was amazing!" Maggie clapped.

Ellie smiled and did a little curtsy before sitting down. "Thank you. That song always kills it in karaoke. The only thing better is when a hairy fat guy sings it."

I shook my head, laughing. "I swear you were a stripper in your past life."

"I can't help it. I've got all this to work with." She motioned to her curvy body. "Like, do you know how easy it is for me to twerk? Look, I'll show you." She started to get up, and we laughed even harder.

I touched her arm. "Later. When you have pants on."

"Pfft." She waved her hand, not the least bit ashamed, though she did sit back down.

The next singer came on, and she was *really* good, belting out "Barracuda" like an absolute pro. Maggie and Ellie shimmied in their seats to the beat, singing along.

Lily took a minute to leaned into me. "Feel any better?"

I smirked and held up my drink. "Once again, you were right. Karaoke solves problems."

"Or at least puts a little distance between you and them for a while."

I booped her nose. "Aww, a Drily truth nugget."

She nodded seriously. "When Drunk Lily advances to Drily status, important conversations are had."

"It's so true. Liquor affects your filter in the best way."

She chuckled and picked up her gin and tonic. "Drosie's not so bad herself."

I shrugged, unimpressed. "Drosie's workable. I will say though that I'm a little worried about keeping Drellie's clothes on."

"Yeah, you may not be wrong there." She raised her glass to toast mine. "Tricky, who?"

"Tricky, who," I chimed and clinked my glass to hers.

"Any ideas on what to do next about all of this?"

I sniffed and made a face. "Not really. I guess get through the weird and hope someday we can be around each other again. But right now, I don't really want to see him."

She leaned in, eyes squinted like she couldn't see me. "Is that true? Like, really real true?"

"Yes and no, I guess. Part of me wants to see him and pretend everything is fine and then fuck his brains out. The other part never wants to lay eyes on him again and really, really wants to forget he ever existed." I took another drink. "I guess it's entirely possible that we won't see each other much, now that he's staying with Seth." The pit in my stomach could have echoed, it was so black and dark.

She sighed. "The whole thing just sucks. After everything, you guys staying together, almost getting back together. I mean, what a fucking tease."

"I know."

Lily nibbled on her lip. "I feel partially responsible."

"Why would you feel responsible? It had nothing to do with you." I touched her arm.

She gave me puppy dog eyes, and my lips pressed flat.

"What did you do?"

She grabbed the end of her hair and twisted it around her finger. "Well, it was West's idea."

My eyes narrowed. "What was West's idea?"

"Well, I'm getting there, if you'd let me talk."

I sat back in my chair and picked up my drink, folding my arm under my elbow, feeling prickly. "Please. Be my guest." I gestured with my glass.

She took a drink and then she took a breath. "So, we obviously know how you two feel about each other, and the … *challenges* you face. You know, the whole not talking to each other situation."

"I'm aware."

She looked guilty as hell. "Well, we maybe, sort of, kind of, were faking the whole loud sex thing."

I blinked. "What?"

"I mean, it wasn't always fake," she clarified. "Sometimes it was *very* real." She snickered.

I held up a hand and made a face. "Ew."

"Anyway, I suggested to Patrick that he should sleep in my bed, and then West and I set an alarm every night to wake up and bang on the walls. West even sabotaged all those fans and white noise machines he kept buying in the hopes he would start sleeping over there, and that you guys would … I don't know. Be forced to make amends."

My mouth was hanging open. "Lilith Jane Thomas. I cannot fucking believe you."

"Well, it worked, didn't it?" she said, defensively, in part in pleading.

"You lied to me, you ass!"

"Yeah, because I love you, which makes it okay," she said sternly. "Anyway, you would have done the same thing if the tables were turned."

I opened my mouth to protest, but closed it again. "Yeah, probably. But dammit, Lily. That was way out of bounds."

"I know. I'm sorry. I really am. I love you, Rosie, and I want you to be happy and I thought I could help. My heart was in the right place."

I scowled. "Which is the only reason why I'm not taking out my earrings to deck you."

She smiled apologetically. "Will you promise to yell at West too?"

"Oh, believe me, his will be worse." I took a drink.

"Well, that makes me feel better," she said happily. "I still think you should go talk to Patrick about all of this."

"I don't know what to say." I leaned on the table and shook the ice in my drink that was already almost empty again.

"Do you want to talk to him?"

I rolled my eyes. "Ugh, Lily. I don't know."

"Okay, okay. Let's go simpler. Do you miss him?"

I paused. "Yes."

"Well, that's something." Lily motioned for two more drinks as the waitress walked by.

I pursed my lips, even though I couldn't feel them. My thoughts stumbled and tripped over each other, just like Patrick and I always did. "Patrick is big and scary and messy. I don't even know how to deal with all the things I feel for him — hurt, betrayal, lust, friendship, amusement, everything. He makes me feel everything, which is why I'd been avoiding it all this time. Starting over just seemed so much cleaner. Easier."

"Except it's not."

"Because we've been around each other all this time. Maybe with him gone, I can get over him."

"Do you want to get over him?"

I took a long drink and set down my glass. "Yes."

"No, you don't."

I sighed. "No, I don't. But I don't know how to handle any of this."

She gave me a look my mother used to give me. "I think you need to start by apologizing."

"For what?" I shot.

Lily rolled her eyes. "Gee, Rose. I don't know. Rejecting him? Hurting him?"

In a split second, my cheeks were on fire. "But *he* rejected *me. He* hurt *me.*"

"You hurt *each other*. So start the conversation by apologizing for your part in that."

I didn't answer for a second, surprised. She was right, and I hadn't even considered the concept. *This is why I suck at relationships.* "And then what?"

"Hope he apologizes back and that you can actually talk about all the things you're afraid of without running for cover." She took a drink.

"And if not?"

"Then, you know. You will have tried. Minimize your regret by doing whatever you can to mend things."

The waitress brought our drinks by, and I picked up the fresh one, promising myself idly that it would be my last. "Is it even smart to mend things? Maybe we're just bad for each other."

"You're not bad for each other. You just need to figure out how to communicate. It's pretty simple. You just go …" She grabbed my chin and moved my bottom lip with her thumb. "Hey, Tricky, ya big stud. I'm sorry I was a smelly bag of fried dicks to you, but I can't stand being apart, so how's about we kiss and make up?" She made wet kissy noises, and a laugh burst out of me. She shrugged. "See? Easy."

I stared down into my amber whiskey. "So, just apologize and see what happens?"

"You want him. He wants you. It's really all you can do, Rosie. You just have to check your ego at the door and do a little groveling."

I made a face. "Why does that make me feel itchy?"

"Probably because you avoid instead of grovel. But if you want to get the guy, you've got to suck it up, Buttercup. You let him walk away thinking you didn't care about him when the exact opposite is true. You need to tell him that. You need to tell him the truth about how you feel about him. He's been waiting to hear it this whole time, forever. And now's your last chance to say it."

The thought of declaring my feelings sent a bolt of excitement and dread through me, followed by flashes of images — rejection, acceptance, kissing, crying. Both. "You're right," I said quietly.

"I know. Drily is always right." She reached for my hand and peered into my eyes. "It's going to be okay. You know that, right?"

"Well, it can't really get any worse."

"Never say that, Rose," she chided. "The night is still young, and Ellie just ordered another martini."

I looked over at Ellie, who was dancing like Molly Ringwald to Karma Chameleon as her jugs bounced around, dangerously close to popping out of her dress by sheer force.

"Oh, God," I said with a laugh.

"See?" she said, enjoying being right again. "It could *always* be worse."

Once & For All

PATRICK

dipped my brush in the tar black paint before pressing the heavy bristles to the canvas, dragging it down. Pressure. A curve. A line. And then the paint was gone, without enough to do what I wanted, which was fill the canvas with darkness. I loaded the brush again.

Nothing was simple except this.

I'd drawn her face a thousand times. Some days, it was all I could see. But she and I weren't meant to be. The distance between us wasn't a straight line. It was a series of winding corridors, lit by harsh, naked bulbs. We didn't know the way through, couldn't find the exits.

Lost. Rose and I were lost to each other.

I painted the canvas black, all but where the light touched her profile, the negative space creating the features that made up the face that haunted me. But she was just a ghost, made of mist and smoke.

I thought I heard a knock at the door and turned my head to the sound, wiping my hand on my jeans before reaching for my phone to turn down the music, listening. The knock came again, and I stood, making my way to the door to pull it open curiously.

I never expected to find Rose on the other side of it.

My breath stopped as my eyes roamed over her. She looked small, shoulders bent in a gentle slope, lip caught between her teeth. Her dark eyes seemed endless as they met mine.

"Hey," she said, the single word heavy with nerves and hope and dread.

My heart hammered as I stood in the doorway, hand on the knob, staring at her. "Hey," was all I could muster.

"Can I come in?"

I nodded and stepped out of the way, and she passed like she was afraid to touch anything, hands her in her pockets, eyes on the ground. I closed the door and turned to face her, not sure what I should say, not sure what she'd say.

She looked up again, her face more determined than a moment before. "I … I owe you an apology, Patrick. I'm sorry for the way we ended things. Not just now, but before."

I nodded and said quietly, "So am I."

She took a breath. "I wasn't the only one who got hurt, but I never acknowledged that, never told you that I'm sorry for hurting you. I'm sorry I pushed you away. I'm sorry I punished you, but I never enjoyed it. Not for a single minute did I feel less pain because of yours." She swallowed. "All of our problems stem from one snag, and it unraveled the whole sweater."

"And what's that?"

"We can't be honest with each other about how we feel. I didn't ask you to stay when you left me. I didn't stop you from leaving the other night. I didn't tell you the truth. And the truth is, I didn't want you to go. The truth is that I miss you and I need you and I want you.

That I'm glad you lied to me and snuck into my apartment to sleep. Because if it weren't for that, I wouldn't have found you again. I'm just … I'm sorry that I let you down. I'm sorry I'm scared."

I stepped into her, slipped a hand into her hair. Her hand found my waist, resting just over the roses there. Just over the thorns. "I was scared too, Rose. Scared you'd leave. Scared you'd hurt me. So I hurt you first."

She closed her eyes and covered my hand with hers.

"But," I started.

Her eyes opened again, shining with tears as fear flitted behind them.

The words caught in my throat, and I swallowed them down, knowing the truth of the matter. Knowing what I had to do, for both of us. "I've waited so long to be here, in this place, in the same place. But it's too late."

Her chin quivered, and she lowered it. I pressed my lips to her forehead.

"Rose … we're no good together. We'll only keep hurting each other, over and over again. It's vicious and destructive. Look at what we've done to each other. We don't know another way, but I don't want to hurt you anymore. I don't want to hurt. I'm sorry, Rose," I whispered, nose burning, voice thick as I closed my eyes. "I'm so sorry."

She said nothing, only took a shaky breath.

A hot tear rolled onto my hand, still cupping her cheek. There was only one thing left to say, the words I'd never said, the words she needed to hear, needed to know. So I took a breath and whispered, "I love you, you know."

"I know," she whispered back, still for a long moment before she stepped back, swiping a tear off her cheek. "I should go."

I nodded, throat tight, taking a step away to put more distance between us. And then she walked away, and I closed the door, completely empty.

trotted down the stairs in Seth's building, sucking in breaths like I was breathing through a straw. I couldn't get enough air, not even when I broke out onto the sidewalk, winding my way through people, blurred by my tears.

I'd been stupid to come. Stupid to think we could make it work, because he was right. I'd known it all along.

The thought wasn't a comfort.

I wished I was home in my bed, where I could break completely, as I walked the blocks in a whirl, choking down sobs as they bubbled up in my throat, brushing away the tears that had no care for privacy.

I unlocked my door with relief coursing through me, breaking down my shredded veil of composure. My hands shook. A sob escaped. And then I was inside.

Ellie glanced over her shoulder at me, though I only saw her out of my hazy periphery as I hurried through the living room and into my room, closing my door behind me to the sound of my name as a question.

I shed my shoes. I climbed in bed. I clutched a pillow. And then, I cried.

It was my soul exposed, the raw ends frayed and nerves screaming. I'd lost. I didn't know if there'd ever been a chance I might have won.

It was over. We told the truth — not the truth we wanted, but the truth of reality — and the truth was that we were better off apart.

I didn't know which was worse. The truth, or the lie we'd been telling ourselves.

The tears slowed after a while, the pain burned down to smoldering embers. My door creaked open.

"Hey. Can I come in?" Lily asked.

I didn't move.

"I'm going to take that as a yes." The door closed, and she lay down next to me. I couldn't meet her eyes as she looked me over. "Oh, Rosie," she said softly, touching the cold tears on my cheeks.

And then the tears were back, pressing at the backs of my eyes, spilling from the corners, the proximity to someone who loved me more than I could stand as the muddy wall I'd built to hold it all back broke down.

"Shh," she soothed and wrapped her arms around me. I curled into her. "I'm so sorry, Rose."

So was I.

She stroked my hair as I cried myself dry once more, the second wave passed, leaving me flat and gray.

"He said we were better off apart," I finally said, my throat raw.

She didn't say anything, though her hand paused in its slow track across my hair.

"I thought it would be easy. I thought I'd just go over there and say I was sorry and it would be okay. But it wasn't, and I can't blame him. He's right, you know. We're both so bad at this. We'll just keep hurting each other, over and over again. It's best to end it once and for all."

"Not that it makes it easier."

"No. Definitely not."

We lay there in silence for a few minutes before she asked, "Are you glad you told him how you felt?"

I took a breath and thought about it, took a body assessment. Nose burning. Head pounding. Eyes stinging and swollen.

Heart shredded.

"At least I have an answer," was as much as I could commit to. "What's done is done. Now I just have to find a way to move on.

Really move on, not whatever we were doing before. There's no saving what we had before all of this." My chin quivered. I closed my eyes. "It doesn't matter that I think I'm in love with him, does it?"

"I guess sometimes it doesn't, as much as we want it to. Maybe, sometimes, love just isn't enough."

"He … he told me he loved me, like he just wanted me to know before he said goodbye. But I already knew."

She pulled in a heavy breath and let it out slow as I lay in the arms of my best friend, wishing I could turn the man I loved back into a stranger.

Things You Can Count On

ROSE

I **stared at the blank canvas,** feet hooked on the bottom rung of my stool, just like I had been for the last hour, the last day. I didn't know what else to do with myself. It was the only way I knew how to get what was inside of me out.

My thoughts stumbled around and around in circles, replaying everything that had happened with Rose in a loop from beginning to end.

Calling it was the smart thing to do. The right thing. I knew that, even though it felt wrong.

I'd dodged West and Cooper easily enough, though only under the promise that I'd meet them at the courts that afternoon. No one else had texted or called, and I'd kept myself locked in my room, leaving only for work. That was where Max told me what he knew, unsolicited. He'd cornered me, really, said that Rose wasn't okay. I tried to downplay it — he was known well for his flair for the dramatic. But I knew she was hurting, because so was I.

I sighed and flipped my pencil around in my fingers. She was all I could see. I opened them, seeing the blank canvas once more.

I needed to clear my head.

I abandoned my stool and my easel to dig around in my duffle bag for a shirt and basketball shorts, changing quickly and putting my sneakers on. The canvas screamed at me, the crisp whiteness, the deep *nothingness* of it overwhelming. I gave it a long, final look before leaving the apartment.

It was one of the warmest days we'd had that summer, muggy and heavy, the kind of day that leaves you sweating and tired, even if all you'd done was tie your shoes and venture out to get your mail. The blacktop sweltered in the heat, and small waves radiated up gently, making things low in the distance look like a mirage.

I spotted West and Cooper at one of the far courts, smiling at me as I approached.

"Hey, man," West said from the bench when I reached them.

"What's up?" I set down my bag.

"Not much. Glad you came willingly," he added with a smirk. "I didn't want to have to show up at Seth's and drag you down here like I did Cooper when Maggie left."

I chuckled. "Am I going to get 'talked to?'"

"Not by me. Not unless you want to be, in which case I'm sure I can find a thing or two to say."

"I'm sure."

Cooper smirked. "Well, now I'm curious."

West shrugged. "I mean, I'd probably say something like …" He glanced at me. "Nah. Tricky doesn't want to hear it, Coop."

Cooper sat down and retied his laces. "Yeah, probably not."

"You guys have zero stealth." I stretched out a leg and leaned on my knee.

Cooper leaned back on the bench, his face more serious. "What happened, man?"

I shifted to stretch the other leg, unable to answer for a moment. "We're bad for each other. Why keep fighting the inevitable?"

"Because you love her," Cooper said.

"That's why I'm walking away. Someone has to put an end to it once and for all or we'll just keep doing this."

"So you're stopping it right when she finally said all the things you've been waiting to hear? I fail to see the logic here." Cooper stretched his arms over his head, threading his fingers as he reached to the side.

My brow dropped as I pushed the stretch until it burned. "It's not that simple."

"Sure it is," West said. "The two of you want to be together, but you're not, and why? Because of some perceived, make-believe fear that one of you will hurt the other?"

"It's all we've ever done. We don't know anything else."

Cooper shook his head and leaned in the other direction. "Not in the beginning."

"Yeah, well, I fucked that up, and we've been on the merry-go-round ever since."

"I'm just saying," Cooper pressed, "if happiness existed for you two once, it could happen again."

The frustration binding my chest tightened, and my voice carried an unintentional edge. "With everything hanging between us, I don't know how to find happy with her. The issue is trust. I don't trust myself not to freak out when things get real and run again. I don't trust that she'll fight for me, for us. I can't be sure that I'll be strong when she's weak, or that she'll be strong for me."

West's lips were flat. "No one ever has that guarantee, Tricky."

"I'm not asking for a guarantee. But she and I have done this before, and we have a shitty track record."

"You can't give up," he said plainly.

I threw up my hands with a huff. "Fuck, dude. I'm trying to do the right thing here. Walk away and save us both the pain."

"Yeah, well, love isn't always responsible."

I had no argument. "You sound like a fortune cookie."

West kept going. "So you could get hurt. She's willing to risk it, but it won't work if you've got one foot out."

"So I go all in? Bet it all even though it's been falling apart since it started?"

His face was earnest, pleading. "You go all in and fight for her when shit goes down. Don't let her walk away. Don't walk away from her. Love her, man. Love her like you do."

I shook my head. "It's not enough."

"Of course it's enough."

"No, it's not. You don't understand, West. My life … my life isn't simple. It never has been. As much as I want her, I can't have her because I'm poisonous. I'm toxic. And at the end of the day, I'll never be good enough for her. I don't deserve her or any of you — I'm just lucky that I had you all for the time I have."

West's eyes narrowed. "Is that what this is about?"

I let out a breath, lips flat.

He put a hand on my shoulder and gave me a hard look. "Patrick, listen to me. Rose isn't your dad. Rose isn't Seth. Rose doesn't love you for any reason other than that she does. You didn't have to *do* anything. Don't you get it? Fight because you want it. You fought to get straight. You fought to get away from your dad. You fight when you want something, and you want her, so why aren't you fighting for her?"

My throat burned. "I … I don't know."

"Isn't having Rose — even if it'll end someday — isn't having her enough to swallow your fear?"

I couldn't speak.

"She wants to try. If you want to try, if you want her, then fucking go get her. Don't let anything stand in your way."

I nodded, my voice rough when I answered, "You're right."

"Of course I'm right." He smiled easily and picked up the ball. "Now come on, Tricky. Let's burn you down. Set you to rights."

And we did — we played until I'd sweat out my doubt, burned through my fear, and in the ashes of that, I found Rose once again.

Patrick

Dusk had fallen, and the only light was pointed at the canvas. I guided the brush, knowing where the black watercolor would drip, where the brushstrokes would be visible. The idea had struck me on the way home from the courts, and the minute I sat down, the painting poured out of me. I hadn't moved since.

I loaded the brush and held out a hand, tapping the base against the flat of my palm to knock the paint onto the canvas in splatters. And then I sat back and looked it over.

It was perfect, or as close to perfect as I could ever get. Now, I'd let it dry, get cleaned up, and make my way back to my old building so I could start to make it right.

I stood and stretched, rinsed my brushes and laid them out to dry.

Someone knocked on the door.

Rose, I thought as I walked through the living room with my heart aching.

When I pulled open the door and found Jared standing there, cold adrenaline pumped through me. He looked much the same as he did years ago, back when we used together, back when he started selling dope. Seth and I were his first customers.

"Tricky?" He looked me over in disbelief. "What the fuck, man." He came in for a hug, clapping me on the shoulder. I didn't reciprocate, and he pulled back, smile fading. "Long time. Seth here?"

"He's at work." I hadn't let him in.

He stepped back into the hallway. "Ah, yeah. The old grind, right? He didn't tell me you were moving back in. You start it up again too? Nobody can stay away from the white nurse too long, am I right?" he asked with a chuckle.

My jaw flexed, lips flat, heart banging like a war drum. "I'm clean, and Seth isn't here."

He nodded and looked up and down the hallway. "All right, it's cool. Just give him this for me?" He pulled a bundle of plastic and white powder out of his pocket and extended it to me.

I couldn't hear for the blood rushing in my ears. I hadn't seen any in years, and time had only made the shock that much greater, reverberating through my mind.

"Give it to him yourself."

Jared's face hardened, and he closed his fingers around the bag, slipping it back into his pocket. I felt relief almost immediately. "Take it easy, Tricky. Don't think you're better than us just because you got out. I don't doubt for a second that you'll be back one day. Not one second." His eyes narrowed as he looked me over before turning and walking away.

I closed the door, hoping I was wrong. That Jared coming over was an attempt to get Seth back in. That he hadn't started up again

— he hadn't. He couldn't. — that it was some horrible mistake. A vulture picking at the bones of the damaged.

My heart didn't slow as I walked through the apartment and opened his bedroom door, stepping into it, feeling like a traitor and a thief. I knew him well enough to know his hiding places. I checked the hollow book on his bookshelf to find it empty. I found the wooden box in the back of his closet with the devil burned into the lid, but there was nothing there but some old photos. And then I looked behind his bed where I found the cigar box.

It was a box I knew well.

My hands shook, the black wolf on the label snarling at me, the words *Big Wolf* in block letters across the top. I flipped open the lid, knowing exactly what I'd find. Needles. Tubing and cotton. A spoon and a lighter. A small bag of white powder.

I closed my eyes and took a breath. I hadn't seen his needle kit in so long, but the sight of it brought back the memories in a wave, followed by a flash of need, of want. Even after all these years, my body remembered.

I shut the lid with a snap

I was still trembling as I walked into the kitchen and set the kit on the table, leaning on the counter with my hand over my mouth, arm tucked under my elbow, eyes on that fucking wolf.

Seth hadn't changed.

I should have known. I wanted so badly to believe he could, believe that he was different this time, and in the end, he'd lied to me. Again.

I don't know how long I stood there in his kitchen with shock and anger and fear tumbling through me. Time stretched to a crawl, snapping back to speed when I heard Seth's key in the door.

He smiled at me when he walked in, though it slid off his face when he saw his kit on the table. He looked back up at me warily.

"Jared came by for you," I said flatly."

He put out a hand. "It's not what it looks like, Tricky."

"Then enlighten me."

He set down his bag, his eyes wide as he tried to convince me. "I've got a handle on it, man. It's not like it was before — I only use on the weekends, just for fun. It's not interfering with my job or my life, I won't let it. I've been down that road before."

I laughed, sharp and loud and without a hint of joy. "Yeah, you have. *Just for fun?*" I shook my head. "I cannot fucking believe you. This is how it starts. This is how it *always* starts — you know that. But you have no control. You *never* have control. None of us do, not when it comes to this. How is it that you didn't get rid of your needle kit? That should have been the *first* thing you did. There is no halfway with this. There's no sometimes, and you're lying to yourself if you believe otherwise."

He hurried to the table with conviction across his face, in his voice. "It's different now," he pleaded. "I know I can handle it, Patrick. I'm stronger than I've ever been. I still don't drink. I don't even smoke weed. But this … I don't know who I am without this."

"I know. But I know who I am without it. Did you think I wouldn't figure it out? Don't you realize I can't be around this? I can't even *see* this fucking box, Seth."

"You weren't supposed to."

"Well, I fucking did. You lied to me, Seth, and this time is the last time. This ends here." I pushed off the counter and made my way to my room.

"I didn't lie to you. When you asked me, I was clean. I didn't ask you to move in here, and when you offered, I didn't think you'd take me up on it."

I didn't answer as I blew through the apartment with him on my heels.

"Dammit, Tricky," he huffed. "I always knew you thought you were better than me. Like you're strong and I'm weak. You've got the answers and I'm some dumbfuck screw-up who can't get his shit together."

I turned on him, brow low. "I don't think I'm better than anybody. But as much as I want more for you, I can't help you. I never could. And I can't give anymore."

He ran a hand through his hair. "You can't leave, man. What am I going to do if you leave?" His chest heaved as he begged. "What do I have to do to make you stay?"

But I shook my head. "Nothing. There's nothing you can do."

His face bent in anger, neck taught as he pulled back a fist and slammed it into the drywall, popping a hole in it the size of a softball. He breathed heavy as he leaned against the wall, pressed his forehead to the sheetrock, voice ragged, body ragged. "I tried. I've been trying. I don't know what more you want from me."

"I want you to want to quit. But you don't. You never will. You have to quit for you, not for me, not for anything but yourself."

His voice cracked. "I don't know how."

"I know," I said sadly. "But I can't stay. I can't, Seth. I can't know that's within reach. I can't walk in to find you with a needle in your arm. I just … I can't. You have to understand that, if nothing else."

Seth stood and looked me over, his face thin and ashen, lined with pain and regret. "I can't understand anything." He turned and walked out of the apartment.

I trudged into my room and began to pack my bag, stowing away supplies in their boxes, carrying them down the stairs and ultimately to the cab I called. And then, I went home.

What Could Have Been

ROSE

The bar was steady enough that night to keep my thoughts occupied, and I was so grateful. I did my crying, and then I hitched up my britches and went to work. Red, red lipstick and black, black liner helped my mood considerably, or at least helped me hide it a little.

I'd been far too busy to think about Patrick. Until Seth walked in.

I couldn't puzzle out why he was there as I walked over. Maybe he wanted to talk to me on Patrick's behalf. But as I looked him over, I knew that wasn't the case. He took a seat near the end of the bar, smiling at me, but that smile left me unsettled. There was something feral about him tonight — he looked more like the Seth I used to know than he had lately.

I headed down to greet him with my best fake smile on. "Hey,

Seth. What's up?"

"Oh, you know. Just living," he said flatly.

I tossed a cocktail napkin in front of him. "What can I get you?"

"Jack on the rocks."

"Sure," I said, glancing at him as I filled the glass with ice. "I thought Tricky said you'd quit drinking."

"Yeah, well. Guess he doesn't know everything." The words were wry and cold.

Unease slipped through me. "Yeah. Guess not."

He seemed to try to shake off whatever was on his mind. "It's been really good seeing you lately. I'm sorry about everything that happened with him."

I smiled and passed the drink over. "Thanks. Just one tonight? Or did you want me to start a tab?"

He picked it up, his eyes hungry as he looked into the glass. "A tab would be great."

I glanced at the time. It was eight, early enough in the night to see what would happen with Seth. If he got tanked, I'd text Patrick. Maybe he'd behave himself and split after a drink or two, and I wouldn't have to.

But somehow, I doubted that.

Patrick

t took me two trips to get everything from Seth's, including the painting I'd done that afternoon. And just like that, I was back in my old room, feeling more sure of myself than I had in ages, though still shaken from Seth. It was like being slapped back into reality, from a dark room to a light one, and I could see, even if not all that I saw was pretty.

I set the painting down in my room, and Lily spent a long time looking at it with her fingers on her lips and her eyes shining.

"It's perfect," she'd whispered as Lily, West, and I stood around it quietly.

A little while later, I showered and changed, then sat down at my desk and wrote a note. It was the first step. The first word to tell her what she meant to me, and I wouldn't stop until she was mine. Not this time.

I would fight for her. For us.

My phone buzzed in my pocket, and I pulled it out to find a text from Rose.

Hey. I'm sorry to bother you with this, but Seth is at Habits, and he's been drinking for a few hours alone. I'm not sure if he's okay.

I texted her back as my heart sped up. *I'll be right there.*

Thanks, Patrick.

I stood and left the painting where it was in my room, no longer having time to leave it in her apartment, my fears about what was next with us replaced by something far worse as I hurried across the blocks to her.

I *should have called Patrick sooner.*

It was getting late, late enough that the bar had cleared out, even Bob who paid his tab with a smile, nodding to Seth as he asked if I wanted him to stay. But I sent him on his way, sure Seth was harmless. I texted Patrick anyway, though, uncertain what else to do.

When I made it back behind the bar, Seth sagged over his drink, shoulders sloped. He spun the glass around by the rim.

"Doing okay, Seth?" I asked in my bartender voice.

He smiled. "Great. Better than ever." The glass spun around again, and he watched his fingers. "You know, I've been wondering about something."

"Oh?"

Seth looked up at me, half smiling, half something else. "How come you and I never hooked up?"

I chuckled uneasily. "Well, I did have a boyfriend when you lived with Tricky."

"Yeah, but I mean, I always thought we had the vibe, you know?"

I shrugged. "To be honest, knowing your past was always chasing you was kind of a turn off." It was honest, all right. Too honest, and the moment it left my lips, I wish I'd made up a lie or a joke or anything.

He shook his head at me, eyes hard. "Tricky had the same past." It was almost an accusation.

"Not many people are like Tricky, though. You know he's different."

"Right." The word was bitter, and he picked up his drink and killed it. "Can I get another?"

I laughed gently, looking for footing, trying to diffuse the tension, giving him whatever he wanted to buy time until Patrick showed up. "It's late, Seth. Don't you have work in the morning?"

He shrugged. "I guess."

I watched him for a moment. "Are you sure you're okay?"

"Yeah, I'm good. How about that drink?" The words were sharper than before, so I smiled and picked up the bottle.

"Sure." I poured him another drink with my mind screaming, wondering when Patrick would get there. "Hey, I'll be right back.

Gonna grab a couple of things from the back."

"All right."

I walked past the bathrooms and into the stock room, propping the door open with the doorstop, letting out a breath as I walked toward the back wall.

"You know," Seth started, and I jolted, spinning around to find him blocking the doorway. "The first time I ever saw you, I was sure you and I would be a thing." He took a step into the room, and I took an instinctive step back. "I wish Tricky hadn't made me leave, but he always was the golden boy, you know? He got the job." He took another step. "He got the girl, even if he lost her." The corner of his lip curled into a smile. "Twice."

"He earned all that. No one gave it to him."

He took another step, and so did I. "He and I came from the same circumstances, but somehow he gets it all, and I get nothing. I tried, Rosie. I tried so hard. But it's never good enough. It's never enough."

Seth moved, and when I took a step back, my back hit the shelves, sending the bottles clinking into each other gently. I had nowhere to go as he closed in on me. "Seth—"

He was close enough now that I could smell the whiskey on his breath as he reached out to touch my hair, running a strand through his fingers. "I'm not gonna hurt you, Rosie."

I didn't believe that for a second. "What happened to you?"

He shrugged as his eyes ran over my face, assessing me. "I'm not clean enough for Tricky, so he left. Moved out."

"Patrick only wants to help you. You know that." *Where is he?*

A shadow passed across his face. "Maybe I don't want any help. Maybe I'm tired of bending myself into a shape that doesn't fit. Maybe I'm tired of fighting what I want. I should just take what I want instead. Like you, Rose."

He pressed his body into mine, slipped a hand into my hair and squeezed until I cried out in pain. My arms were by my side, fingers gently groping for anything on the shelf that I could use as a weapon. They brushed the neck of a bottle, and I fumbled with it until I could grip it with my heart thumping so hard, so loud. I squeezed my fist around the neck and snarled.

"Get the fuck off me, you son of a bitch."

But the angle was odd and slow, the bottle heavier than I thought as I brought it up, and I knew through every millisecond that it wouldn't be enough. His face twisted, full of rage when he realized what I was doing, shifting into shock as he flew backwards, then sideways into the shelves against the other wall.

Patrick stood in Seth's place, staring at his back with his body tight, jaw firm and lip curled, voice dangerously low. "Don't you ever put your fucking hands on her again."

Seth pushed off the shelves, roaring as he flew at Patrick. But Seth was too slow. Patrick barely moved, didn't even flinch, just shifted and threw out a fist, catching Seth in the jaw.

Seth spun around and hit the ground, lying there moaning for a second.

I looked up just as Patrick stepped into me, cupping my face in his hand, searching it with his dark eyes. "Are you all right? Did he hurt you?"

"N-no. I'm all right." My eyes moved back to the floor where Seth looked over his shoulder at us.

"It's okay. You're safe. I won't let him hurt you, Rose."

And when I looked up at him, looked into his eyes, I knew. He wouldn't let anyone hurt me, not even himself.

Seth tried to get up, but faltered. "Fuck you guys."

Patrick turned around, shielding me from Seth. "What do you want to do with him?" he asked me, though he stared down at Seth still, waiting. "Call the cops? Let him go?"

"I … I don't know."

"I can call them to pick him up, if you want."

Seth's eyes flashed. "You can't do that. I could lose my job."

Patrick's face was hard and still as stone. "Maybe you should have thought about that before you came here tonight."

"I won't come back. I shouldn't have come here. I was just ..." He looked down at his hands splayed on the ground, bracing him. The fight had slipped out of him, leaving him empty, a shell of a man on the floor in the back of a bar. He didn't look up as he spoke, seemingly to himself. "I don't know how many times I have to hit the bottom before I learn. Maybe I'll never learn."

Patrick still didn't move. "You're the only one who can make that choice, but I don't want anything to do with it." He looked back to me. "What do you want to do, Rose?"

I glanced at Seth, knowing that if he went to jail for this, it would be the end of him. Even if he didn't, it might be the end. But I couldn't be the reason. "I don't want to press charges or call the cops, as long as he doesn't come back."

"Go. Stay gone. If you come back I swear to God, I'll ..." His voice trembled, fists clenched by his side. "Just don't come back."

Seth nodded, looking ten years older than he had only a few hours before. He hauled himself up and walked toward the door, turning just before he passed through. "I'm sorry."

"So am I," he said.

And we watched him walk away.

The minute he was out of sight, Patrick turned again and pulled me into him. The adrenaline had waned, leaving me shaking, thankful for his arms around me.

"I'm sorry, Rose. I'm so sorry," he whispered into my hair.

"You can't apologize for Seth."

"I'm not."

I pulled back to look up at him, his face full of apologies and forgiveness.

He touched my cheek. "I know I said we'd only keep hurting each other, and I may not be wrong. But my mistake was letting you walk away without fighting for you. I won't let you slip away again, Rose, even if hanging onto you means I bleed from the thorns."

"Patrick …" I whispered.

"I love you, Rose."

A tear slipped down my cheek. "I love you. Even when it hurts."

His eyes closed, brows knit with emotion as his nose brushed mine. "Don't leave me."

"I won't. Not again. "

And then, he kissed me.

His familiar lips, the sweet softness that demanded and gave all at once — it was a kiss that erased what had happened before. It was the kiss of my dreams, except this wasn't a dream. I could feel his warm fingers against my cheek, feel his solid chest under my palms, his heart beating against my skin.

It was real.

No more walking away. No more fighting him, fighting us. I saw the path behind us, saw the path that lay before us, and I knew we would survive, as long as we never gave up.

He kissed me until I was breathless, and when he pulled away, I lowered my head to his chest. He wrapped me in his arms, and we stood for a long moment, just being.

Patrick moved first, shifting to look down at me. "What now?"

"Now, we move forward. Together."

And he smiled, one of the rare ones. "Together."

Anything

PATRICK

I sat at the bar, sipping my whiskey, still shaken, as we waited for Sheila and Brent to come down. Rose poured herself her second shot and slammed it, wincing as she set the glass on the bar top with a clink and got back to cleaning up. Keeping her hands busy made her feel better, she said, and I couldn't argue with that.

It was a half an hour before they got there, haphazardly dressed with worry all over their faces. They embraced her for a moment before the questions flew — Was she all right? Should they call the police? Who was he? Will he come back? Rose answered them calmly before they ordered her home and to take as much time off as she'd like, thanking me over and over again, telling me how glad they were that I'd shown up when I did.

They weren't the only ones.

I pulled her into my side as we walked home, wrapped my arm around her shoulder to keep her close, as if I could protect her from the world. I watched every person as they passed, suspicious.

We climbed the steps to her apartment, stepped inside in the dark. Ellie was gone, the apartment empty other than Valentino. We found him perched on the back of the couch when she turned on the light, though he jumped down, purring as he wound his way through our legs.

Rose turned to me, buried herself in my chest. I cradled her in my arms.

"What do you need, Rosie? What can I give you?"

She sighed. "This is a good start."

"Anything," I whispered, chest aching. I closed my eyes.

"I already have all that I need."

I squeezed her tighter, smoothed her hair, kissed her temple. Her eyes when she looked up at me were bright, clear, though they disappeared behind dark lashes as she kissed my lips sweetly, deeply. She took my hand and led me to the bathroom.

Instead of turning on the light, she opened the cabinet under the sink and pulled out a few candles that the girls seemed to stow there for baths, along with a lighter.

"I just want to wash all the bad off of me," she said as she lit the first.

I smiled and nodded. "I'll leave you to it."

She lit the second. "No. Stay. Please?"

I nodded again, stepping past her to run the water.

When I turned around, she was pulling off her shirt, black hair against her creamy white skin. She unhooked her bra, undressing without care that I was there, without intent to seduce or lure. It was more intimate than that.

I undressed too, simply, quietly as the water rushed, echoing off the walls of the small room.

She reached under the sink again, coming back with something in her hand that looked like a scoop of ice cream. When she dropped it into the claw foot tub, it fizzed and bubbled, and I watched her step in after it gently.

Rose looked back over her shoulder and reached for my hand. I took it, her fingers warm and slender in mine, and we sat together —her body nestled between my legs, the tops of her knees peeking out of the water, her arms resting on my thighs. Her skin shone in the candlelight.

She sighed. The water was a soft, milky blue, and the scent of lavender and lemon hung in the humid air as she reached out a foot to turn the squeaking faucet until the water stopped.

We lay that way for a long while, long enough for me to close my eyes, head resting against the curling edge of the tub, letting a little bit of everything go with every slow breath. She sighed against me again. Neither of us seemed to want to speak, lost in our thoughts as they wound around each other.

Her hair hung over her shoulder, the tail floating in the water like a ghost, and I gathered it all in my hands, twisting it until it was a rope as she angled her long neck. I tied her hair in a knot that slipped loose once I let it go, and she rested her head in the crook of my neck, her fingers idly traced the mandala on my knee.

"Promise me something," she said softly.

"Anything."

"You have to talk to me. Even when you think you know better. Even when you think you're doing the right thing by saying nothing."

"Promise me the same."

She took a breath. "I will. I do."

"I will. I do." The words were quiet, reverent.

"Promise me you won't run away," she said.

"I'll never leave you, not unless you tell me to go. Never again.

I know now. I know what I stand to lose, what I didn't understand before. I'm not afraid of you, of us. I'm not afraid of anything except losing you." I wrapped my arms around her shoulders, kissed her hair, willing her to understand, to know how much I meant it. How much she meant to me.

I could see part of her face when I kissed her hair — eyes pinned shut, chin trembling. A tear escaped, rolled over her cheekbone as she hung her hands on my forearms and squeezed.

"Shhh. Don't cry. I love you, don't cry," I whispered, my lips near her ear, hand moving to her cheek.

She turned in my arms, tucking her head under my chin as her arms wound around my waist. Her breath was heavy, shuddering in through her nose, a sob racking through her chest as she tried to hold it in. And I held her while she cried, stroking her hair, waiting until she calmed.

"I'm sorry," she said after a while.

"No. You don't have to be sorry for anything, Rose. Nothing. Everything we've been through, these months … it's my fault. It's my fault, and I'm sorry, but you've already forgiven me for that. So I don't want to think about it anymore. I don't want to think about life without you. I just want to love you, and I want you to love me. I trust you, and I want you to trust me. And if you do, if you really do, then I believe we'll always survive. We'll always find a way through. Because there's no one, Rose — not one person in the world who I could ever love like I love you."

Her breath hitched, and she whispered the promise, "I will. I do."

"Then *we* will. Always."

It was a long time before we moved. I felt her breathing against me. My gaze rested on her hip, rising out of the water in a soft slope, like an island in the milky water, her ribs, the curve of her breast like the shore of a beach in an ocean. It wasn't until the water had chilled that she turned and pressed her lips to my chest and reached for the plug. We stood and found towels, dried off in silence. She blew out the candles, and we found ourselves in the dark once again.

Rose took my hand and led me into her room, which looked as it always did — rumpled bed, dark other than the light next to her bed, small piles of black clothes like islands on the floor. She turned off the light as we slipped into her bed, towels discarded, legs still wet and sticking to the sheets as they searched for the other's, winding together when found. She nestled into my chest, the warmth of her pressed against me.

My body was heavy, wishing for sleep, wanting to stay in the moment always. Rose, in my arms. Rose, mine. She was mine. I had always been hers.

I thought she was asleep, but she shifted, leaned back. I could see nothing but the deepest shades of blue, the glint of light on her eyes. My hand found her jaw, thumb grazed her lip, and she closed them against my skin, pressing a kiss to the pad. I angled her face, breathing in as I kissed her.

She came to me gently, gave herself to me softly. It had nothing to do with need, the way we touched. It was an exchange of hearts. It was a promise.

Her lips composed the sum of my world as my hand trailed down her chest, traced the soft curve of her breast, then down her ribs, over her hip, down her thigh as it hooked on mine. I gripped and pulled, bringing her body flush against me.

I dragged my hand around the back of her thigh and up until it found the warmth of her, until my finger was cradled in her. I trailed it up, then down — she stopped kissing me to sigh — then up again before slipping a finger inside, stretching the other so it grazed the sensitive spot. Every flex of my hand arched her back more until her neck was long, stretched out in the darkness before me. I leaned in to lay a hot kiss on the skin offered to me.

"Patrick …" It was a whispered plea, a declaration, a prayer.

The moment I let her go, her hips swung into me, leg wrapped around my waist, and I met her with a long kiss. She rolled, pulling me with her, my hand on her hip as she spread her thighs, and I pressed against her, our lips only parting when I flexed, my forehead against hers, eyes closed as I filled her until her thighs trembled.

She was everywhere.

Her arms around my neck.

Her lips against mine.

Her legs around my waist.

My name riding her breath.

My heart beating her name.

My thoughts tumbled away from me with every thrust until it all fell away, and there was nothing except Rose.

this time

ROSE

When the morning came and my mind began to stretch into awareness, I thought at first it had all been a dream. Maybe it was the fall and the last nine months had been a nightmare. Maybe it was a few days ago, before the fight, a fight that never happened.

But, no, it was real. The steady rise and fall of his chest was real. His arms around me, heavy and warm. The smile that showed a sliver of his perfect teeth when he woke. It was all real, and somehow we'd survived. We found a way through when my pride stood in our way, when I fought and pushed and denied him everything.

Emotion rolled through me again as the night before crawled its way through my memory, and he turned on the light, casting light and shadow across the room, across our bodies —his dark with ink and mine smooth and white.

I lay on his chest, chin on my hands as he propped his head and smiled with the smile he only gave to me.

"How did we do it?" I asked in wonder.

He seemed to know what I meant without needing an explanation. "There were a lot of things, I think, but in the end, it was us. Just us."

"All this time, we've just been in our own way."

He smirked. "Well, mostly you."

I chuckled. "Yes, mostly me."

He touched my face. "I should have gone after you sooner."

"I wouldn't have budged."

"Maybe. But I still should have."

My smile softened. "Why didn't you?"

"Because I wanted to respect how you felt, what you asked of me. Because I didn't think I deserved to be happy."

"How could you think that?" I asked, heart aching.

He shook his head and swallowed. "I don't think I'd ever been happy before I moved here. Met you, West, everyone. I just didn't see it lasting, you know? It was a gift I cherished every day that I had it, knowing it'd be gone, eventually."

"Patrick …"

But he smiled and cupped my cheek. "It's okay. I'm okay."

I leaned into his hand.

His thumb shifted against my skin. "West said something that resonated. He said that I've fought for everything, fought my way through life, but I wasn't fighting for you. I thought I was doing the right thing by doing what you asked, but I was wrong. Letting you go so easy denied everything I wanted." He shook his head. "I don't mean that I would have given up my respect for your wishes to get what I wanted, but I didn't even try, Rose. I didn't even try, not really, and I regret it. Because if I'd fought for you, we could have been here, where we are right now, a long time ago."

I nodded as his hand slipped away from my face and to my arm, and I shifted to press a kiss into the soft skin of his chest. "But we're here now. So, what should we do with our second chance?"

"Oh, well, that's easy."

I raised an eyebrow, amused. "Care to share?"

But before he answered, he sat, smiling, wrapping his arms around my back to hold me to him until I was cradled in his arms, looking up at his beautiful face, full of so much adoration and love that I knew he'd make me happy forever, if I'd let him. And I would.

"This time," he said, "we do it right."

Epilogue

ROSE

Music played softly in the next room as I looked in the bathroom mirror, leaning in to slip my earring on. My palms were a little sweaty, and I smoothed my black dress down my thighs, stepping back to check myself out one last time.

I took a deep breath. This was it. I'd been working nonstop for the last three months to get to this moment — the opening of Wasted Words.

I'd arrived.

My lips curled into a smile, and I let the breath out, venting a bit of my nerves along with it.

I walked out of the bathroom with every intention of going into my room to grab my heels, but when I saw Patrick painting, I couldn't help but stop and watch him.

We'd converted Lily's old room into a studio just after he'd moved

STACI HART

in, which was just after Ellie moved in with Max. If Ellie had been anyone but Ellie, I would have been worried, but not only was this exactly her modus operandi, but she and Max were good together. Happy. The two of them just made perfect sense, much like the rest of us.

Patrick sat on his stool in the center of the room where I found him so often. But rather than jeans and tee, which he usually wore, he was in suit pants and a white button-down, sleeves rolled up so he wouldn't get paint on it, exposing the tattoos all over his forearms. The light was slipping away as dusk fell, painting the room in oranges and yellow, illuminating the white walls with fire. I watched his back as he painted, his shoulders, his head turned just at an angle, looking at the canvas like he could see something that wasn't visible to me.

I leaned against the doorframe for a few minutes, the beauty of his movement captivating, the fluidity of every motion like that of a dancer. He turned to look back at me when I sighed contentedly.

Patrick smiled back and began cleaning the rest of his brushes. "How long have you been there?"

"Not long enough."

He chuckled. "What time is it?"

I shrugged. "We've got a little time."

"You can't be late to your own party."

"Why not? It's mine, isn't it?"

Patrick stood as he finished cleaning up and rolled down his sleeves, buttoning the cuffs as he made his way over to me. "You've been working all day, every day for this. Even today, you've been at the bar since seven this morning. Who would have thought you'd be willingly getting up so early every day?"

My smile stretched wider as he stepped into me, slipping his arms around my waist, smiling down at me. "Not me."

"Me neither. I'm proud of you, Rosie. You did it."

My arms wound around his neck. "I did it."

"Even when it was hard."

I nodded. "That was weirdly when it was the most fun."

"Do you feel ready?"

My mind skipped down the to-do list that was now a constant part of my brain. "I think we've done everything we can do. The last few days have just been hammering down the tiniest of details, but everything else has been decided. When we started this — really started it — I couldn't have imagined that I'd know this much. Like, I can put together an invoice in a snap. I can call a distributor and bitch them out when my shipment doesn't get here on time."

"As long as it's not in China."

I laughed. "Yeah, I don't know how to argue in Mandarin yet. But Cam does. And thank God for her."

"Cooper wasn't kidding when he said he had experts."

"I certainly didn't expect a nerd girl genius in a flannel and a Hulk T-shirt, but that's exactly what I got, and she's perfect. And the store's perfect. And everything's kind of perfect."

His smile pulled up at one corner, turning it into a little bit of a smirk. "It is kind of perfect, isn't it?"

"Mmhmm." I nodded, really wanting to kiss him, but really *not* wanting to smear my lipstick all over my face, or worse — his. "Patrick?"

His eyes were on my lips like he wanted to kiss me too. "Yeah?"

"Thank you."

"What for?"

My hands slipped down his chest and to his tie, and I fiddled with it, avoiding his eyes. "Everything. But mostly for coming back for me. For staying. For loving me."

"You don't have to thank me for that. You make it easy."

"But I didn't always."

"No, but neither did I."

"But we found a way," I said. "And now, here we are. Are you scared?"

"No," he said quietly. "Are you?"

I shook my head and looked up at him, meeting his eyes, eyes that burned like embers. "No. Not anymore. I love you. Even when we were apart, I loved you every minute of every lonely day. And I know I'll always love you. No matter what happens."

His hand found my cheek, slipped into my hair. "Then I'll always be yours, Rose. Forever."

And his lips brushed mine, the softest, gentlest of kisses, as if to seal the promise.

Within a half an hour, we were in a cab on our way to Wasted Words, getting there before everyone arrived. Nerves fluttered around in my ribcage, occasionally shooting through me in bursts, starting when I saw the sign to my bar, lit up in the twilight. Or when Cam rushed out and grabbed me, dragging me inside to approve the last minute shipment of liquor that had come in the eleventh hour. And when I saw the painting Patrick made for me hanging over the bar, right in the front where everyone would see it when they walked in.

He'd given it to me the day after Seth — a black, dripping and splattered watercolor rose at first glance, but it was also *me*. I could see myself in the negative space of the petals, my nose, my lashes, my lips and chin. It was the most beautiful, meaningful thing anyone had ever given to me.

I might have cried. A lot. It was perfect. He was perfect.

The last months had been everything I'd imagined. It was so easy, being with him. It always had been, but now, after everything we went through to find each other, now I knew. He said forever and meant it, and so did I.

I'd fight for him. We'd fight for each other.

Within an hour, we were greeting our friends. The music played — a real DJ with vinyl and everything — and I stood in my bar, surrounded by books and friends and love and happiness. And everything was exactly as it should be.

Patrick was at my arm all night as we made our way around the bar. All of our friends were there — the Habits gang, everyone from Tonic, Cooper's socialite friends — the familiar faces making the night that much more meaningful. There were some less familiar people there too — book bloggers and publishers, editors and some indie writers we'd partnered with, plus my new staff.

But not Seth. He'd kept his promise to stay gone, though we all wondered about him. Worried about him. But Patrick had let him go, and for good this time. There was no going back.

The next day marked our grand opening, so the night wasn't overly long, just a little bit of time to celebrate the end of the hard work. Some of us would need to be there early, definitely me, possibly puking, and definitely Cam, possibly holding back my hair. But just before the party was over, Cooper stepped up to the bar and rang the brass bell.

Everyone quieted and turned to where he stood at the front of the bar.

"I wanted to thank you all for coming tonight and kicking off our newest adventure. This is a bit of of a dream come true for Rosie and me, an amalgamation of ideas and passions that turned into what you see here. But I'm only the muscle in the operation. The brains, the charm, and definitely the style is all Rose. Come on up here, Rosie, and say hi."

Everyone turned to me, and I blushed and waved him off.

"You're not getting off so easy," he said, smirking, that asshole. "Come on, Rose."

My cheeks were on fire, frozen in a smile as I made my way up to stand next to him and face all the people who were there for us, for me. I took a breath and raised my glass.

"I'm not one for big fancy speeches, so instead, I propose a toast."

Everyone raised their glasses, waiting for me to speak, and I was filled with emotion, swallowing it down so I could speak.

"Cheers to the end, because every story that ends begins another. Cheers to beginnings, that they may be full of hope and love. And cheers to you, my friends, for being a part of ours."

Here, here, waved through the crowd, and we drank to our future.

Cooper pulled me into him and pressed a kiss into my temple. "We did it," he said, and I beamed, disbelieving that it was real, that it was happening, right then. And it was ours.

I walked through the crowd, first hugging Lily, the best friend I'd ever have, and she laughed, swiping at her tears as they fell. I hugged West, the beaming lumberjack, and he kissed my cheek and told me how proud he was. Then Maggie and Ellie as I passed, accepting their well wishes and congratulations, and a half dozen more people in a whirl as I made my way back to Patrick.

I found him at the edge of the crowd, standing in the middle of my universe. And when I stepped into him gently, looked up into his eyes — eyes that saw me, all of me, and loved me still — I took a body assessment.

Knees: weak.

Cheeks: flushed.

Stomach: flipped.

Eyes: glistening.

Heart: full.

And the moment he bent to kiss me was the moment that marked the beginning of the rest of my life.

Acknowledgments

Of course my first thank you goes, as usual, to my husband, Jeff Brillhart. This was a rough one, and you picked up my slack without a complaint, at least not an audible one. Without you believing in me *so* much, without your sacrifice, I couldn't be doing this very hard thing that I love so very much. So, thank you. I love you.

My second and third thank yous are combined into one super thank you, the likes of which only the Three Brosketeers can achieve. To the other two wheels in my tricycle, Becca Mysoor and Kandi Steiner — there's legitimately no way I can repay you for being here for me. If it weren't for you two cheering me on, I may not have made it to the end. You've held me and loved me and cried with me. You've told me like it is. You've given me hope when I had none. And I love the two of you so, so very much. #Brochachosforlyfe

To my beta readers: Zoe Streiker-Howard, Melissa Lynn, Brie Burgess, Lex Martin, Miranda Arnold, Terry Maggert, Monique Boone, Jen Miller, Beth Cranford, Jenni Moen, Tina Lynne, and Angie McKeon. You, my dearest crew, are invaluable. I told you when I sent the manuscript that it was a mess, and your comments helped me sort through it and turn it into something I'm proud of. So thank you for your honesty and criticism because without it, I wouldn't the writer I am.

To Lauren Perry — You are absolute magic. This cover is my favorite so far, and that's thanks to you, Chelsee Spinello, and Jesse

Sykes. The three of you made the most beautiful art together, and I just can't thank you enough.

To Christine Stanley — You've always got my back, ready to go when I need you with a smile and a hug and a smack on the ass. Never leave me!

To Kiezha Smith Ferrell — Thank you for taking my work and polishing it up until it shines. It brings me immense relief to know my book is in such capable hands.

And to you, dear readers. Thank you for reading this story. Thank you for your love and support of me, of these books, and the characters in them. We do this for you, and we couldn't do it without you. So raise your glass to beginnings disguised as endings.

About Staci

Staci has been a lot of things up to this point in her life: a graphic designer, an entrepreneur, a seamstress, a clothing and handbag designer, a waitress. Can't forget that. She's also been a mom to three little girls who are sure to grow up to break a number of hearts. She's been a wife, even though she's certainly not the cleanest, or the best cook. She's also super, duper fun at a party, especially if she's been drinking whiskey, and her favorite word starts with f, ends with k.

From roots in Houston, to a seven year stint in Southern California, Staci and her family ended up settling somewhere in between and equally north, in Denver. They are new enough that snow is still magical. When she's not writing, she's gaming, cleaning, or designing graphics.

FOLLOW STACI HART:

Website: Stacihartnovels.com
Facebook: Facebook.com/stacihartnovels
Twitter: Twitter.com/imaquirkybird
Pinterest: pinterest.com/imaquirkybird

Enjoy a sneak peek of...

WHEREVER IT LEADS

BY ADRIANA LOCKE

*USA Today bestselling author of **Sacrifice** & **The Exception Series***

WWW.ADRIANALOCKE.COM

FENTON

*"**Tell him I got his** message yesterday and I don't need him to blow me. But thank him for the offer."*

Grabbing the nearest shopping cart and sliding it in front of me, I toggle the phone against my shoulder. It nearly slides off my rigid muscles, a mix of workout fatigue and work stress setting up shop across my back.

Duke sighs through the phone, not even pretending to hide his frustration. "Fenton, that's not true," he says, exasperation thick in his voice. "He didn't ask to blow you."

"Obviously it's not fucking true. I just want to hear him have to deny it."

"You know what? Just forget I called. I'll come up with a response myself."

"That's probably the best idea you've had yet."

Duke sighs again, louder this time. I'm sure I've been an asshole to deal with since I hired him, but I gave him plenty of warning what he was getting into. This entire situation, the one he was hired to deal with, has been a complete clusterfuck from the start. There's nothing more vexing than not being able to fix a problem and having your hands tied behind your back while being needled that the problem exists. I know it exists. I'm keenly aware and no one wants it fixed more than me.

"I'll just tell them the status hasn't changed."

"I could've taken care of this," I bite out.

"I know. I know."

"And they wouldn't let me."

"I. Know."

"I know *you* know. Try to impart some of that knowledge to *them*. I'm playing by their rules right now, but I'm starting to lose patience with their—"

"Fenton, you have to play by their rules. Otherwise—"

"I'm heading into the store," I interrupt. "The service is going to get shitty."

"Talk soon," Duke says, ready to end the conversation anyway, and the line clicks off. I shove my phone into the pocket of my black athletic pants. My jaw pulses, the buzz from this morning's workout now vanished.

Ignoring the eyes of an uptight man perusing the apples, I skirt my cart left to avoid interaction. I have no idea why I chose today of all days to do my own grocery shopping. I could've waited three damn days until my housekeeper gets back from vacation.

Steering clear of the apples and the negative energy rolling off the shopper, I head towards the bananas. I need to find the optimism I had five minutes ago before Duke called from the office and ruined my Saturday morning.

The bananas are organic and perfectly ripe, so I pluck a bunch off the podium. I start to push away, but the hairs on the back of my neck stand on end. A ruffle of unease scatters through my subconscious.

I pause mid-step and glance around the store. People mill about, minding their own business, nothing out of the ordinary. I start to push away again when I spy the offender. A black piece of plastic peeks out from behind a bundle of bananas, the overhead light ricocheting off it and catching my eye.

I reach behind the produce and pull out a black cell phone. Turning it over in my hand, it looks no worse for wear. I press the round button on the bottom and the screen lights up.

Staring back at me are two gorgeous girls, probably a couple of years younger than me. Mid-twenties, I'd say. The dark-headed one is flashing a peace sign in a barely there white bikini. She's hot as fuck. But it's the blonde that draws my attention. She sits crossed-legged in shorts and a tank top on the beach, her hair falling around her narrow shoulders. Her body is covered, her stance demure, but there's something striking about her that I can't pinpoint. I almost can't look away. Her blue-green eyes taunt me, tease me with a look that's downright beguiling. The touches of vulnerability hidden behind her confidence intrigue me, make me want to hear her voice and know what she's thinking.

Laughing at my ridiculousness despite the heat roiling in my blood, I skim the store again. No one seems to be searching for the phone.

I glance back at the screen and my gaze goes immediately to the blonde. The curve of her hip has my thumb gliding over the screen.

I should turn the phone in to management. It's the logical, responsible thing to do.

My feet don't move.

Losing your phone in the bananas doesn't exactly shout responsibility.

Taking a deep breath, I ponder my options. I can turn it in to Lost and Found and hope that they actually give it to her if she comes looking. Or … I could try to get in touch with her myself.

Keep telling yourself you're playing the Good Samaritan.

Leaning against the produce display, I do a quick analysis. The odds of her finding it at the Help Desk aren't great. Maybe fifty-fifty. Some bagger boy will probably see the lock screen and take it to the bathroom and jerk off. The odds of *that* are phenomenal. The odds of me breaking the passcode aren't great either, but if possible, would greatly increase her chances of getting it back.

And the chance for me to see those eyes in person.

I type in 0000.

"Try again" flashes on the screen.

1234.

"Try again."

Steering the cart with my elbows towards the customer service desk, I run through possible passwords before I commit to my final try. I have one more chance before it locks me out for good and I have no choice but to turn it over to Bagger Boy and his bathroom break.

I go for 1111, another overused password.

It makes a clicking sound and the lock screen opens. The phone toggles in my hands, my jaw dropping in disbelief. It worked. The home screen is filled with apps over shiny gold wallpaper, waiting to be explored.

Should I or shouldn't I?

My thumb glances over the photo album and I see the first photo.

I definitely should.

Made in the USA
Monee, IL
28 July 2021